TRAPPED—
AND ON THE RUN!

rified voice tore through the night, and with each piercing syllable, a red pang of fear shot through Jim.

He had fallen back and now he half-turned, his gun poised; but the girl at whose side he had been tore at his arm.

"You fool! Do you want to hang?" she gasped.

Suddenly, there were noises everywhere. Men shouted, dogs barked or howled wildly. But Long Tom, in the thick heart of the alley's darkness, halted his band.

Then the big man struck terror to every soul by saying swiftly: "We're cut off from Charlie and the horses. They're clean on the other side of town. Boys, God knows what we can do. I haven't a plan!"

Books by Max Brand

Ambush at Torture Canyon
The Bandit of the Black Hills
The Bells of San Filipo
Black Jack
Blood on the Trail
The Blue Jay
The Border Kid
Danger Trail
Destry Rides Again
The False Rider
Fightin' Fool
Fightin' Four
Flaming Irons
Ghost Rider
  (Original title: Clung)
The Gun Tamer
Gunman's Reckoning
Harrigan
Hired Guns
Hunted Riders
The Jackson Trail
Larromee's Ranch
The Longhorn's Ranch
The Longhorn Feud
The Long, Long Trail

The Man from Mustang
On the Trail of Four
The Outlaw of Buffalo Flat
The Phantom Spy
Pillar Mountain
Pleasant Jim
The Reward
Ride the Wild Trail
Rippon Rides Double
Rustlers of Beacon Creek
Seven Trails
Singing Guns
Steve Train's Ordeal
The Stingaree
The Stolen Stallion
The Streak
The Tenderfoot
Thunder Moon
Tragedy Trail
Trouble Kid
The Untamed
Valley of the
  Vanishing Men
Valley of Thieves
Vengeance Trail

Published by POCKET BOOKS

Max Brand

PLEASANT JIM

A KANGAROO BOOK
PUBLISHED BY POCKET BOOKS NEW YORK

POCKET BOOKS, a Simon & Schuster division of
GULF & WESTERN CORPORATION
1230 Avenue of the Americas, New York, N.Y. 10020

ISBN 0-671-81759-0

First Pocket Books printing September, 1978

Trademarks registered in the United States and other countries.

Printed in the U.S.A.

PLEASANT JIM

CHAPTER 1

ALL that Jim Pleasant had been, all that he had done, amounted to nothing. His life, for our purposes, begins with the moment when he ran down Charlie Rizdal in the mountains behind King's River. It would have been a pity for either of those expert fighters to have a real advantage over the other, but the God of Battle provided that they should meet fairly and squarely on the elbow turn of a narrow trail with a two-thousand-foot outer edge. If there were any disadvantage, it hung upon Jim Pleasant, for at that moment he was busily studying the sky, not regarding the imaginary rings of the poet's paradise but more profoundly interested in the polycyclic flight of a buzzard which was throwing its broad loops between the peaks that looked into the valley. The conclusion of Jim Pleasant or Pleasant Jim, as he was ironically and punningly nicknamed most of the time—was that it would be a vast advantage for a fellow on a man-trail to be able to live like a buzzard on the wing. For his own part, he had not tasted of any food for two days and the ache of his stomach made him frown a little; moreover, a terrible sit-fast was forming on his pony's back, and so Pleasant Jim rode under the burden of many clouds, at the very moment when he turned the corner of the trail and ran into that delightful gun-fighter, Charlie Rizdal.

Accordingly, Jim was slow. He was no quicker, say, than a scared wolf or a startled cat; as a matter of fact, his bullet flew wide and only pierced the shoulder of Rizdal, but since it arrived at its mark just a hundredth part of a second before Rizdal pulled his trigger, the latter incontinently fired into the ground. At the same time the impact thrust him half around in the saddle.

He was a man of parts, however, as a man must be who has a

reward of eight thousand dollars hanging over his head, and even when he was thrown off balance and thoroughly staggered by the impact of that forty-five caliber slug, he had the presence of mind to observe that his horse was much bulkier than Jim Pleasant's and that it was, moreover, on the inside of the trail. Accordingly, as he fell back, he clutched the flanks of his good horse with the spurs, and the frantic gelding leaped straight ahead into Pleasant's mustang.

The latter shot into open space like a pebble snapped from the fingers; but Pleasant had seen the meaning of that charge just in time, and while the poor little mustang spun head over heels towards the canyon floor two thousand feet below, his master was clinging to the body of Rizdal.

One of Mr. Rizdal's arms was useless now, of course, but with his other hand he picked from the top of his riding boot a long knife which he wore there much as a Highlander wears his skean dhu. Pleasant, in the meantime, was clinging to Rizdal, while the frightened horse plunged madly along the winding curves of the trail and at every corner the body of Pleasant sailed out like the boy who is snapper in the game of "crack the whip."

He saw the glitter of Rizdal's knife, but he was not startled into the commission of an act of folly. Rizdal deserved death, beyond doubt, but dead he was worth only five thousand, while, living, he was worth eight; for some people thought that if the bank robber were captured alive he might be induced to surrender some of his old spoils for the sake of a lighter sentence. Pleasant thought in time, and instead of pulling the trigger a second time, he used the long barrel of the Colt to tap the robber on the head.

Rizdal fell from his horse and so did Pleasant, but the latter fell on top. When Rizdal's wits returned to him, he found his captor sitting cross-legged beside him on the trail, weighing in his hand a scarcely ponderable bit of stone.

"Well?" said Rizdal, sitting up, and clasping his wounded shoulder. "You came out best, as usual."

Pleasant decided to overlook the compliment.

"I've been wondering if it's worth while, Charlie," said he. "It's a long trip; and there'll have to be a wait, first, while your shoulder is healing; and after you arrive at Fisher Falls, of course they'll simply hang you. Whachu think?"

"That's one thing that might happen," agreed Rizdal calmly. "What's the other?"

"The other is neater, a lot," declared the victor. "Here's two of us to ride one horse. Well, if you was to step over the edge, here, we wouldn't have to ride double, you wouldn't have to hang, and I wouldn't have all the bother of watching over you and nursing you in camp while your damn shoulder gets sound, and while you figure ways to cut my throat at night."

"I always heard you was a reasonable man, Pleasant," answered Rizdal, "and now I see it for myself. Besides, if you fuss around a couple of weeks with me in the mountains, here, the greasers that are working your place for you may run off most of your good stock."

"They won't do that," answered Pleasant Jim, without hesitation. "Three years back, when I was just starting, a couple of the boys decided to crook the game on me while I was away on a trip. I had to chase them almost to the Rio, but since then I ain't had any trouble."

"You brought back the stolen horses, eh?"

"All except one. One of those greasers had been a prizefighter and he had a cauliflower ear. Well, I brought back that ear, too, and nailed it into a post on my range. It's a funny thing how I been able to trust my punchers from that time on."

Mr. Rizdal nodded, caressing his bleeding shoulder.

"Well, Pleasant," said he, "you could put a bullet through me and say it was done during the fight. But speakin' personal, I don't aim to step off that edge of the trail."

Mr. Pleasant looked up to the mountain heads, from the southern sides of which the tractile clouds were being drawn out upon the wind.

"As I was sayin' before," he remarked absently, "there's three grand more in you alive than dead. I think I'll take you in, Charlie. Now, lemme have a look at that shoulder, will you?"

They patched up the shoulder between them, working industriously, chatting of odds and ends. From Rizdal's pack they got iodine and poured it into the wound, while the wounded man's face went white; yet he did not falter in his sentence.

When the wound was dressed, they moved half a mile down the trail to a little glacial meadow, and there they camped for the next three weeks while the wound closed and healed with magic speed. It was easy to get food. With little snares they caught birds and squirrels for the pot, and once the rifle of Pleasant dropped a deer on the farther side of the little lake. It was grueling and nervous work, for not a minute of the day did the

captor dare to turn his back upon the robber; and at night he put
aside his weapons in the fork of a tree and tied himself to the
body of Rizdal. If he kept so much as a knife on him, that knife
might get into the clever fingers of the captive, and Pleasant
would be minus eight thousand dollars, and life as well; but when
they had nothing but bare hands to use, Pleasant had no doubt
of how a contest would terminate. Apparently, Rizdal had no
doubt either; he decided to try another method.

On an evening, a lobo at the edge of the trees raised a long,
ululant cry, and the two sat up and listened to the ghostly
wailing.

"This is the right sort of a place for that devil," remarked
Pleasant.

"Well, the place don't matter so much," decided Rizdal. "Put
him in a kennel and teach him to wag his tail, he'd still be a wolf.
You're like that, old timer. They've kenneled you up, they think,
but you're still a wolf, and one morning they'll wake up and find
that you've slaughtered a flock of the greyhounds and the
lapdogs and the poodles. You're like the wolf, all the time; it's
work for your teeth that you want."

"Because I go a-man hunting," remarked the other. "No, it's
just that I want extra cash to clear my farm ranch. This here job
will about shove me into the open, Charlie."

"If you want the cash," said Rizdal, "I could show you a
quicker way."

"I'm listening."

"Look how you're fixed. You turn me in and get the blood
money and I hang. All right. Then you have my brother on your
neck, and Long Tom ain't a joke to play the cards against."

"We gotta take chances," philosophized Pleasant.

"Sure. I ain't trying to scare you. Just reasoning. But you
admit that Long Tom is quite a man?"

"He is," replied Pleasant, with quiet decision.

"Now, what a cinch it would be, Jim, to just meet up with
Tom and let him drop a chunk of banknotes into your pocket.
Eight thousand you get from some damned Pooh-Bah who'll
make a speech to you and then forget you. Say you take fifteen
thousand from Tom   who *won't* forget. That's logic, I say; what
do you think?"

"Sure it's logic," nodded the other. "The slickest I ever heard.
But I don't like floating funds, old boy. I put my money in the
bank, and I play dog till somebody makes me play wolf."

A skein of birds slipped in a long line above the trees, and the robber paused to watch them disappear down the wind.

"All right," he said. "Only, if ever you're trimmed, remember what you missed. Also, I don't hold no malice, particular. But Long Tom is different. Well, you think it over."

But if Pleasant thought the matter over, he said no word concerning it, and five weeks later, when the pink was just beginning to mix with the gray of the dawnlight, he rode with his prisoner into Fisher Falls and tapped at the door of the jail.

The jailer opened the heavy, creaking door with an oath and a yawn.

"What damn foolishness is up now?" he asked.

But presently his mind cleared.

"Come right in, Jim," said he. "This here bank is always open, and we'll honor your check."

CHAPTER 2

A DRIVING tramontana came down from the white-headed upper range that morning, and Pleasant was glad to step out of the wind and inside the snug doors of the bank. The clerks looked up and smiled at him   they knew why he was there   and Lewis Fisher, the president, came in with the broadest of smiles, also.

"Three years ago, Jim," said he, in his private office, "there was fifteen thousand against you. Now there's barely twenty-five hundred. That's progress, my boy. Only twenty-five hundred between you and freedom!"

Mr. Fisher was not yet sixty, but he was the father of the town, had given it being and name, and he looked upon the place and all the people in it partly with a child's delight in a toy and partly with a sense of unreality, as though they were rather his dream than a fact. He was a public-spirited man. He had built Fisher's Theater; he had established Fisher's *Evening Democrat*; and he had allowed the town fathers to buy a central tract which was to be turned into a park, one day, though so far nothing had been done to ornament the sandy waste beyond the erection of a lofty stone statue which showed Lewis Fisher mounted upon a fiery steed of rather odd proportions. This was the man who smiled on young Jim Pleasant, who answered: "I'm free enough, Mr. Fisher."

"Never so long as you owe money," said the banker. "That's the penalty of speculation. Money makes strength; also, it makes slavery. Credit is the blood in the veins of the commercial giant; it forms the shackles, also. So clear yourself of debt, my boy. I have an interest in your progress. I want to see you get on. That's why I give you this advice."

He patted and smoothed the top of his desk as he spoke. He

12

could not touch that radiant, red-shot mahogany without feeling his strength renewed and his faith in himself reinforced. As he spoke, he did not look young Pleasant in the eye but regarded his own hand traveling softly across the polished wood, and the reflection traveling beside it, lit with a green spark from his emerald ring. Pleasant had nothing to say. He merely folded and tucked into his wallet the release which sliced away so large a part of his mortgage and then stood up.

"I'll be going along," said he.

"So soon? So soon?" asked the amiable Mr. Fisher. "Not even wait for a little celebration? Not sit in the sun for even a moment not even wait for an *Evening Democrat* reporter to get the true story of the capture?"

Pleasant tossed his head, and quivered like an unbacked colt at sight of a halter. "Newspapers make nothin' but trouble," said he; "and I got to get back to the place."

The president of the bank stood up and shook hands.

"It's a fine thing to have done what you've done," said he, "for a few men like you make an entire community rest at ease!"

He glanced over his shoulder at the face of the great blue-black safe which filled in the corner of his office. Men said that a great fortune was locked behind its doors continually, in cash and in securities.

"Only," continued Lewis Fisher, a benevolent smile on his rosy, fatherly face, "don't forget that all work and no play makes Jack a dull boy!"

A group of admiring townsfolk had gathered around Pleasant Jim's horse—the one, of course, which he had taken from Rizdal on the trail—but he stepped through the midst of their questions and congratulations and swung into the saddle. An active young man caught the bridle and held the tall horse.

"I'm from the *Evening Democrat*," said he, "and I got a couple of questions to ask you, Mr. Pleasant. First, what "

Never did the Pope of Geneva look more grimly upon a critic than Mr. Pleasant looked upon the reporter.

"Just slack off on that bridle, friend," said he. "I'm busy."

And, deftly, he twitched the horse through the group and sent him pelting down the street. By the time the last house of the village jerked away behind him, he had forgotten Fisher Falls and the considerable glory of his last adventure; that was put resolutely to the rear of his mind. There remained in front of him only twenty-five hundred dollars in debt; that paid, his ranch and all that was upon it would be his. In a word, he stood only around the corner from assured success!

Eight miles separated him from his farm, and he made the good gelding turn off that distance at a dizzy speed until he topped the last hill on the verge of his domain. There he drew rein and went on softly, his eyes busy. It was no great tract but all of it was good. Let others have their sweeping acres of desert, pricked with a scattering of bunch grass here and there, burned crisp by summer heat and whipped and beaten by the white winter storms; he preferred this sheltered little valley   it was small, to be sure, but all his from the roots of the stream that ran through it to the widening mouth of the hollow. The self-satisfied skipjacks of the town might sit in their offices and draw down a weekly pay envelope, but he preferred the longer work and the greater gamble with its larger reward. No water famine could destroy his stock and where could better pasturage be found than the short, thick grass which grew here? He did not waste his energies on the maintenance of a clumsy herd of cows, neither did he run a ragged band of mustangs, or keep goats or sheep or swine; instead, his fortune was invested in a glorious bit of saddle stock, tough and hardy with the broncho strain but made taller and swifter by constant crossing upon hot blood. A "flush" cowpuncher knew where to come when he wanted between his knees something that could throw dust in the eyes of nearly every other horse on the range. He journeyed to the valley of Pleasant Jim and picked a mount there. The prices were high, but the quality was unquestionable and a guaranty went with every sale. There were a few instances when the most delightful picture horses had turned out "high-headed fools," or proved lacking in bottom; Pleasant took back these failures and gave sound stock in exchange, and though this policy cost him somewhat at the moment, it enabled him to push up his prices still farther, for when this solid policy transpired and was talked about, horselovers came from still greater distances with wallets stuffed more thickly.

So Pleasant Jim reviewed his past and his present as he jogged his horse up the valley. It might be christened "Pleasant Valley" one of these days. A prickling sense of joy ran up his spine at the thought, for it was, in fact, Pleasant Valley to him.

When he came through the southern gate, a gray two-year-old came dancing to inspect him, then in alarm shot away like a bolt, glancing over the good green turf and disappearing into the shadows of a coppice. There would be a mount for some one bone and substance enough to please one of those Montana fellows who want a mountain of horseflesh under them! He jogged on beside the creek, taking keen note that the fences were in good repair and all as it should be. Plainly the Mexicans had not been idle in his absence! So he passed the little river pasture where half a dozen brood mares, their foals beside them, lifted their heads and looked at him with recognition in their gentle eyes. A lump formed in the throat of Pleasant Jim, and he breathed rapidly. He had lived with enough bitter hardness to appreciate what is good in life; and looking about him, he was content. Some day he might be able to push his holdings farther up the hills on either side; he could get that land cheap, because he owned the available water beneath it. Some day he might step farther down into the broadness of Fisher's Valley, too; but in the meantime, this was very good, and he told himself that he was content.

The house itself was tucked between two big trees on a hill near the creek; one room for the kitchen stove and the greasers, one room for himself. In a way, that little place was a fort; the log walls were safe protection, and the four small windows looked out like eyes to every quarter of the valley. So, like a landholder returning to his land, like a herdsman to his herd, like a general to his fort, Pleasant Jim came home.

There was only one stain of unhappiness. Twenty-five hundred dollars remained unpaid, and Banker Fisher had declared that a man in debt is in part a slave.

He quickened his horse, now, for he could see at the hitching rack before his cabin a fine, tall bay, with silverwork on his saddle glinting in the sun. He who owned such a horse as that would be most likely to have an open heart and an open purse to buy another of like quality.

Clattering noises came from the kitchen, and looking through the door, Pleasant saw that the stranger was helping himself to a cup of coffee and frying a few slices of bacon, now smoking in a pan.

"Howdy," said Pleasant, throwing his reins.

"Howdy," said the other, without turning around, for at that moment the coffee came to a boil and had to be snaked from the fire with care. He was a big fellow, wide and heavy in the shoulders, gaunt about the waist—the very type of Pleasant himself. Then he turned, and the host instinctively went for his gun, for he found himself looking into the brown face and the keen gray eyes of that undergod of smugglers, robbers, and gunfighters, the brother of Charlie Rizdal   Long Tom in the flesh!

CHAPTER 3

LONG TOM showed no alarm whatever, as though realizing that the sanctity of a guest armed him against all danger. He put the coffee pot on the back of the stove and extended his hand.

"Before we shake," suggested Pleasant, "tell me if you know about Charlie?"

"Sure do I know about him," nodded the other.

And at that, since his smile of good will persisted, their hands closed together.

"Had your breakfast, Jim?"

"No."

"Sit down to this. I'll drop some more bacon in the pan."

"Sit down and rest yourself, Tom. This is my business."

He went to the stove, and a little shudder went through him as he turned his back on the long-rider. With such a man, one never could tell. Perhaps all would be well; perhaps not and if not, a well placed forty-five caliber bullet would end the dreams of Pleasant Jim!

However, Long Tom was talking of cheerful odds and ends how well the valley looked; how the water from the limestone mountains put bone on the yearlings; and there was a brown mare whose cut appealed to Long Tom; perhaps she was for sale?

They were opposite one another at the table, at last, taking stock, letting their imaginations have some scope. To Long Tom it seemed that never before had he seen a man so fit; and there was something about the wrists and the fingers of the rancher that promised speed and power in equal proportion. To Pleasant Jim came the feeling that his match sat before him. Whether hand to hand or gun to gun, for deftness or for strength, Long Tom was a formidable man, and would have been judged so even without the past which was attributed to him. His jaws were somewhat underhung and his expression, perhaps on account of that peculiar feature, was a trifle grim in ordinary moments of repose, though at other times his gay manner and a suggestion of libertinage in his air counteracted the impression. In the meantime, Pleasant determined to give away nothing and to watch every motion of his dangerous guest. At the same time, it was not altogether unpleasant to be near this famous brigand who stood out among other men as a gigantic menhir rises over a ruined city.

"I haven't come about Charlie," said Long Tom, dropping suddenly to business, "but I've come to see the man who was good enough to take him. Ten hands, they generally have to have; you needed only two. Well, Pleasant, I'm going to use you!"

Pleasant Jim smiled a little.

"All right," said he.

"I want," said the other, "anywhere from five days to a week of your time. You'll need two fast horses   your place is full of them   and you'll have to have your wits about you. What money do you want for a job like that?"

"Go on," said Pleasant Jim.

"You have a price on your time. If somebody wanted an extra puncher in your off season, what would you work for?"

"I'd never leave my place for less than fifty a week."

"I want you to ride two days from here and light a fire on a mountain. Up at the top. There are people who don't want that fire to be lighted. They might try to give you a bad time coming away. Dangerous, but not too dangerous for you, I'd take it. Well, what would you say to that?"

"A little off the line of punching."

"Yes. A little. What would you name as a price for that?"

"About five hundred dollars," said the rancher, striking out at a bold figure.

"I'll make it a thousand," replied Long Tom instantly.

"Mind you, if there's anything crooked about it, I'll have nothing to do with it."

"Why should you care, Pleasant, if you're well paid?"

"Nobody can pay me high enough for a thug's job. I've got my work cut out for me here and what if I have to lose this for the sake of a thousand or two that looks easy but ain't?"

"You're tied to this racket?"

"Yes."

"It's a snug little valley," replied the bandit. "I'd choke without a bigger horizon than this, but every man to his own likings and now I'll tell you: All you'd have to do would be to take this matchbox, you see? Filled with these same matches which you're not to use on your cigarettes because, as you may notice" here he opened the little metal box "the heads of these here ain't apt to light very well! You take this along, and when you get to the place you're bound for, you light a fire and hang around for a while. Maybe you'll see a fire blaze up to answer you on one of the nearest peaks. If you do, just put your fire out, and a few inches under the ashes, you bury this here matchbox. After that you can come home."

"If there was no answering fire?"

"Then you go back to the top of the mountain three nights running and you light the fire every night. If there's no answer after that, you come back here to me, and you bring the box and the matches with you. I'd do this job myself," went on Long Tom "but I got to get Charlie out."

"You'll manage that?" grinned Pleasant Jim.

"It's nothing at all except a little time and money," replied the outlaw. "But look at your own part: All you know is, if you're caught, that somebody gave you this box of matches and told you what to do with it. Nobody can hang you for that, I suppose?"

"I suppose not."

"Then what do you say?"

One thousand from twenty-five hundred would leave fifteen hundred. There was nothing niggling or obscure about the thinking of Pleasant. He took out a bonehandled bowie knife and began to carve the edge of the table, already much nicked from similar absent-minded whittlings.

"Them that ask too many questions could be damned, I suppose," said Pleasant Jim.

"Naturally."

One thousand from twenty-five hundred would leave fifteen hundred another stroke or two, or a few good sales of horses, and he could pay off Lewis Fisher and thereafter look the world in the face.

He rammed the knife back into its holster.

"Sometimes," said Pleasant Jim, "you fellows ring in somebody and try to work him all the time afterwards. Now I'll tell you. I fall for this job; but it's the last one. I see no harm in it. I don't stick up anybody. I don't touch a match to anybody's barn or reputation. But tell me who the gents will be that might try to snag me?"

"Four chances out of five, you won't be bothered. The fifth chance is that a lot of hard-boiled gents with a United States marshal at their head may try to lag you."

Pleasant Jim whistled softly.

"A marshal?" he echoed.

"Does that come too high? You see, I put the cards on the table."

Pleasant Jim looked slowly around him—but he failed to see the dingy room, the bunk with the tangle of soiled blankets in it, the heap of broken saddles, bridles, spurs, bits, old clothes, worn-out shoes, and a hundred other odds and ends in the corner; he did not notice the staggering, lopsided little table, the stove which leaned wearily to one side, the window, with thin boards from cracker boxes taking the place of planes in several instances, or the footworn boards of the flooring. Instead, he saw a vision of a strong-walled house of stone, thick, soft rugs under foot, fireplaces yawning for the logs piled in the woodshed, and a breath of sweetness and cleanliness through the entire place. Some day all of this vision would come to pass, assuredly, and in that good time, he would have a wife, no doubt, and children to care for, and a high place in the community, and no man on the face of the earth could look up higher than to Pleasant Jim, in the height of his self-respect. Behind him lay the dark years of labor and struggle, of saving of money and spending of soul and body, of all that lay upon his consciousness, as remembered night terrors lie on the spirit of a child.

One thousand dollars for a week's work lifted him closer to the ideal! And if it were work done for a criminal, could he not close his eyes to that fact? Whatever the crime might be, it was hidden from his eyes, and he could say that his only knowledge was of a box of matches to be buried in the hot ashes of a fire!

He turned back to Long Tom; and he saw that though the face of his companion was calm, yet there was a tenseness about the mouth and a grimness about the eyes, so that it was plain that the outlaw set much upon his decision. Well, perhaps Tom felt that this was the beginning of a long association, but as for the illusions of the bandit, let them take care of themselves; they had no part in the life of Pleasant Jim, and they were no portion of his care.

"I'll take the job," said he.

Long Tom paused to swallow a mouthful of hot coffee, and as it went down he looked at the other with eyes pleasantly misted by the strength of the drink.

"All right," he nodded.

He took out a wallet without hesitation and opened it. Pleasant Jim saw within a giddy prospect of banknotes crowded together as thickly as they could be pressed, a veritable book of wealth. The outlaw took forth a slender sheaf   a mere fraction of the whole! He counted out ten one-hundred-dollar bills and laid them upon the table under the edge of the plate.

"There you are," he said.

"No C.O.D. business with you, I see," murmured Pleasant Jim, highly gratified.

"If you want to play crooked," said the other, "of course you can. But I trust you, Pleasant. Got anything stronger than coffee, here?"

Jim, without a word, brought from behind the door a small jug of whiskey and poured a liberal dram into a tin cup.

"And you?" asked the other.

"I ain't sick; and otherwise I don't take it."

"You play safe," remarked Long Tom.

He tossed off his potion and stood up.

"But you've done your stepping?" he suggested.

"I've done my stepping," answered Pleasant. "You can't step and work at the same time, I take it."

Long Tom walked out. Only at the door he paused and turned again.

"You know Black Mountain?"

"I know it."

"You might as well start to-day. To-morrow night there may be somebody watching to see a fire, Pleasant. Good luck to you."

From the saddle he spoke again.

"If you have to shoot at all, I advise you to shoot straight. Second thoughts ain't worth a damn at a time like that. So long!"

Straight down the valley he galloped his horse with the freedom of one who spent horseflesh as readily as he spent money. The strength of oil-tempered steel was in him; for how readily he had made this gamble and trusted his thousand to one who might keep it and make no return! A touch of envy mingled with Pleasant's admiration and not for the first time he felt that there was little freedom in his lot. Yonder man lived, but he in his shanty was like a corpse in the lich gate.

CHAPTER 4

HE WAITED only to see the two Mexicans, get their report of the happenings on the farm during his absence, and call for two horses. They brought him what he asked for, a ten-year-old mare, a seasoned traveler and like the wind for a short burst, together with a white-stockinged gelding that went a bit lame in the morning but could gallop the rest of the day. His pack was quickly made, and then with the meridional sun at his back, he went north towards Black Mountain.

He camped that night at the foot of the range, a tired man, but well ahead of his schedule. He was glad of that, for it gave him time to sleep himself out that night, and all of the next day he had before him to let the horses rest and graze while he wandered slowly up the grades, pausing at every prominent place to scan the surrounding country with his glass before he went on.

So he slept that night, seeing the broad, bright face of the Nile star in the heavens as he closed his eyes. In the gray of the morning he was up again. He made a small fire with care, taking only the dryest of twigs so that there might be a flame with no smoke. On that fire he made coffee; hardtack and dried figs were his food; and when he had finished eating he took pains to destroy every vestige of the blackened site of the fire.

The horses had done well. They had grazed on good bunch grass, than which no fodder is more nutritious except grain itself; and they were keen for whatever work lay before them.

There was little labor for them that day. What he wanted was a pair of fresh animals for the possible danger of the night; therefore he went on foot, leading the horses slowly on from ridge to ridge as he approached Black Mountain. There was good reason for its name; it stood like a dusky shadow among the sunlit peaks, bare-headed, gloomy, and seeming alone in spite of much noble company. Pleasant stalked it like an enemy, keeping careful ward on every hand, but in spite of himself he could not mark a sign of man or horse. There were only a few old cattle trails, made during the August heats when enterprising cowmen pushed their stock up into the heights where they would find not much grass, to be sure, but coolness of night, shade by day, and plenty of the best of pure water.

Those old trails he searched with careful eyes but could not read any new sign upon them. For his own part, he avoided going along them, but picked his way instead over the roughest rock-faces where the shod hoofs of his pair would leave no marks, however slight.

Before evening, he had run a loop around the mountain and fairly assured himself that Long Tom's expectations of danger must be wrong. Then, when the dusk began, he wound slowly up towards the height.

He had measured every inch of the landscape. He knew, to the north and south and east and west, what made the best terrain for swift flight in case of an emergency; his guns were cleaned and loaded; and he was prepared even against the danger he did not expect.

He reached the top and found that he had climbed into the last of the afterglow. All the valleys below him were pooled with thick darkness, but the final glow covered the tall peaks that went up on all sides of him like spear-points raised above a shadowy army. It was a grave sight, which might have suggested strange thoughts to a more philosophical mind; but Pleasant Jim took more notice of his immediate surroundings, picking out a stretch of good grass just below the summit where the horses could graze during the night, and then taking note of a circle of old stones upon the very crest. Perhaps it was the remains of an impromptu fort built here by Indians in ancient times. He was more sure of that when he found the half-buried shard of an olla within the circle.

The discovery pleased him; it gave him a weird sense of companionship upon the bleak height, and he set about cheerfully gathering the materials for a bonfire among the brush which grew on every hand brush large enough, he noted grimly, to mask the cautious approach of twenty men if they cared to steal up the height.

When he had seen these things, and stacked up his pile to a

considerable size, he waited a little longer. Night thickened gradually, stirred up from below, and the keen stars pressed lower in the heavens. It was complete dark, at last, and when that time had come, he lighted the fire and stood back among the brush to watch the conflagration.

He had put on much green foliage; the result was at first a heavy smudge rolling straight upward through the windless sky, but presently the heat grew greater, a yellow point appeared in the center of the brush pile, and finally a strong head of flame leaped up, died and rose again, and then with a roar raised a twenty-foot arm of crimson high above Black Mountain.

The big man watched this display with much satisfaction and smiled as the brush crackled. So furiously did it burn that little twigs and then skeleton fragments of the bushes soared upward and fell down slowly after the sparks which had accompanied them died in the black air above.

If a signal were waited for, such a column of terror as this could not fail to be seen from any of the neighboring summits. But though Pleasant swept all sides of the mountains near by with a ceaseless vigilance, he discovered not so much as one glimmer of answering light. So he took a quantity of rocks and sand which he had prepared beforehand and flung them on the core of the fire. For he had done enough to show friends that he was there. Why should he make a greater disturbance, which might attract any curious eyes besides those for whom it was intended?

The fire smoked and fumed for some time. He had to stamp over some of the embers and beat out others, but in a very few seconds the light was gone, and the density of darkness seemed now doubly great. Even the stars had nearly disappeared, and only by degrees they began to shine once more for his dazzled eyes.

After that, by turns he watched the mountains and harked and peered down the slopes of the Black Peak; but there was not the slightest token either of signal from beyond the valleys or of any approach towards him.

He was by no means without suspicions, and peering down into the hollows, he felt that danger lay covert there, as a trout lies in the shadows of the pool, waiting for a fly to fleck the surface of the water.

However, there was nothing further for him to do. And since it was foolish to waste sleeping hours, he prepared for bed, making down his blankets on the edge of the small pasture where he had left the horses. He did that for two reasons. One was that there was danger, otherwise, that wild animals might stampede his mounts; the second was that in case some human tried to stalk him the beasts were apt to alarm him in time to allow him to defend himself and them. It had turned bitterly cold, with a rising wind cutting across from the loftier snow summits, so he took a noggin of brandy to warm his blood, then rolled in his blankets and was instantly asleep.

The first sign of light wakened him, as usual, for he was trained in the observance of day and night like any bird of prey. He washed his face and methodically shaved in a little spring head which had been bubbling gently beside him all the night. After that, he scrubbed a pair of extra woolen socks with a bit of yellow laundry soap, washed out a bandanna and a suit of underwear, and so prepared himself for the day with what would have seemed to most frontiersmen a most finicky waste of time and labor.

After this, he made his breakfast fire with all due care and finished off a brief meal, covering the traces of the little fire with all of the precautions which he had used before. That done, it occurred to him that the two horses might not be concealed sufficiently by the shrubbery and the low trees among which he had tied them for the day. With his own strong glasses he could study many small traces and trees upon the faces of the neighboring slopes, and it appeared likely that the horses could be seen by a similar survey.

He conducted them deeper into the woods, therefore, and when he had done that, he went back to the summit, moving as cautiously as if rifles, and not merely field glasses, might be picking him off from one of the near-by heights. There on the top, he continued to scan all of the landscape around him.

All was crystal clear. The wind had fallen away again, as it had done in the early evening. There was not a trace of dust and there was not a breath of mist, not so much as would have stained the face of a mirror. So he could see ten thousand details with his naked eye, but he preferred to study the important points with the glass. It was a lesson in patience to watch him probing every suspicious patch of shadow which might be a cave mouth, and every oddly shaped bowlder. Once his heart leaped into his mouth, for he indubitably saw something stir on the shoulder far down a southern peak. Yet when he fixed the glass upon the spot, he could make out that it was no more than a deer, walking, and then trotting softly out of sight among the stones.

He waited to make sure that the creature had not been moving because danger was coming behind it, but nothing more came in sight for a full quarter of an hour, and he relaxed his vigilance in that direction.

Still he was by no means at rest, for a twitching of the nerves and a peculiar keenness in his senses and a vague shadow of fear continually disturbed him, like the pressure of another mind upon his own. He was no believer in metapsychosis, but he told himself that all was not well.

And at length, turning his attention from the distance to the summit on which he stood, he found first-hand evidence that danger actually was around him. For in a patch of soft earth at the very edge of a rock, he saw the distinct outline of a shoe heel and sole   and such a shoe as he himself never had worn in all his days.

CHAPTER 5

PLEASANT was no typical cowpuncher. Above all, he refused to crowd his feet into the narrow-toed and high-heeled boots which may hold a stirrup well enough but which leave one floundering on dry land like some foolish amphibian. He searched hastily for more signs, but he who had made that impression had done the rest of his walking with the greatest of care upon the rocks, so that no spoor remained. It was possible that the footmark might have been made days and days before, preserved there in the softness of the ground. Pleasant dropped on his knees and pored over the imprint. However, he could see the small, wiry grasses, some no larger than a dowl, gradually rising themselves a small, stealthy movement, yet it told him what he wanted to know: that the man who trod there had been on the mountain surely during the night!

Perhaps he was still here, lurking behind the rocks, hidden in the brush; perhaps he had gone down to warn his companions that Black Mountain was occupied; perhaps at this moment he was in the act of stealing the two horses! In a panic, Pleasant hurried to them and breathed more easily as he stood between them, glaring about at every shadow; and whatever fear was in him was accented by the idle curiosity of the horses, lifting their heads and nudging him with their soft muzzles.

He picked up a saddle, and slowly equipped each of the horses for the trail, fighting out his own problem as he did so. But he could see no purpose in immediate flight. If hostile eyes were watching the summit, what could be easier than for them to spot him if he tried to get down with two horses? So he decided to wait for night, which would give him another chance at the signal sending—and the earning of the thousand.

It was a mortally long and weary day; his rifle was never out of his hand while he gathered the second pile of brush, making it even larger than the first; and every time a branch crackled in his hands, he paused to listen and to watch.

The dull eternity of the afternoon went by at last and his heart began to return with the dusk. As the shadows deepened, he strained his eyes the more through his glass, for with the coming of evening his enemies, whoever they might be, were more apt to show themselves. All the side of Black Mountain which he could view he scanned, and studied to blindness the hollows at its base with never a sign of man or horse.

So the darkness grew and once more he was standing in the rose of the afterglow in an upper world above the flat fields of the night. Again he kindled the fire, taking care, this time, to apply the match to a section of dry leaves and twigs; his reward was an instant up-burst of flame and in a few moments the shaking arm of red was brandishing above Black Mountain. It was at its very height when an eye of crimson looked at him across the valley from a lower peak—one that he had noted before as being no rock-mass but rather a great cromlech of piled stones. That winking point of light towered presently into a bonfire, and the moment he was sure of it, Pleasant flung on his own blaze a few large rocks and then a tarpaulin loaded with pebbles and carefully gathered sand. His blaze was not extinguished save at one side, but into the sand he thrust the little metal matchsafe and then sprang back to the heads of his horses.

He had kept them behind a bowlder so that when he retreated to them he would be in shadow from his fire, and here he waited a moment, his heart beating fast. All below him the slope was regularly studded with big rocks like the crenelated top of a wall, and through one of the embrasures he now saw a shadowy form moving swiftly upward. Another shadow appeared beyond a second opening between the great stones, and Pleasant could guess that he had not seen all of the party. Leading the horses, he hurried to the farther side of the peak and there he saw nothing immediately beneath him. It was the roughest and least practicable way down the slope, but he knew that he must go that way. So he sprang into the saddle on the mare. She had the quick, sure footing that was most useful for such work as this. The gelding he cast loose, well knowing that that good natured and faithful animal would follow him unless a bullet stopped it.

Then, not twenty yards behind him, he heard the rolling of a

rock and a stifled curse. That was his signal. The least touch of
the spur sent the good mare forward and he urged her like a
bounding stone, headlong down the steep slope.

No men on that side? She had not made three strides when
two voices shouted at him from a clump of shrubbery to halt.
For answer, to unsettle their aim, he tried a snapshot above their
heads and in return two rifles clanged.

He heard not even the whistle of the bullets; the mare did not
wince, and by that he knew that he had gone by unscathed.

No men on that side?

He heard a half dozen they seemed a half hundred to
Pleasant as a crescent fear mastered him shouting to one
another: "It's Long Tom Rizdal! This way! Shoot, shoot, for
God's sake! Watch for him, you below!"

So they yelled. From behind rocks and bushes the odd
shadows leaped out and rifles swung in a long gleam to their
shoulders. But they had only the night to shoot by, and they were
firing at a target that moved downward like an avalanche. As
well be crushed in the jaws of rock as in the jaws of the law, it
seemed to Pleasant; moreover, the mare had gained such
momentum that it seemed impossible to stop her. She darted
through a broken maze of bowlders and brush, grazing death a
score of times, and so came to a long plunge of stone rubble and
gravel. Sitting well back on her haunches, she tobogganed down
the fall; and at the bottom of it the gelding with a snort of fear
shot past them, staggered as he reached more level going, and
then tumbled head over heels. He was up again like a cat, and
galloping at the side of the mare across the lower reaches of
Black Mountain; all of the noise was far behind them, and it
came from men on foot!

So Pleasant rated the mare at an easy canter. They had
descended the upper parapet of the mountain—when he looked
back it seemed a sheer wall and they were dropping more
gradually now into the hollow of the valley. Danger, no doubt,
was safely distanced, but if enemies lay before him they now
would have something better than starlight to shoot by, for a
treacherous moon now stood up on the shoulder of an eastern
peak and turned the valley pale. It was an open stretch, only
cross-hatched by low-lying streaks of brush. The slope was not
sharp and Pleasant made the grade easier by running quartering
down it towards the bottom of the valley; the footing was good;

and the mare ran kindly with the gelding high-headed beside her, apparently none the worse for his fall.

Nevertheless, Pleasant checked her, and sitting still in the saddle he cupped his ear against the wind and listened. The rabbit is a foolish creature, but it knows that the hearing often may be trusted beyond the sight; Pleasant had learned this trick from the cotton-tail and now his caution quickly rewarded him, for straight before him, muffled as they came up the wind, he heard the dull beating of hoofs.

He twitched the mare about and barely had started her north when half a dozen riders bent around the foot of Black Mountain in single file and came pouring after him. A full gallop could not drop them; glancing over his shoulder he saw them gaining, so he settled the mare into a racing stride. With flattened ears she steadied to her work; the gelding, despite his empty saddle, was jerked away to the rear, and for a full mile they flew before Pleasant looked back again and chuckled grimly when he saw the gap he had opened.

But he kept her at her labor until her head began to come up and the gelding drew alongside once more. Then—he had practiced it many a time—he changed to the saddle of his spare horse.

Two horses are better than one. The posse rode gallantly and well, regardless of broken ground, tearing thorns, and dangerous, sharp-edged rocks that reached for them on either side; but they failed behind the good gelding. He was warmed and ready, by this time, and in half an hour up the hard grade of White's Ravine he left the pursuit out of hearing, out of sight. Pleasant began to take the worst uppitches at a walk; he knew that he was saved. And whether or not the six threw up their work on the spot or toiled vainly in his rear, he had no further sight of them.

All night he headed steadily through the lower valleys and into the foothills. There, at dawn, he made camp, slept for three hours, and took up the trail again. In the dusk of that evening he made the head of Fisher's Valley, and so came to his own lower gate. The weary horses pricked their ears, and with a lighter step they climbed the last path. Before the barn Pleasant dismounted, unsaddled, and then stood awhile smoking a cigarette and looking genially forth upon the world. The sky was a dark blue bowl touched with points of gold, and nowhere within the lips of that broad grail, he felt, was there a happier man than he.

He listened to the eager munching of the tired horses as they fell to upon their oats, grinding their teeth down against the bottom of the feed box. Above his head a bat with staggering flight followed the swarming insects. Even for the flittermouse there was a place and a need in this best of all possible worlds.

And a thousand from twenty-five hundred left fifteen hundred to go!

Well, that was only a step, and once the debt was raised, he promised himself a little ease and pleasure instead of endless labor, endless thought; he could trust himself in a poker game now and again, perhaps; he could grant himself the joy of drawing the plans, at least, of the new and big house; he could start work upon the valley road, now so full of bogs and pitches; and he could buy that pair of pearl-handled guns in the window of Cross-Thomas & Hardy's store!

He felt very tired; he felt the honest satisfaction that only comes with weariness and labor well ended, and so he walked slowly towards his shanty with no shadow whatever upon his conscience.

CHAPTER 6

THE following morning, he sent in Pedro with the thousand dollars to the bank. He knew that Pedro loved money and that a thousand dollars would be to him as a million to another, but he also knew that Pedro feared his master more utterly than he feared death. He merely scribbled a note to send along, a note to the great banker saying that he wished to have this coin deposited not in his drawing account but against the mortgage. In the meantime, he had other work at hand on the ranch, requiring his presence, and having been away from active labor for such a long time, he was hungry to fill his hands. It is one thing to labor for hire; it is another to be occupied with one's own possessions, renewing this, creating another, whether it be a broken fence or a new manger. So, from a cloud of dust of his own raising within the barn, he looked up from no jerry-built manger which he was completing and saw that he had guests two at the rear door of the barn, and another couple striding down towards him.

Suddenly Pleasant leaped out of the manger and sat on the edge of it, alert. One of those visitors was Sam Lee, Federal Marshal for the district!

"Well, Sam," said he, "what are you trailing through my diggings?"

Sam Lee was a little man, rather withered, ever smiling; one never caught him with a serious expression, so that to some people his smile seemed a grimace.

He came at his meaning, wherever possible, by dint of many circumlocutions and he was so almost femininely gentle that strangers were apt to despise him. Pleasant never could make a mistake like that but once—it was after his old bunkie, Dill Peters, was arrested for running guns into Mexico he had stood in the street of Fisher Falls and damned Federal Marshal Sam Lee and all his kin for ages back and dared the marshal to step out into the street and begged him to come with rifle, shotgun, or revolver, he cared not which. Sam Lee had not stepped forth; he never sought quarrels; he merely accepted them in the line of his work, and when some fool asked him why he did not face Pleasant: "Because I'm afraid, of course," said the marshal with his smile.

That speech and that answer had been repeated to Pleasant, and he was well aware that the marshal did not love him; which was now his reason for bringing himself on guard with such abruptness out of the manger.

"I'm a mortal weary man, Jim," said the marshal, pausing to pass a red and white bandanna across his forehead. "I'm dragged back and forth across the country the way you wouldn't work a dog, and I'm going to quit, I am. I ain't gonna stand it no longer."

"Sit down and rest your feet," suggested Pleasant, not a whit off guard. "You boys sit down, too."

The two from the rear door had sauntered inwards and now were joining the marshal. They were exactly the type that Sam Lee loved to use, low-bred, black-browed fellows, rejoicing in the terror they inspired, and hating those who feared them not.

Sam Lee accepted the invitation with a grateful wave of the hand; but the other three did not stir. Their gloomy eyes remained fixed upon the rancher with the never filled hunger of kestrels. Fear began to grow stronger in Pleasant Jim but he maintained his insouciant air. Besides, even if there were four of them, he wore two guns; he could use them both; and every man of these knew his skill.

"And what you been doing, Sam?" he asked, as Lee settled himself on the barley bin.

The marshal sighed and shook his head, which thrust forward on his skinny neck as his back slumped into a curve of weak relaxation. He looked more like a bird than like a man; or if a man, more a beggar than an important and well-paid official. For he was famously ill-garbed and careless of his clothes. It was said that one suit had lasted the hard-riding little man a full ten years and the garments he wore now looked the part for the kirkah or no dervish ever was more full of patches.

"I been chasing, and chasing," said the marshal, "and I got

nothing to show for it. Riding my head off after ghosts, you might say. I kind of think I'm getting old!"

"Chasing what?"

"At Black Mountain," said the sheriff　was it possible that he brought out the words rather more quickly and sharply?　"I was trying to run down a job!"

Pleasant Jim rolled a cigarette, but his eyes never left the face of the marshal. He nodded with interest.

"That's rough country," said he. "What sort of a job?"

"The worst kind," said the officer gravely. "Someone hooked up with that snaky devil, Tom Rizdal, that smart, gun-running hound! I went for a man, but all that I got was this!"

And he took from his pocket a small, metal matchbox and showed it; opened it, and shook the matches out into his hand. Then his bird-like eyes flashed up at the face of Pleasant Jim.

He could see the latter only through a cloud of smoke, that moment puffed forth.

"Maybe you can find the gent that owned it," said Pleasant. "That ought to be a clew to a smart fellow like you, Sam."

"The gent that owned it? Oh, Rizdal owned it, of course. And what good are clews so far as he goes?" went on Sam Lee with much bitterness. "He's a ghost; fades out into solid stone, you might say; got his friends salted away in every corner of the hills; fellows that would sell their skins for him; Chuck, here, was one of them, till I showed him the light."

He hooked a thumb at one of the three black-browed men, and the rascal grinned sourly.

"Well," said Jim, "I don't suppose that matches tell much of a yarn, at that."

"Don't you?" murmured the marshal. "No, you wouldn't　a good, square, honest, law-abidin' fellow like you wouldn't think much of 'em, Pleasant, but me, I been forced to be suspicious of everything, y'understand? So I put these matches under a glass and what do you think I seen?"

Jim was frozen with interest.

"Little pricks all running down the sides of 'em. Telegraphic letters, you see; and arranged in code; maybe ten words on one of those little matches. Well, well, the tricks that the crooks are up to!"

He shook his head in sad wonder; and Pleasant Jim swallowed hard.

"We pelted after him that left this matchbox on the top of Black Mountain," continued the sheriff, "but he skinned right away from us. He had two horses, and none of us had more'n one. Right through the hands of about twelve men he slipped, and then walked away and thumbed his nose at six of us that tried to bag him down in the valley. It was a good trick, eh? Enough to make the reputation of any—crook. And the way those horses of his ran was a caution. I never hope to see their like again—unless it was right here on your fine hoss-ranch, Pleasant!"

The blow came quickly and sharply home, but Pleasant Jim stirred not a muscle of his face. In the little pause that followed he felt their four pairs of eyes upon him, and the wind blew sweetly in to them the fragrance of the jessamine that grew at the corner of the corral fence.

"Yes, I'd like to match any pair that runs in these parts," observed Pleasant Jim. "You had a hard ride, Sam?"

"When I see him going like a bird, I just pulled up and knew that the game had gone bust. Back I comes to Fisher Falls with nothin' but a matchbox to show for the work of nigh twenty men for two days; and no sooner back in Fisher Falls than I get more work to do. A different kind. I go past Mr. Tucker, the cashier of the bank; he's setting under the marquee on his front porch during the noon hour. And he says: 'What you think of this?' and he handed me a little envelope. This here one."

Sam Lee took the envelope, accordingly, from his pocket, and from it he took a little sheaf of greenbacks—even at the distance Pleasant could see the corner figures—one hundred dollars. His throat became exceedingly dry; he could not help measuring the distance to the door, and now he noticed that the three deputies had arranged themselves with care so that they blocked his way to either exit.

"This here money," said Sam Lee, "looks good, it feels good, and it's printed with a lot of care, but the trouble is that it's queer, y'understand? And I come out here to ask you where you got it, Pleasant."

There was not even a rising inflection of the voice as he asked that question, but the shock to the other was just as great.

"Is that my money?" he asked hoarsely. "Lemme see!"

"It's your money," said the marshal softly. "There ain't any doubt about that, because as soon as the cashier seen it, he labeled it quick and put it right back into the sealed envelope that you'd sent it in. There couldn't be any doubt about that. And so the main thing is just to find out where you got this coin? What horses have you been selling lately, Pleasant?"

Pleasant Jim raked his invention. Absurd fancies leaped into his mind. He would say that it was paid to him for an old debt; he would say that he had received it through the mail; he would say well, he would say anything rather than that he had taken this money for work performed at the bidding of famous Tom Rizdal. The marshal, having finished his own jeremiad, waited.

He said quietly: "Think it over; let's have the real facts, Pleasant."

"Matter of fact," said Pleasant Jim, "that money came to me through the mail."

"When?"

"There was a batch waiting for me when I got back from the Charlie Rizdal trail."

"A fine, proud job you done on that trail," said the marshal. "Well, it come while you was away? Maybe you saved the letter that it come in?"

"No."

"An old debt, I guess?" said the sympathetic marshal.

"Yes."

"Lucky devil!" sighed Sam Lee. "I would wish to be picking a thousand out of the mail, some day. But I got to wait and work for my coin!"

The voice of the marshal was almost lachrymose. "What was the money owned you for?"

"Oh, a couple of horses that I sold a while back."

"Two?"

"Yes."

"They must of been bang up fine ones for that price! Eh? Which ones was they? I've known most of your stock since you set up. Ah, it was that pair of bays that you sold two years back to..."

"No," said Pleasant Jim.

"No? Lemme think! Five hundred apiece! Who did you make the sale to, Pleasant?"

"A gent that was passing through; stranger."

"Hello! You give a stranger a couple of fine horses on trust? You're a believin' man when it comes to human nature, Jim. I got to say that!"

So spoke the marshal, gently, but the three assistants grinned widely, their evil thoughts printed plainly upon their faces.

"No, I didn't trust him. He gave me a deposit, y'understand?"

He felt that he was being cornered, but still he was bound to fight well and valiantly.

"Ah, he'd paid some money beforehand. And now a thousand more—and for two horses!"

Pleasant suddenly began to sweat. He felt that the perspiration betrayed him, but he could not prevent it from rolling down his forehead without wiping his brow with his handkerchief.

"Ay, it's a hot place—this here barn!" said the marshal.

"It wasn't money that he left me. He left me a ring. You see? That was my security. I was to keep it a year, and if he didn't send the money by that time—"

"Was it a year ago that he passed through?"

"Yes. About."

"Along about this time of the year?"

"Yes."

"I thought you said it was two years ago this happened? Sort of seemed to me that you said two, but no matter. It takes a good ring to be worth a thousand, don't it?"

"Sure. This here was a ruby and a grand big one."

"I'd like to have a look at it," said the marshal.

"Can't show it to you."

"You can't. But why not?"

"I sent it away, you see."

"Ah?"

"Yes, sent it away after I got the money."

The marshal nodded in perfect agreement. "Wouldn't want to have a valuable thing like that lying around loose, of course. What sort of a looking fellow was this one?"

"Dark-haired fellow. Very black looking. I suspect Mexican blood. Looked a good deal like Chuck, there."

He could not help sharing his own misery with another, and under this thrust Chuck started and cursed.

"I'll have you know—" he began.

"Pipe down! Pipe down!" said Pleasant Jim smoothly. "I hate loud talk, young man!"

"You, Chuck, shut your face," said the marshal peremptorily. "You'll be getting yourself accused of suicide, one of these days, if you start in picking fights with men like Pleasant. Doggone me, Jim, if it ain't a shame the way that these kids will shoot off their faces! Now, let's hear some more about the crook that beat you, if you don't mind. Because beat you he has, and trimmed you right out of a thousand dollars. Kind of makes a fellow squirm just to think of it. But you got an iron nerve, old man, and you take your beatings without whining. You remember his name?"

It was jeopardous work; but Pleasant felt that the trail was turning away from him and towards his man of fiction. He went on agreeably enough, his heart warming with his imagination: "Bentley was his name. J. H. Bentley, I think. And his address was some place in Brooklyn; 917 Fourth Avenue, Brooklyn. No, maybe that street address is wrong. I got no head for figures. Maybe I got his address in my note book, though."

"Most likely you have," agreed the marshal. "I'll tell you what, Pleasant, with your help we're going to run down this dirty pusher of the queer! And I hate a counterfeiter worse than I hate any snake! Let's get down again to what he looked like. Middle aged, you said?"

"Yes."

"And gray hair."

"Yes," answered Pleasant.

There was a loud, snarling laugh from Chuck, and Pleasant looked across at the deputy with an eye as cold as iron.

"He looked like me, a minute ago," said Chuck, "and now he's middle aged and got gray hair."

"By jiminy," murmured Sam Lee, "that's right."

He slipped from the barley box.

"I'm afraid you'll have to explain that to the judge, Pleasant. Mind you, now, you'll probably come out of this, all right; but I'll have to take you in and let you see the judge. And in the meantime, I got to ask you for your guns. It's my duty!"

Had Sam Lee turned into a bristling *loup-garou* at that moment, he could not have seemed a more disgusting or astonishing spectacle to Pleasant.

"Don't draw, boys!" snapped Lee. "Pleasant ain't going to be a fool; he knows that four agin one is too much odds. Besides, he ain't any crook. I know that you just been bamboozled in this counterfeit deal, old son. Just lemme have those guns, will you?"

CHAPTER 7

So Jim Pleasant went to jail. He had a man on either side of him, and two men behind him, and in this fashion they walked their horses down the main street of Fisher Falls.

"Kind of making a little show of me, ain't you?" said Pleasant to the marshal.

Sam Lee turned his head and blinked a little, for the eye of Pleasant Jim, at certain times, was not as kindly as his name.

"Why, Pleasant," said he, "the jail is on this street, ain't it? I could of taken you around the back way, though. Doggone me for not thinking of it! No malice, Jim!"

But malice there was, Pleasant could not help feeling, and he lodged the grudge deep in his heart, where such matters never were forgotten. On either side he had spectators. The blacksmith and both his apprentices ran out, hammer or tongs in hand, to view the procession; Mr. Jackson, the grocer, came to his door with his hands white with flour, and gaped widely, his innocent face turning pale; and trailing behind them, and then running ahead, six, a dozen, twenty boys and girls scampered, shouting, calling, pointing.

Dull red began to rise in the face of Pleasant Jim, and he sat straighter in his saddle; for he felt a weight settling upon him as the ox-bow settles over the neck of the ox. Not faces only, but words were spoken which he never would forget. Men, he thanked his proud gods, dared not say them, but the women found their tongues readily enough, calling to one another from their doorsteps:

"It takes a thief to catch a thief!"

"I knew no good never would come out of him. No good never comes out of a killer!"

He turned grimly to the marshal.

"Did you hear that?"

"Don't you mind 'em, Jim. They think you're down. But you ain't. You been a little careless; that's all. And when you're out, they'll grin at you again."

"They called me a killer. Why, I never killed a man in my life!"

"No?" said the marshal, raising his eyebrows. "I was thinking about the three half breeds that came down from Fort Mason to hunt you—that was five years back, wasn't it?"

"Half breeds!" sneered Pleasant.

"And the Mexicans that cornered you in Phoenix?"

"Maybe you could find a nigger or two to add to the list," said Pleasant angrily, "but I'm talking about white men, Sam! I never killed one in my life!"

"Now, that's a true thing," said the marshal. "Mighty true. There is some that shoot straight enough to kill; but there is some that shoot so much straighter that they don't have to kill. And I wonder, Pleasant, how many fellows you've dropped with a slug through the shoulder or the hip? Yes, sir, that straight shooting of yours has saved many a man his life! Take young Charlie Rizdal, for instance!"

To this the prisoner made no answer, for he suspected that there was more than a touch of irony in the speeches of the marshal. They came before the jail, and over the door, upon the eaves, a maize bird sat, tiling in the wind and eyeing Pleasant Jim, as he thought, like a little red-stained spirit of darkness.

He held back at the door for an instant; but the three deputies closed up instantly behind him; the jailer was standing before him, grinning broadly, and trying to mask his malice behind an insufficient hand. He was too close to the trap and he must enter.

He stood in a little room and had to answer questions: "What was his full name? Where was he born? When was he born? What was his occupation? Had he ever been in jail before and if so for what offence?"

"Hell, Danny," said he to the jailer, "you can answer all those questions about as good as I can. Why do you ask 'em?"

"Matter of form," said the other. "I dunno; I'd get fired if I didn't do it this way."

Pleasant answered grudgingly, for he had an increasing desire to make trouble; but now he was to be searched, and a thorough job they made of it, going through every stitch of his clothes, taking away his knife, his wallet, even his comb.

"It's made of steel," said the jailer in explanation.

"You hound!" exploded Pleasant. "I'll make you sweat for this!"

"Will you?" sneered the other. He stepped up close and looked his prisoner closely in the eye. "You'll sing smaller before you get out of this," he suggested.

For the first time, Pleasant was thoroughly frightened, for since he came to manhood all men in this district had known and feared him; this jailer, for instance, would sooner have twitched the beard of a lion than badgered Jim Pleasant the day before. But now the jailer was something more; he was magnified by the power of the law which lay like a shadow behind him, and out of the excess of that power, he could afford to sneer at his new prisoner.

CHAPTER 8

THE marshal explained that Pleasant must be lodged not alone, but in a cell with some other prisoner. "I've got a full house, here," he explained. "The sheriff, he's doing quite a business himself, and by the time that I've got through bringing in my free boarders, why, it sort of crowds things. But I'll see that you're fixed up with a good, clean, decent, up-standin' sort of a gent for a cell-mate."

"You're going to shove me into a cell, are you, without letting me talk to the judge and have a hearing?" asked Pleasant, his heart swelling with helpless indignation.

The marshal was full of sympathy.

"I'd like to do it," he explained. "I know just how you feel. Understand exactly! But you don't know the way that the judge is. Everything has to be regular with him; suppose that I went to him and asked him to see you now. 'Is court open? Is this the proper time to bring a man into court? Don't talk like a fool, Marshal Lee!' He has a tongue that a man won't forget in a hurry, Pleasant! I hope you never have to have a taste of it the way that I have!"

The lambent whimsicality of the marshal had no ending; and Pleasant felt that it was useless to try to bring him to a truly serious consciousness.

"Here's a place for him," the marshal was saying. "Here's a man in your jail that's as clean, up-standing, and intelligent as you've ever had here, I suppose. And the best of it is that Pleasant knows him already!"

He had paused before the barred door behind which sat none other than Charlie Rizdal.

"You're going to put me in here?" asked Pleasant, grimly.

"You wouldn't want to be put in with some dirty hobo, would

43

you?" asked Sam Lee. "You wouldn't want that, old-timer, would you? No, you couldn't have a better cell-mate than Charlie Rizdal. Besides, Pleasant, of course it'll only be a day or two before you're out of this!"

Pleasant Jim said no more; he saw that argument was foolish, and now the door swung softly open upon oiled hinges and he had stepped inside. The marshal paused before him.

"If there's anything that I can do for you," he said, "let me know before I go and   "

"There's nothing," answered Pleasant bitterly.

"Hold on!" cried young Rizdal. "Are you going to keep me here with this damned bloodsucker and head-hunter? If you do, by God, I'll throttle him, one of these nights!"

"Friendly, ain't they? Like a pair of Kilkenny cats!" said the jailer, grinning in a broader self-content. "Marshal, you're a wonder!"

"Why, Charlie, I'm surprised at you," answered the marshal with a deprecatory gesture. "Would you want a finer fellow to swap yarns with than Jim Pleasant? Well, boys, so long. Best of luck to you!"

"Mark you me!" shouted Rizdal, leaping at the bars and shaking them furiously. "There'll be trouble out of this! There'll be damned bad trouble!"

The mocking laughter of the jailer floated back at him; Rizdal burst into a passion of cursing that raised a murmur of interest from the adjoining cells; and then, as though realizing that nothing could be gained by mere talk, he stopped abruptly, and turning towards his companion, who stood stiffly on the defensive, he winked broadly.

Pleasant, amazed, stared at him.

Rizdal continued in a loud voice: "Pleasant, it was you that landed me in this hell-hole; and I'll have your heart out for that little trick, one of these days. They've put us together, now. Well, you keep to that cot and that side of the room; and I'll keep to this; and if you cross the center line, by God, I'll tackle you! You understand?"

"I'm a peaceful man," said Pleasant through his teeth. "I don't hunt trouble. But when it comes my way I aim to use both hands on it; and if you raise a hand on me Rizdal, I'll break you open like a damned nut!"

A fury of anger had mastered him and his voice as he came to this conclusion; and he was more amazed than ever when, after his outburst, he saw Rizdal nod commendation and smile. The latter sat down on his cot and took from his pocket a little ivory trinket—the roughly worked shape of an ape, which he set up in the palm of his hand and admired for a moment.

When he spoke again, his voice was so carefully modulated that it could reach to his companion, but no farther.

"I knew the old juju would bring me luck before the finish," said he, "but I never guessed that they'd be fools enough to put the pair of us in one cell! Why, Pleasant, we'll crack out of this place almost any time that we want to, now that the two of us are together!"

He added: "But play up, for God's sake. The minute they guess we're pals, they'll separate us. But while they think we want to kill each other, they'll figure that we don't need any guard more than one another. Sam Lee is smart, but here's a trick that he's missed!"

The pleasure of Rizdal was so great that he sat back against the wall of the cell and almost closed his eyes with silent laughter. But his meaning was clear to Pleasant. He answered gravely and softly: "It's all right, Charlie. I'd never stand in your way, but it's not my game to break jail; I couldn't stand outlawry."

"Wait till they're through with you," said Rizdal calmly. "You'll get a new idea!"

With that, he picked up a book which he had been reading, and opening it again, he went through the pages quite rapidly, and now and again he seemed to be making a covert notation with a pencil which he held. Pleasant, however, was tired, rather bewildered, and felt that he had been committed to a trail of which he had no knowledge. So, following his usual rule, he stretched himself on his cot, folded his powerful arms beneath his head, and fell instantly asleep. A rested brain is better than a fagged one, no matter what the emergency.

He dreamed that he was back on the farm again, breaking a colt and trying to make a mouth on it—a fiery, springing, wild-hearted devil of a two-year-old such as he loved to handle. Too much force and the youngster would have a mouth of brass; but just the requisite power and play combined would keep it sensitive and tender as velvet. He had a theory that thought runs down the reins from the hands of the man to the lips of his mount, and so from the human to the equine brain; accordingly, he broke every colt reverently, carefully, with pains and with love, so that the saying arose: "On a Pleasant Jim horse, a wish is as good as a Spanish bit!" But this animal in his dreams was like a winged spirit and a heart of mounting flame; struggle as he might he could not rein it; and a vague and vast sense of fear began to oppress him.

He was wakened by the loud voice of Charlie Rizdal, calling: "Hey, you!"

Pleasant Jim wakened with sweat on his brow, and turning his head, he was aware of Charlie at the barred door of the cell, talking to a girl who carried a bucket in one hand and a mop in the other.

It seemed strange to Pleasant that a woman should be allowed in a common jail, but after all, where would a man be found to do the drudgery of cleaning at any ordinary wage; and it was plain that this simple creature could not be offended or give offense. She had a white, rather round face, which possessed a certain prettiness of feature, but her hair was twisted into a tight knot, high on her head, her nose was pink as though from the effect of a perpetual cold in the head; and above all the eye was open, round, blank, unthinking. Never a colt had been foaled on the farm of Pleasant Jim, surely, with so little of spirit. There was scant trace of mind stuff in her; she was body and body alone.

Rizdal spoke to her in a tone of good-natured contempt: "This is a rotten book that you gave me," said he. "Nothing happens in it. Chuck it for me, will you? And here's a quarter. Pick up something that's got a little action, kid! What's your name, anyway?"

"Sally's my name."

"Hey, Sally!" bawled the voice of the jailer. "Ain't I told you not to talk to nobody in here? Come here, you fool!"

Pleasant Jim sat upright on his cot. He was no lover of the ladies, but a certain tone was not permissible when one addressed them, and now he looked down at his hard knuckles and thought of the broad, soft face of the jailer — a fighting man who had grown pulpy in easy jobs.

"Comin'!" called Sally.

"You poor sap!" shouted Charlie Rizdal. "D'you think I'm trying to make a crush on this cartoon? I just asked her to buy me a book. Here's the quarter I'm givin' her. Bite it and see if it's lead, will you?"

"Swallow your lip, Rizdal!" boomed the jailer. "All right, let her take the quarter. But she's likely to quit work if she sees that much money all in one piece."

"Now, Sally," said Rizdal, "don't forget."

"No, sir," said she.

"And if there's a nickel left over, buy yourself a ribbon or something."

"I seen a lovely one in the store for five cents," said Sally, and she rubbed the back of her hand across her nose and sniffed.

"Run along, kid. Your boss is calling you."

"Yes, sir," and away shuffled Sally, the heels of her over-large shoes trailing and scratching on the stone floor as she went.

Mr. Rizdal watched her going, and then he turned sharply on his cell-companion.

"She's our bet, old man," he said rather with his lips than with his voice. "Wait till the middle watch, and I'll tell you why!"

Pleasant smiled again. Never in his life had he seen a tool less likely to be of use for breaking from such a strongly modern jail as this.

CHAPTER 9

In the hush of the night, Pleasant wakened to a touch on his arm, and the whisper of Rizdal: "Listen, Jim. Are you awake?"

"I'm awake."

"I have the stuff here, now. That gem of a girl—that Sally she gave me the last installment to-day. I've got the layout complete—the saws, the oil, and all. Shall we start now, Jim?"

Pleasant sat up in the dark; his brain was spinning a little. The faint, sick odor of the jail oppressed his nostrils.

"To cut our way out?"

"What else?"

The thrill leaped down the veins of Pleasant, and he swung an arm through the darkness, like a sabreman making a moulinet.

"But wait a minute; no, I can't do it. It would be junking my life's work. My years on the farm would be chucked, and because of what? Because your brother crooked me with a dirty deal!"

"He'd give a hand to have the doing of that over again."

"How do you know what he'd give?"

"Old fellow, I hear from him every day, and he hears from me. The point is—you won't believe it of a man like Long Tom he didn't dream that the stuff was queer; it was passed on him by an old pal."

"Well," said Pleasant, thinking the matter over, "I'm inclined to believe that he wouldn't have played the sneak like that. But I'll pull out of this without jumping into outlawry."

"How? Will you go to prison?"

"Go to prison for what? For riding to Black Mountain and planting a matchsafe in some sand?"

"Pleasant, they know that you carried the safe; now they're trying to make out the code that was used on the matches; and in

48

any event, you can't make them feel that you haven't been deep with Long Tom."

"After my job with you, Charlie? Does that seem like being deep with him?"

"They figure it simply enough. They think that you're sore at me and deep with Tom. That might happen. But I'll tell you, they've written you down one of my brother's men, and you'll see a fiver, for this."

"You mean that they'd send me up for five years?"

"Or ten."

"By God, they can't! It's not justice!"

"They're looking for convictions, not for justice. And by the time that you got out of prison, what would be left of your farm?"

Pleasant, breathing hard, grasped the side of his cot and set his teeth.

"I'll wait and see it through," he declared at last.

"You're a crazy man, Jim."

"I can't chuck the place."

Rizdal was silent, after a time, and then his dim shadow rose and melted away in the darkness as he crossed the floor in his stockinged feet. And Pleasant found that his cot was shuddering like quake ooze beneath him; it was the tremor of his own body that caused the disturbance. He stood up, and mopped his wet forehead. Somewhere in the jail a prisoner was maundering in his sleep and now and again his voice rose to little mouse-like squeaks of terror, and aimless gibberings.

"That's little Pete Marley," murmured Rizdal, coming back to his cell-mate. "He did a stretch; and it broke his nerve. He was a regular rakehell in the old days, but he's nothing, now. Listen to him crying in his sleep, poor little rat! But prison ain't any sweet song, man."

Pleasant noticed that there was no further attempt at persuasion, and he could not help saying: "If you have the stuff for cutting through, go ahead. I won't make a noise about it."

"Old son," chuckled Rizdal, "Long Tom gave me my marching orders in the book that Sally brought to-day. I'm not to step out of this here jail unless I take you with me; that's his last word."

"How could he send a message in a book?"

"Little system of checking off the words. Very easy when you know the key. We're here together, and he says that he'll never stop working if it takes the rest of his life and every penny of his money until he's got you out of this mess."

He dwelt no longer on the subject, but Pleasant was touched. This was a sort of faith which he could understand.

So he asked about Sally, and it was a subject which seemed a favorite with his companion.

She was, according to Charlie Rizdal, the smartest woman in the entire universe, and of all the associates of Long Tom she was the most capable and the most trusted by her chief. He had sent her into Fisher Falls the instant that his brother was jailed there; and of her own devices she had managed the disguise which, so quickly, took her into the jail not for an occasional visit, but as a constant worker there.

Pleasant Jim remembered the white, round face, and the blank eyes, and he wondered, for he saw that he had come upon the verge of a world of new things. And deep into the dark of the morning his companion talked, picking out details, painting them with skill and devising before the imagination of Pleasant an existence where joy was merely deliciously spiced with danger, and where all one's chosen companions were true to the death; where there was no labor but play; where the good deed of to-day was never forgotten to-morrow; where men stood to men as brothers.

"Put on quarter boots, Charlie," said the listener, at length. "You're overreaching yourself a little."

"All right, Jim," replied the other. "You'll see that I haven't lied. You'll see when you're one of us."

And as Rizdal went away, Pleasant said gravely to himself that that day never should come. Somehow there was justice in the law; and if he had made one vital error in serving the will of a notorious outlaw, had he not paid enough for the single slip? And had he not been sorely tempted for the mere bearing of a trinket to a mountain top?

The first stroke was not delayed beyond the next day. First, on that day he asked to see the judge and was told that the "old man" had a full day. Secondly, he received a little message from bank president Lewis Fisher, a courteous little note, but one which drove home its point with much precision. Mr. Fisher had come upon evil days, said the note, and he was forced to protect important interests by calling in every outstanding loan. Among the rest, he was sorry he had to ask for Pleasant's twenty-five hundred, still outstanding. Of course Pleasant would have no difficulty in raising the money on such a fine property as was his; and Mr. Fisher would not press at once for payment. He would allow three days of grace!

In the meantime, he was sorry to hear of the plight of his young friend, but he knew that Jim Pleasant was far too much a man to have been beguiled into any dealings with that human viper, Tom Rizdal.

So all would come out well in the end.

And was there anything he could do to serve Mr. Pleasant during his confinement?

That letter slipped from the numb fingers of Pleasant and whisked across the floor to Rizdal, who made no pretense of not reading it as he picked it up. Having glanced through the contents, he nodded.

"He'll have the farm in a week, then," said Charlie Rizdal.

"I dunno what you mean," murmured Pleasant. "But it looks queer. How *can* he need money? He's rich   his safe is full of cash securities all the time, as every one knows!"

"Of course it is," remarked the other, "but the old boy has a taste for horses, and of course he's glad not to have to pay for them."

The eye of Pleasant was utterly blank.

"You see, of course?"

"Not a damn thing!"

"Why, they'll foreclose on you, you see? Then they'll auction off everything that you've got!"

"I'd have their blood, if they dared. It's not possible, besides!"

"It's the law, partner!"

Pleasant groaned, but then he took new hope out of despair. "If they wiped out my work, still they'd have to leave me with a good deal of cash!"

"You'll probably get about twenty-five hundred   enough to pay Fisher's note."

"I see," chuckled Pleasant, greatly relieved. "But you don't understand. I was offered twenty thousand dollars flat, no longer than three months back, and I laughed in the face of old Grindle when he made the offer. Well, he'd bid the place up that high, at least. And then he'd have Young, and Chalmers. They would like my farm, too. You see, Rizdal?"

The latter paused to drum his fingers lightly on the edge of his cot.

"You ain't young," he explained to himself, "but just kind of

innocent. Why, son, if Fisher started bidding on that place of
yours, there ain't a wealthy man in the range that would dare to
bid against him."

"Will you tell me why?"

"Because it's understood. They keep their hands off when
Fisher goes after something, and then he keeps his hands off
when you've got a plum in the wind. So they play for each other.
He does the financing—at damned fat interest—and they all get
rich. Why, Jim, you didn't think that old Fisher got his coin
squarely, did you? He was a money-lender in St. Louis before he
came out here, for his health!"

It brought Pleasant to such a nervous tension that for eight
days he hardly slept, but walked ceaselessly up and down the cell
like an impatient tiger. And the rest of the time, he busily wrote
letters   wild appeals to this friend and to that. Ah, how bitterly
he wished, now, that he had invested a little more time in human
friends, and a little less in horses! For his bosom cronies and old
companions were far away, their addresses uncertain, and as for
the few he knew here in the valley, what one of them could
advance him twenty-five hundred dollars?

In the meantime, he was made to taste the first sting of the
law.

CHAPTER 10

HE often had passed the judge on the street; they had exchanged cheerful greetings; and he had looked upon the man of the law as rather a good-natured but weak person. On the morning of his examination he changed his mind. It was simply an informal test to discover whether or not the prisoner should remain in jail or be admitted to bail. For Pleasant there appeared a gray-headed lawyer who had dropped into the horizon of Fisher Falls from some far greater city. It was the work of the great Tom Rizdal, of course, which procured such a defender. He sat down with Pleasant and had the entire story straight from him; after which, he frowned sadly. In his opinion, he declared, what Pleasant needed was a fine and a sharp lecture; but he pointed out that it was apt to go very hard with him. In spite of that opinion, he defended Pleasant with vigor and with wonderful skill, but all was no good. The judge battered through all of the frail fences which the lawyer reared and brought down his remorseless finger upon certain disagreeable facts. The fugitive of Black Mountain looked like Pleasant, rode like Pleasant and upon just such horses; and Pleasant himself had been absent from his home, as the Mexican cowpuncher testified, at exactly that time. So much for that, but then there was the matter of the thousand dollars of bad money. Undoubtedly it looked as though Pleasant had allied himself with the famous forger, robber, and smuggler, and counterfeiter, Long Tom Rizdal, or at least the judge was determined that the prisoner should not slip through his fingers without a thorough trial. He fixed the bail at ten thousand; bail in that sum instantly was offered by the lawyer, but the judge calmly declared that he needed twenty thousand, and that if twenty thousand were brought, he would demand a hundred thousand. In a word, he intended to keep Pleasant in jail until the trial, which was illegal and unfair enough, but the judge was a veteran of the Western bar, which knows odd expedients and makes nearly as much law as it reads! And when Pleasant's lawyer raged and quoted authorities, book and page, the judge sat still and grinned like a mugger on Ganges bank.

"Young man!" said his defender to Pleasant afterwards, "unless I'm very much mistaken, you are in to catch hell for this little tangle."

That was not a cheerful speech, but the lawyer was so well paid and esteemed that he did not have to lie; but the second blow was far more serious than the first. It came not from the court but from the soft hand of Lewis Fisher, for all that Charlie Rizdal prophesied came to pass swiftly and surely, as though he had written out the course to which action must conform.

The news came in the form of a cheerful little note from Lewis Fisher:

"Dear Jim Pleasant,

"How regrettable it all is! Your place was auctioned off this morning and I'm sitting down at your own table this instant to tell you what happened. You will be as astonished as I to learn that although several people came to look on, there really was no bidding whatever. I think that the farm and everything on it would have gone for fifteen hundred. I didn't want the place myself, because as you must know, I don't want my hands encumbered with different kinds of business. However, I simply couldn't sit by and see your place sacrificed so utterly. It would have left you a thousand in my debt after losing your farm. Therefore I bid it in. What I'll do with it, I don't know. But as soon as you're out of your little difficulties of the present, no doubt you'll agree to manage the property for me. We could arrange a handsome salary, of course. Much more than the usual cowpuncher gets!

"Let me know when I may be of assistance, and believe my heartiest good wishes go with this note.

                              "Yours most sincerely,
                                        "LEWIS FISHER."

When Pleasant read the thing, he staggered like a horse that strikes poachy ground at full gallop. Then, turning his back sharply upon Rizdal, he went to the window and rested his elbows on the sill. The wall was thick, the window not over large, but through the checking of the bars, he could see a corner of the distant range, three noble heads of white and in the center something like a great shadow. It was Black Mountain again; it seemed to Pleasant Jim that there was something fatal in the very sight or the mere name of the peak.

"Poor devil," said a whisper at his door.

He turned his head in time to hear the rustle of a skirt, and knew that Sally had gone by; Charlie Rizdal was studying the floor; the whole world knew that he was a ruined man! So he stared back through the window again, loving Rizdal for his silence. For an hour he stood by the window, fighting himself, for the passion started somewhere in his heart and ran up into his brain in thin red lines of fire. He wanted to rush to the bars and see if he might not tear one of them down; once through and armed with such a weapon—The savage joy of the thought choked him.

But he kept fighting, for a voice inside his soul told him that madness was just around the corner or such things as these.

He began to set his hands hard and forced his thoughts away from the farm, for all those thoughts were madness-making. Anything else would do—the way the cottonwood shook in the wind, yonder, or the manner of that foolish rooster, strutting through the dust and showing the seed or the worm to hens before he ate his prize. However, no matter where he fixed his mind or where he began, presently into his imagination the picture of the little valley farm came back, and the soft-eyed brood mares, and the wild colts, and the "made" horses walked across his mind's eye   walked across his heart.

The sun dropped lower and turned red in the west, and as its cheeks began to puff out, a ruche of crimson and purple cloud came around it, so that it had the look of a drunken clown in a clown's collar. At that, Pleasant began to laugh, and turned from the window still laughing until he saw Charlie Rizdal shrink away with fear and horror.

"It's all right, Charlie," said he. "I ain't crazy. I won't do any harm to you. No, nor to anybody else. Why, hell, I ain't got the brains to do any harm, for I'm simply a dumb fool that anybody could wrap around their little finger. But, oh, God, Rizdal, one of these days I'm going to get my hands on President Lewis Fisher and I'll make his windpipe crackle under my thumb."

"If you want to do that," said Rizdal quietly, "I have the stuff still waiting. We can start to-night to cut through, old man. Or are you going to wait to serve the prison term?"

Pleasant replied with a glance; he dared not trust himself to speech for once his voice began he could not say where it would take him. He was trying to keep himself in hand and steer a straight and manly course; he was trying almost with a physical effort, and it reminded him of the labor of holding the ploughtail steady when the share is in rough ground.

That night they started work with the saws.

What miracles of art were each of the little strips of steel, edged with a diamond hardness, and they ate into the well-proved steel of the window bars almost as though it were wood. Eased with the finest of oil, the little blades still worked on softly and silently, yet now and again there was a thin scream as a flexible blade was stuck in the cut it had made. At those times, the two stopped work, gasping with excitement, but no alarm came to them.

For a full three hours they worked, when it became apparent that they could not finish the task before the morning was on them. It was a double trellis which secured that window, the inner one made of mere strips, the outer of greater bars; and altogether, as Rizdal pointed out, it was a case rather for a work bench and large circular saws than for two prisoners and their sadly cramped fingers. However, they had made good progress, and Rizdal announced that he would send word that they were coming through the next night. As he declared this, he could not help making a little speech on the subject: "You're down, old fellow, I know. But you'll be up before long. You've had a good many things in your life, I know, with plenty of excitement thrown in, but you've never had friends, Pleasant! You're going to find that you have them now, and that they'll never let you down. Try us before you trust us. You'll find, as the Mexicans say, that when a friend asks there is no to-morrow. Well, Jim, damme if I don't get a little sentimental about it all, but I can't help feeling that the happiest day in your life will be the one when you join up with Long Tom Rizdal!"

There seemed to be no room in the heart of Pleasant even for hope or a kindly touch of excitement; for all his emotions, now, were bitter, savagely straightforward. He was like a dog that has found a blood trail but is held hard upon a leash. Rizdal could not help noticing.

"When you get Fisher   what'll you really do to him?" he asked.

And Pleasant Jim smiled, and then passed the tip of his tongue over his dry lips.

That night they finished the inside cut and lifted out the square segment of the bars; the outer trellis had been cut also, only a few shreds of steel remaining to hold the work in place until the last moment.

Rizdal climbed up with the aid of Pleasant Jim, and his shoulders would not go through the gap! He got down and tried again to wriggle through on his side, but all he managed to do was to tear his coat and bruise his side badly.

He got down again, gasping and groaning until Pleasant had to warn him that he was sure to rouse the whole jail. It was simply clear that they had made a mistake in their measurement. The hole would have to be enlarged; it could not be done in the remainder of that short night; and in the meantime, how were they to replace, for the day, the section which they had taken from the grating?

CHAPTER 11

ANY casual passer-by might glance up from the street and take heed of the gap in the inner bars of that window, and no one could enter the cell without seeing instantly what was wrong. Their reactions, now, were oddly characteristic, for Charlie Rizdal, gritting his teeth, picked up the square of bars and held it into the place from which it had been taken. But Pleasant sat down on his cot and turned the matter gravely in his mind. They had nothing of which a cement of any kind could be made; not even the slightest adhesive substance was in their hands. A possible solution came to him then and they acted upon it instantly, cutting small, thin, wedge-shaped slivers from the legs of the cots and then driving these into two of the opposite cracks which were left when the section had been fitted into place as nearly as possible. The tapping in of one wedge dislodged the sliver at the farther end; a dozen times they failed; the light of the day had commenced long ago; and now a sharp whistling went up the street.

A boy of fourteen or fifteen idled past, his hands in his pockets, all eyes— and therefore how could his glance fail to spot famous Jim Pleasant who was observed in the gray of the dawn with his face at the window, and his hands, apparently, desperately clutching the bars of his window.

"Hello, Jim!" called the passer-by. "Can I do anything for you, Jim?"

Greatly Pleasant strove for some word to say, some casual thing which would dismiss the boy and send him down the street, but not a syllable could he speak and the youngster, looking up into that fierce and silent face, suddenly was overcome with a nameless fear, and scampered down the street.

Pale and stern-lipped now, the two resumed their efforts.

58

What must be shall be; and the section of grating was in place at last. After that, they gathered dust from the floor, working cement from between the cracks of the stones, and thus they managed to smear the saw cuts with an improvised mud. But how insecure was their work! With every breath of wind that day they expected the grating to fall clanging from its place, and yet they dared not make any further attempts to strengthen the fastenings, for fear lest the very first hammering would dislodge the insecure wedges which held the bars in place.

However, as the hours went past, their confidence returned; and then in the mid-afternoon Jailer Danny Rankin suddenly appeared before them and said sullenly: "What was you doing at the bars of that window this morning, you   Pleasant?"

"I was looking at the sky and the street and wishing I was out of this damned hole. What else?" said Pleasant.

"I got almost an idea that you   " began Danny Rankin, and he walked straight towards the window. Pleasant turned too white and sick to speak, but Rizdal called: "Rankin! Come here, will you?"

At the abrupt challenge, Rankin turned and scowled.

"What in hell is biting you?" he asked amiably.

"I'm fed up with this cell," said Rizdal, falling into an apparent passion. "I'm fed up, I tell you, and worse than that I'm tired of this here wooden Indian, Pleasant. I tell you, he looks at me like a snake at a rabbit, as if he'd like to swallow me. One of these nights I'm going to brain him—and it'll be self-defense   I warn you beforehand!"

"What happens to either of you," said the uncourteous Rankin, "ain't a bit of difference to me, or how you get yourselves knocked on the head or hung. But you," he added, turning and pointing a stubby finger at Pleasant, "you quit tryin' to scare the kids in the street! Now mind you, I run this jail, and I'm gunna keep a hand over everybody!"

So saying, still scowling over his shoulder, he turned and walked from the cell. Pleasant leaned back against the wall, almost overcome, his heart hammering, and his breath gone. But the peril of the moment was past, and now they could prepare for the new effort.

A new book came for Rizdal that afternoon, interleaved with new saw blades! Pleasant wondered at the carelessness of Rankin in allowing such a traffic, but after all it was the stupid eye of Sally that disarmed suspicion. As she passed in the book

she murmured   and Pleasant heard it: "You've bluffed too
hard. Rankin will separate you to-morrow. To-night or never,
Charlie!"

Dusk had scarcely fallen when with Rizdal watching at the
door, Pleasant fell vigorously to work making the new cut. Too
vigorously, for at the second stroke, a saw blade snapped, and
fell tingling into the yard below them. For a desperate five
minutes they waited; then rapid steps came up the jail aisle
towards their cell   with set faces the two stared at one another,
feeling that the end had come. But the steps passed briskly by,
and Pleasant refitted a blade and began work once more.

By midnight the cut was complete, and taking down the inner
bars, with a bed leg they pried away the outer ones which were
secured only by the threads of steel which they had left after their
cutting. Rizdal had prepared two blankets knotted together, and
it was he who slipped through the window first and dropped to
the ground below. Pleasant followed, and they moved softly
around to the rear of the building. There, standing close in the
shadow of the wall, they took stock of their surroundings.

A rear window was lighted and threw a broad shaft of
illumination across the backyard of the bu''ding, dimly
sketching the outlines of the tree-masses beyond. The night was
warm; many people were still up, as the lighted houses showed,
in spite of the fact that it was midnight; and in this little, waking
city, a sudden alarm sounded from the jail behind them   a loud
shouting, and then the trampling of feet. The front door was cast
open, and voices descended into the open night.

Rizdal took the lead, and brought them quickly into the deep
shadow of the trees.

"Now horses?" asked Pleasant. "Have you thought of that,
Charlie?"

"Don't worry," replied the other. "You don't have to. We've
done our part. Long Tom will have to do the rest."

"But where shall we go?"

"Not a step from here. I sent word that we'd be here about
midnight. Here we are, and that lets us out, of course. But   "

There was a rush of three horsemen down the street, shouting
wildly that the jail was broken, and calling on every man to arm
for the pursuit. "They'll have us like fish in a net," suggested
Pleasant nervously.

"Here comes our help now," answered Rizdal, and through
the shadows beneath the trees came two men, each leading a

span of saddle horses. "It's Christy," went on Rizdal with satisfaction. "We couldn't have a better man. Christy! Here we are!"

Mr. Christy, a short and broad-built silhouette, said with unnecessary loudness: "Tumble aboard, mates. Here, Charlie, this is for you. And here's something special for Pleasant."

Pleasant Jim, in the very act of taking the reins and throwing himself into the saddle on a big gray horse that was led to him, checked himself with an exclamation. "By the Eternal and seven thousand devils!" said Pleasant. "It's the Leinster Gray! Tell me, how did you—"

"Take now and talk later," urged Christy. "Give way, boys. We got to cut out of this town; it's beginning to swarm for us!"

There seemed to be fifty men who had responded to the call of the jailers and who had saddled horses and turned themselves into wild cavalry at a moment's notice. They were scurrying everywhere; the acrid alkali dust began to taint all of the air; and Pleasant heard the sharp, almost whining voice of Marshal Sam Lee raised like a piercing trumpet, calling every one together to take his orders and so organize the search.

"Take it slow and easy," urged Pleasant. "Ride up the street with the first swarm of gents that passes. They'll never recognize us in the dark."

So they came out of the trees and joined a flurry of riders who were pounding hard through the dust. And one of them merely called: "What's up?"

Christy answered in stentorian tones: "Rizdal and Pleasant Jim have busted jail, and hell is loose!"

The riders went on; behind them passed the four, turned to the side through the first alley and "Who's there!" called a voice, and a shadow stepped from the brush into the alleyway and the long barrel of a rifle thrown across his forearm and all the bearing of one prepared for war.

"Get out of the way!" called Christy. "Pleasant and Rizdal have escaped and rode this way."

The other drew unwillingly back.

"I dunno how they could of got by here," he said. But they already were sweeping by him when he shouted: "Jim Pleasant! Halt!"

Something in the outline of Pleasant's head and shoulders against the stars had betrayed him, but the rifleman had made his discovery too late, for the long arm of Jim Pleasant reached for him as a piston reaches in its stroke. The rifle exploded, to be sure, but it was fired blindly and the sentry fell with bleeding face and half-numbed brain in the thick dust.

The four went on.

The racing gallop of the horses pushed Fisher Falls at once behind them; before them they had the narrowing cañon of the upper valley, with the mountains drawing in on either side like arms prepared to gather up the fugitives, so that to Pleasant the jagged outlines of the peaks seemed more delightful than the form of a familiar home. They meant freedom to him; but more eloquent than the sight of the open mountains, almost enough to redeem all of the pains and the losses which he had suffered was the sweeping gait of the horse which carried him, not as with beating wings but like wings. Freedom? He felt that never before had he been free like this, like an eagle! And looking back over his shoulder down the white line of the river, he almost was sorry that he saw no dimly following forms like hawks beating vainly upwind after the king of the air.

CHAPTER 12

THEY turned from the main valley through a narrow-floored ravine, and up this they rode in the center of a little stream. It was great labor for the horses and required an hour for a single mile, but though they frequently fell saddle-deep into holes, and though there was great danger that a horse might break a leg or ruin a hoof on the sharp rocks in the bed of the stream, they stuck to their purpose, for this was a gap in the trail which would defeat the pursuit even if they took dogs up the line.

They left the creek where it diminished to a mere runlet, and bearing to the east up a winding cattle trail, they came in the gray of the morning to a spacious plateau sowed with rocks, clustered with many trees, but affording many patches of excellent grazing land where cattle were scattered and some already browsing. In the midst was a farm-house and Christy, who had maintained the lead, bore boldly ahead for it. Pleasant anxiously asked Rizdal if this were not folly but he was reassured. The farmer was "right" and had been well bribed long before. He was a Rizdal station, so to speak, and Pleasant learned, what he had guessed before, that Long Tom made no effort to work the country with a lone hand. Instead, he made a point of making friends here and there where he could find an outlying small farmer or trapper and hunter who spent much work for small cash returns. These were the hostelries patronized by the long riders of the gang, where food and lodging was paid for at a handsome rate and always in hard cash and where, besides, a small present of money was sure to be seed falling on fertile ground. All that was required of these "station agents" was that they should see nothing, hear nothing, know nothing. Among their mustangs were sure to be found a few horses of a different breed, longer of leg, cleaner of cut, and if those horses were occasionally "borrowed," other animals were left in their place, usually worn down by hard traveling.

The farmer welcomed the party with a grin and a wink and sent his son to go hunting at the head of the ravine and keep a sharp lookout for any pursuit that might head that way. The wife, in the meantime, went into the kitchen to cook, and presently four hungry men sat down to a table covered with fried ham, with baking-powder biscuits, and great cups of coffee.

Over the last cup of coffee and Bull Durham cigarettes, Rizdal completed his introductions.

Christy appeared in the morning light as a sort of pugilistic type, low-browed, deep-chested and with extraordinarily long arms. And Rizdal said of him: "Here's Joe Christy, Jim. He's what Tom calls an all-around man. He can blow a safe, or use a can-opener; he can make soup and use it; he can work inside or out, and if it comes to a pinch, he handles a gun the way that you admire. Now here's Lefty. I dunno just what to say about Lefty. Lefty, what would you say for yourself?"

Lefty was just the opposite of his stocky companion. Pale and thin of face, with lank black hair falling over his forehead, he had a detached and somewhat superior air, and his dull, dark eyes wandered slowly here and there and seemed to see nothing. He was like an artist, whose thoughts are lost in dreams rather than in realities, and like the hands of an artist, his fingers were long and slender, with little strength but much active deftness.

He smiled faintly at the question of Rizdal, but said nothing to explain himself, and the other continued: "Lefty has a talent for listening to a combination and then telling you what's in its mind. You could duplicate the rest of us, but you couldn't duplicate Lefty. In addition, Lefty shoots a little straighter than almost any one else, except Tom or you, Pleasant. That's why he was asked to ride down with the party this evening."

This praise did not seem to be noticed by the pale man, who was lost in an aimless reverie, while Rizdal went on: "Boys, you know Jim Pleasant; everybody does in this part of the range. It was Jim who put me behind the bars and he might have landed the rest of us there if it hadn't been that the fools who could have used him decided that they'd double-cross him. Well, they'll have to pay through the nose for that, and they'll begin to pay pronto. Now, fellows, I know you, and I know Jim. I tell you that he's a man to take to; and I tell you, Pleasant, that Lefty and Joe never will let you down in a pinch. Mix up a bit and get to know one another. It'll pay you in the long run."

Pleasant cleared his throat.

"I like straight talk," he observed, "and I'll give you some. You fellows have taken me out of jail. I'm grateful for what you've done, but I'm not going to throw in with you. I've worked for my living, and it's too late for me to switch callings. What you do for yourselves is all very well. What I do for myself has to be something else. I can't try the new dodge."

In this statement he received sudden confirmation and encouragement in the vigorous voice of Mr. Christy: "There ain't any fool in the world," he declared, "like the sap that goes crooked when he can go straight."

"Sure," agreed Charlie Rizdal. "You're talking like a book, Joe. The point is: How is this bird going to fly straight, again? After busting jail, I mean? Or is he going to take the sentence for pushing the queer on top of the sentence for jail-breaking? Gimme an answer, Joe!"

Joe had no answer. Neither had Jim Pleasant, and the conversation ended for the moment when Rizdal added kindly: "You make up your mind any way that you want to jump, because nobody's going to press you here. Tom thinks the whole world of you and he'd be the last man to want to drag you into anything."

After breakfast, they went to bed, assured by the farmer that fresh horses would be saddled and ready for them, and a strict watch kept in case there should be any need for a hasty departure. "Except," he added, "I guess that the gent that has the gray wouldn't want to change him for another?" And he looked at big Pleasant partly in admiration and partly in malice and envy.

On the way to the beds, upstairs, Pleasant asked cautiously: "What price, Charlie, would your brother put on the gray?"

"Price?" smiled the other. "Why, man, the horse is yours, of course. And by the way—there'll be a thousand of clean money for you, as soon as Tom arrives!"

So Jim Pleasant lay down on the bed which was assigned to him, but he could not sleep at once. In his brain and in his blood was the thought of the gray, hauntingly persistent; for he knew good horses and had lived, in a way, to make them. But never before had he had such a mount between his knees.

By noon he was up and left his three companions snoring while he wandered downstairs and out to the pasture. There

were six well-bred ones there, but the seventh was the gray.
There were six horses of bone and substance with eyes like deer
and muzzles which, like the horse of the Arab poet, could drink
from a pint-pot; but the seventh was the Leinster Gray. With
hungry eyes he devoured the proportions of the tall stallion.
Looked at from behind, his quarters seemed too broad and
gross, like the driving muscles of a draught animal; but viewed
from the side that sense of overweight disappeared. Beautifully
balanced, made like a watch for fineness, he possessed sixteen
hands and a half of go and stamina, and yet Pleasant knew that
the big fellow was as neat-footed as a cat.

This horse, worthy of a king, had been given to him off hand
by a thief, a smuggler, a bank robber! It set his blood on fire, for
the possibilities of such a man were limitless, it appeared to
Pleasant.

In a short time, the others appeared, Christy and Rizdal to
lounge about, but Lefty withdrawing himself to the shade of a
tree where he unwrapped a small bit of machinery and began to
work with it, his ear bent close to it, his eyes half closed like one
listening to the most delicious music. Christy explained to
Pleasant:

"That's a new combination. Loves it, don't he? My God, I've
seen him spend a hundred hours listening to the tumblers fall!
Burglar proof the saps who made that lock call it   the greatest
invention in the world for beating the wise boys; but God help
the joint that trusts to that lock when old Lefty lays hands on it!
He's readin' its mind, and look at him! Ain't he hearing a pretty
story?"

But Pleasant left them and went back to the pasture. He was
sitting on the fence, and the Leinster Gray was eating sugar from
his hand when Long Tom Rizdal appeared in the middle
afternoon. He came on a strong bay, blackened with sweat and
chafed to foam across the shoulders where the reins had been
rubbing. He gave hardly a word to Christy but drew his brother
aside.

"How did he go?" asked Long Tom.

"Steady as a clock," answered Charlie Rizdal. "Twice I
thought we were beat. It was Pleasant's game that pulled us
through. You were right about him, Tom, but I don't think he'll
throw in with us. There he is now—more interested in a horse
than in the rest of us."

Long Tom thrust out his underhung jaw a little and narrowed

his eyes, as though he were looking at the spirit of Pleasant rather than his body.

"You don't understand, Charlie," said he. "You've talked horse and money to him. He needs something else!"

And he went straight to Pleasant and took his hand: "Pleasant, you've been put in hell because of a boner that I pulled. Now you're out, tell me what you want to do?"

"What can I do?" asked the latter rather bitterly. "I've got the law after me!"

"Horses are your job, aren't they?"

"They are."

"Then pick some spot where there's good grass and water. Change your name, and buy the land and stock it with the cash that I'll give you. No man ever lost money through me, and I'm not going to let you be the first. You've lost twenty thousand dollars, Pleasant. You can have thirty from me. Grow a mustache and a beard and talk through your nose; you'll never be spotted, hardly."

"And let Lewis Fisher sit down and laugh at what he did to me? No," exclaimed Pleasant, "they'll have me for murder before I'll let him do that!"

CHAPTER 13

Long Tom sat down on a tree stump and picked a Colt forty-five from the spring-holster beneath his armpit; he began to pass it over his finger-tips, lightly, dexterously, bringing it to point on a white-faced stone twenty yards away; and again and again as he talked the gun covered the mark and recoiled again on the sensitive fingers. Pleasant Jim followed the gun movements with understanding eyes, for he himself had indulged in hours and hours of that not unmeaning play; so that while they spoke the two, no matter to what they were giving their minds, appeared to concentrate all of their attentions on the six-shooter.

"Old Fisher sticks in your craw, then?" said the smuggler. "Well, I'm not surprised. You're not the stuff that lies down when it's kicked, after all. But gun-work   is that the thing for him?"

Pleasant was silent.

"Take a look at him," said Rizdal. "Suppose that you walked in and blew him full of holes. He deserves shooting. Sure he does. Of all the dirty crooks in the world, he's the lowest, because he's the sort that never takes a chance; he never works without having the law between him and trouble. Well, I know of gents that killed themselves because that was all that Fisher left for 'em to do. But suppose you drop him, what's happened? He's got nothing except death, and death comes to everybody some day. He'd leave his money and his land and his work behind him for that chalk-faced sneak of a nephew of his to inherit; and there'd still be the statue in the square to the founder of Fisher Falls. What sort of a real revenge would that be? They'd simply make him out a martyr and write books about the great pioneer!"

Mr. Rizdal spat in the dust, and as though overcome with his disgust and his anger, he fired the Colt suddenly; a sharp

68

shoulder of the white-faced rock disappeared.

Pleasant listened intently, leaning forward a little, his eyes upon the gun but his thoughts in another place.

"Suppose, though, that you were to snake the soul out of that fat-faced hound and leave him alive to groan and yell? That would be something like, Pleasant. You agree?"

"What's his soul?" asked Pleasant Jim bitterly.

"I dunno just how much there is of it," replied the other with a smile, "but I can tell you where it lives. It's in the big safe at the end of his private office where he keeps his cash and his securities not the stuff of the people that have deposited in his bank, but his own. They got their loot in an old cast-iron box that any fool could crack with a can-opener. But he's got something better for his own goods. A hard job, then. But suppose that the doors of that safe swung open, there would be the soul of Mr. Fisher to take out and handle the way we please. You follow me, old son?"

"I follow you fine. You mean to crack that safe, Tom?"

"I mean to crack that safe. Would you want to be in?"

"They've tried the safe three times," remarked Pleasant. "The first time, three of the yeggs were shot and two of 'em died. The second time the whole gang was rounded up, betrayed by somebody that sold the information to old man Fisher. The third time, they got into the office and there they had to fight, not to get into the safe but to get out of the room; and that time two more dead men were left. Well, Tom, you've thought that all over?"

"I've thought it all over," replied Tom Rizdal. "The old man figures that luck is on his side, and he puts everything he's got into that safe. All his convertible bonds, his cash, his family jewels, and everything that's worth stealing is lodged in that safe; in the meantime, the rest of the profession keep away from the place because they figure the way you do—that the place is poison. Well, maybe it is, but if you're willing to work, we'll make the try."

"You've got a crew of experts," observed big Jim Pleasant. "What real use could I be to you?"

"Because," replied the other, "for this job we got to have somebody with no more nerves than a chunk of stone; somebody as steady as a mountain, that'll live every day with the danger of being pinched and shoved into jail. You understand?"

Pleasant shook his head.

And at that, Tom Rizdal took from his pocket a small notebook and a pencil and he drew upon it, rapidly, with an artist's rough surety, a very good facsimile of the front of Fisher's Bank.

"Where's the solar-plexus of that building?" asked he.

"This is a new line of work for me," admitted Pleasant. "You tell me, Tom."

"What's under the bank itself?"

"Why, the old Jew made that row of stores in what used to be the basement. What of that?"

"A lot! Wait a minute and we'll get to it. Three stores, ain't there? That corner one is where the janitor hangs out and sells stationery and odds and ends, isn't it? Here's the watch-maker's and jeweler's place in the center, and down here at this end is the plumber's place and hardware supplies."

"That's right."

"Well, old son, that center store, d'you see? That's right under the office of Fisher his private office, where he has his safe!"

Pleasant sat up straight, but still his fascinated gaze held upon the evolutions of the restless revolver.

"The lease of the jeweler in that shop runs out in three months—no, it's four months, now. I'll put every card on the table and let you see what I have in my mind. Then you can decide. You throw in with me, or you don't. I want a safe man to appear and rent that middle shop, you understand? I want him to keep the place open and appear to run an honest business for a few weeks. Then I want to get into his place and start making a cut up through the floor of the bank and into the office of the president where old Fisher sits every day. Mind you, it'll be damnable work. That floor of the bank is thicker than the wall of a safe, and it's damned near as hard to cut through. It'll mean days of steady work. And every minute we'll have to be sure that the night watchman isn't on the job, and that the people aren't in the janitor's stationery shop, or in the plumber's place next door. And all the while that that work goes on, from day to day, the gent who runs the shop has to be on the job and keeping up a safe front. You understand? His nerves will have to be like steel!

"Well, I know a few men who can do that sort of work in a way, but what are they? Thugs and yeggs, and when we had a passage cut through the floor, those birds would be apt to go through by themselves, make the clean-up, and then make their getaway. You see how it is? What I need to have is a man who can be trusted, and you're the man, Jim!"

Pleasant listened, amazed.

"I know you have some sort of meaning," he declared "but what it is beats me. I'm known in that town, Tom. How the devil could I open up a store there? Sam Lee would nearly die laughing at the idea!"

"You're known, eh?" said the smuggler. "How well are you known?"

"Why, damn well! Not a man or a woman or a child, hardly, that don't know my face. I ain't been living in a hole or dodging the daylight."

"You lived there?"

"No. Always out of town on the farm."

"You got many friends in Fisher Falls?"

"Been too busy to have friends, Rizdal. What of that?"

"It means a lot. People know you. They have a flash of you going by. That's big Jim Pleasant, the horseman, the gunman. Sure, they know your face. What else do they know about you? Nothing, I'll put a bet!"

Pleasant considered.

"But how get by the face?" he asked.

"It ain't so hard. Not half. Two months would grow a beard and mustaches; and you get weak eyes and have to wear big horn-rimmed spectacles."

"My voice, Tom. They'd spot that."

"I don't think so. A mother or a brother or an old pal would spot it, maybe. But not folks that have seen you, but hardly talked to you. They couldn't do it! Besides, in four months you could change your lingo. You've had schooling, Jim."

"High school. That's all."

"That's enough. You talk rough and free and easy not because you have to, but because you've got careless. You concentrate for four months, talking the King's English as if you were a king. You'll begin to change. Right? And speaking a new lingo, who'd spot you with glasses, a beard, and the rest? Who'll be dropping in to finger-print you? And there's something else worth talking about. People see and hear not what's actually in front of 'em but what they expect to see and hear. Suppose that they see you in the store. What they think of Jim Pleasant is of a big gent roaming around somewhere in the open, dodging the law and doing it damn successfully. They think of you with a gun in your hand and a mask on your face, most likely. And there you'll be in Fisher Falls right under the old bank, and getting ready to cash in. They won't have any imagination to fit into a thing like that. Ask yourself, and you'll see that I'm right!"

"Perhaps," murmured the other. "But how the devil could I run a store? What do I know about stores?"

"You know guns, saddles, ropes, everything that goes to a horse or a cowpuncher's outfit, don't you?"

"I know something about those things."

"You know 'em backward, their prices, the best makes, everything. You know rifles and shotguns. You know everything that powder and lead can be fitted into. Why, man, the thing for you to do is to open a gun-shop here in Fisher Falls. For that matter, you ought to make money at it. The thing's never been tried!"

The eyes of Pleasant began to glint, still following the evolutions of the uneasy revolver in the fingers of the master criminal.

"And selling things," he objected. "I never did that."

"You can learn. After a couple of months of hair-raising, you can travel back East and get into a real gunstore as a clerk. I've got a lead that would plant you in a shop, I think. Spend two months there, raising more hair, studying your lingo, learning the system. When you come back, you'll be a first-rate gun salesman. Now, what do you think of the dodge, Pleasant?"

"It makes me sweat," admitted Pleasant Jim, honestly. And he mopped his forehead.

"The hard jobs," replied the philosopher, "are always a damned sight harder in the distance than they are when you're close up to 'em. Those mountains, you look at 'em, and they seem like a solid wall, but you and me know a hundred half-blind trails that run through them. Think it over."

"I'll let you know to-morrow."

"No, let me know in five minutes. To-morrow I'm due a hundred miles from here. And I'll tell you this to help you think. We've got our party for the job here at hand. There's Charlie. You know him. There's me. And besides that, there's Lefty for the fine work on the combination, and Joe Christy to blow the safe, perhaps. Lefty and Joe are strangers in the town. They could work with you in your shop. That's five men. Well, we'd give you two shares on the loot. One-third, old timer, of everything that we take out of the soul of Lewis Fisher."

"I'm kind of shaky about the idea," replied Jim Pleasant.

"You think you are, but you ain't. Try your gun on that rock that I tried to hit a while back, and you'll see how shaky you really are."

Instinctively, Pleasant obeyed. The heavy Colt glided from beneath his loose coat into his hand, and exploded instantly, hip high. The rock jumped into pieces, squarely smitten in the center.

"I told you so!" grinned Long Tom Rizdal.

CHAPTER 14

MR. FISHER was a man who believed that there are few acts in this life of ours when time and thought will not surpass accident and swiftness of decision. Therefore he never was in haste. The center store beneath the bank was vacant and had been vacant for a week with no claimants of the quarters because most of the storekeepers in the town were rather contemptuous of what they termed "cellar stores." However, Mr. Fisher was in no haste to rent according to the proposal which had been committed to paper and lay in a letter upon his desk.

It said simply:

"Dear sir,

"We understand that your bank is located in the central portion of Fisher Falls, and that beneath it there is quarters for a small store. We contemplate opening a gun-shop in Fisher Falls, and we are prepared to offer you thirty dollars a week for the location of which we speak. We understand that it is shortly to be vacant. Will you kindly let us know at an early date if this proposal interests you?

"Yours very truly,
"WILLIAM J. FOXHALL,
"for Greendale, Chase, and Foxhall, Ltd."

The letter was interesting, and the rent offered was some twenty or twenty-five per cent greater than Mr. Fisher had expected to receive; on the other hand, he was not altogether pleased with the idea of a gun-shop beneath the bank. Would there be a shooting gallery attached? Of course that would make the thing impossible, but at any rate it would mean a constant gathering of the idle and the curious cowpunchers who passed through the town and that, he was sure, would detract from the dignity of the bank. That bank, you must understand, was something more than a spaciously arranged piling of stone and brick and mortar; it possessed for Lewis Fisher a soul of mystery and strength. Sometimes he even thought it was his own unfleshed spirit which was housed there, and always he grew increasingly uncertain as to where the boundaries of his self ended and the boundaries of the bank began. So other men worked for immortality by striving to throw themselves into pictures or poetry, but he committed his personality to the bank; and a very great poet it would have to be who should outlive the bank of Fisher Falls. Just as his name must exist forever in this town which he had made; even when the stone statue of him should molder in the park; just so the bank must go on and on. Its fleshly form would change, no doubt. It would advance, at last, to the solemn dignity of Grecian façade, with Doric columns of white marble, tenderly fluted; and not in vain would it have the temple's appearance, for it would be housing a changeless spirit—his own soul! Sometimes he felt an over-whelming wave of self-pity when he thought how utterly he surrendered himself and lived for his bank, for what he performed was done in its name instead of in his own. Reports went out from directors   shadows which he maintained!   and policies were decided by the same board, so that he was concealed in the institution which he had built. But on the other hand, he received from the bank a delicious companionship. He had endowed it so richly with spirit that it had a soul with which it looked back at him; moreover it had other uses and if at times strong and cruel things had to be done, they were not done for Lewis Fisher but for the bank.

Therefore it will be understood why the president considered the letter on his desk for a long time, and every day for a week he glanced at it again, and pondered. It might be a blow to the dignity of the bank; on the other hand, the rent offered was excellent. Compared with the gross bulk of his millions, such trifling sums were negligible, but Mr. Fisher had ever in mind the flowing of a mighty river which is composed of a myriad runlets. So he would have the bank to be—recruited constantly by the trickling of little streams of currency.

He wrote back, at last, asking if they would allow him to see their representative; they replied that a trusted subordinate, Mr. Struthers Holman, who in fact had been selected to open the store in Fisher Falls, would call upon Mr. Fisher in a few days.

Then Mr. Holman called.

Mr. Fisher liked him at once, for he was a tall, solemn, quiet man who wore a short, sharply pointed beard, and closely trimmed mustaches. When he sat down, he looked steadily at Mr. Fisher through great horn-rimmed spectacles.

"Are you," said Fisher, when the other's business had been stated, "are you really qualified to work in the shop with guns?"

He would have guessed, rather, the profession of medicine or of law; there was just a touch of the funereal about this tall fellow. However, Struthers Holman assured the banker that he was in fact qualified to sell guns and other furnishings for cowpunchers. He made a gesture as he spoke, and the banker took note of hands which were long, and covered with sinew and all the signs of great strength. He decided on the spot that he would give the lease. But, first of all, he mentioned his possible objections. He hoped that violent advertisements would not bring crowds to the place; he hoped that the new store manager would have a due regard for the dignity of the environment in which he found himself. Mr. Struthers Holman was the height of consideration. He assured Fisher that Greendale, Chase, and Foxhall, Ltd., never pursued a radical policy. That they carried only the best of guns and the best of ammunition, together with knives, some saddles, and other matters which might be able to please the eye of the Westerner; and Greendale, Chase, and Foxhall, Ltd., really despised violent and acrobatic advertising. They preferred to go steadily and slowly and build up a reputation by letting customers see that their goods were of the best and that they stood behind their goods.

Mr. Fisher was satisfied. He shook hands with Mr. Struthers Holman, and the strong, large hand of the gun merchant amazed him again. Mr. Fisher liked strong men; he was a strong man himself, but of course his strength was rather of the spirit than of the flesh, and from that moment he patronized the new store. He recommended it. He stopped in to see how it was coming on. He took an interest in the large and heavy cases which Greendale, Chase, and Foxhall consigned to their new branch. He was delighted when, behind glass cases, the glimmering shotguns and rifles were displayed in dark and terrible beauty. Whenever he stepped in, the tall and stately Holman was sure to wait upon him with a deferential courtesy. Holman had good manners of a rather clerkish pattern, and above all he knew how to use the little word "sir." It makes such a difference!

"I hope you are going to like Fisher Falls," said Mr. Fisher at length. "Because you are the sort of person we want out here. We want strong men, because we're a strong community. There's a place for you here, Holman, even if you have to write with your left hand."

He laughed at his little jest, and Mr. Holman smiled gravely at this allusion to his infirmity. An accident had happened to his right wrist in a fall and he had lost that delicate control of the fingers which is necessary for the movement of a pen. For that reason, he had had to learn to write with his left hand   a labored matter, and a most scrawling, scratchy signature!

"You are making a good thing of this place," said Mr. Fisher. "But as a matter of fact, you have one weakness. Let an older man tell you what it is."

"You are really kind," said Mr. Holman earnestly. "What is it, sir?"

"You don't know people, Holman! That's your fault. You know guns; you know your business; but you don't know people! Now, you've employed that stodgy, beetle-browed, square-jawed fellow as one clerk, and that thin, pale, absent-minded chap as another. In the third place, you've hired that simple-minded girl who used to do the drudgery at the jail. That creature's a half-wit, Holman. I can read the human eye; trust me when I say it!"

Holman made a deprecatory gesture.

"As for the two clerks—I don't need them. I could get along without them and save a great deal of money, sir. But the firm sent them out to give them experience in a new field. They expect to open other stores through the West. So I have to keep them. As for the girl—what you say is very true, but then you see, she's cheap, and she's too simple-minded to steal!"

"Ah?" said Fisher. "There's sense in that. I always keep my mind open to reason, and I see that you have thought the thing out. And yet there are few people in the world so simple that they may be trusted. Believe me!"

"I do," said Holman with a strange earnestness. "I do, with all my heart, sir!"

CHAPTER 15

When Mr. Fisher left the gun-store, two clerks who had been apparently busy at the gun racks, and a pale-faced drudge who had seemed to be scrubbing in a distant corner, turned to Struthers Holman.

"And now what does the old sap have to say?" asked Joe Christy.

"He just has pointed out," said Struthers Holman, "that you look like a beetle-browed, square-jawed crook, and that Lefty seems to be an absent-minded idiot. He thinks that I ought to fire you and get a new layout. I pointed out that the firm hired you, and it's not my fault."

"He's got your interests at heart," said Joe Christy with a sour grin. "I got a personal interest in trimming the old four-flusher."

"At least," said the girl, "he didn't pick on me."

"Didn't he?" answered Pleasant. "All he said of you was that no one was simple-minded enough to be trusted."

"There's more blood in a turnip than in the brain of that old boy," said the girl. "I'm dead for a smoke, Pleasant. Do I get it?"

"Get out of sight, then," said Pleasant. "Come back here where the crates are."

They sat down in the rear corner of the shop and she lighted a cigarette, sitting cross-legged on a box-head and leaning back against the wall.

"You're tired," suggested Pleasant.

"Tired of my game; tired of my face; tired of everything," said she.

"Suppose that the deal goes through," said he, "what will you do with your split?"

"Me? Oh, I'll pull out and take my share back East. I'll settle down in the village and build mother a new house and make her happy. And maybe I'll marry, Jim. A girl wants to marry and have children. But, oh, how I long for quiet!"

"Go back now!" he exclaimed. "Go back and pull out of this mess now, Sally. You're too good for it. And you've done enough already to deserve your share. I'll personally see to it that you get the coin."

"Will you?" said Sally. "Good old Jim!"

She laid a hand on his arm and smiled at him with such a childish trust and gentleness that suddenly he stood up and walked away to conceal his emotions.

Mr. Joe Christy examined him with a critical eye as he strode past; watched him with attention as he fumbled blindly at a rifle in a rack; and then turned towards Lefty. With deliberation and solemnity Lefty winked.

Christy, however, seemed much excited, and hastily he went and stood before the girl.

He pointed a stubby finger at her, and his face worked with anger.

"You promised the Chief," said he, "and you've busted your word!"

"I don't know what you mean, Christy," said the girl with coldness.

"Aw, hell, Sally," said the yegg, "don't come that over me. You know what I mean. You been making a fool of the Big Boy again."

"What business is it of yours?" asked she with a sudden savagery. "Let me alone. Do you hear?"

"You're heated up about it, too," said he judicially. "All heated up and mean about it. But what surprises me is that you, who always was considered a square-shooter and a fair one, should take it into your head to play a low game on the Big Boy! What chance has he got against you?"

"Am I poisoning his soup?" she asked fiercely.

"You're knocking him cock-eyed," declared the yegg with conviction. "You never miss a chance to hand him a mealy smile or get a calf-look into your eyes. One of these days you'll shake your make-up so that you can hit him harder!"

She smiled faintly, a satisfied smile, and Joe Christy became angrier still.

"I know you like a book," said he, "and every thought in your crooked head. If you can crumble him up in this make-up, what'll you do when you get a chance at him dolled up in something slick, with a gown from old Paree and some fake pearls around your neck? But I'm gunna spoil your little game, kid. I'm gunna blow to the Chief and let him know the entire layout!"

She smiled again, and leisurely blew a long puff of smoke towards the ceiling. The anger of Christy was increased.

"Him too!" said Christy. "You got him twisted around your finger, too!"

He added, with inspiration: "Suppose that I go to Pleasant Jim and let him know the facts about you?"

"Go on," said the girl, unperturbed.

"Suppose I tell him," said the yegg, "that you never been straight, that you started picking pockets when you could walk, and that you passed on to bigger work in the line of bunco steering and smuggling jewels, and finally you graduated right up to the class of Long Tom. I know the line you pull   a little mother waiting for you in a little cottage in a little town back in Connecticut with a little rose vine climbin' over the front door ah, hell, Sally, I know all about you!"

"All right," said the girl, "you go ahead and tell him all that!"

"You ain't afraid even of that?"

"No, but you are. He'd have a gun on you, Christy, before you got halfway through that little recitation, and you know it, friend!"

She picked up a string, and with marvelously dexterous fingers began to tie it in runic knots.

Joe Christy began to perspire. Finally, changing his tone, he said: "Why d'you do it, Sally? You been a square shooter. Why d'you pick on poor Pleasant?"

"I got to have my fun, dearie," answered the girl. "It's a dull life, and it don't last very long. Besides," she added with some heat, "who's Jim Pleasant?"

"I'll tell you if you don't know. He's hell on wheels," replied the yegg, "and if you get him into a tangle, he's gunna bust through and smash things generally when the pinch comes. He ain't a crook at all, Sally, and you know it. But before you get through with him, you'll make him as bad as they come!" He glared at her and then added: "As you've made crooks of plenty before him!"

"You love him, don't you? you bull-faced toad!" said Sally amiably. "You love him so you could hardly live without him! And yet it's you, you sap, that's taking him down the line, you and the rest of you! Who started it? Me? No, but I'm having a bit of fun with a real man, such as comes inside of my eye once in a lifetime. The rest is spent with common yeggs, and dead-beats, and saps, and crooks and long-riding roughs like you! Go tell him that, too! No, I'll beat you to it and tell him what you've told me!"

She slipped from the box and started for the door, but as she moved towards the main store, Joe Christy caught her by the wrists and called to her softly: "Don't you do it, Sally. Don't you, for the love of God, girl. If you start on me, you'll make him kill me; and I never could stand in front of him. No more could I with even Lefty to help me out. You'll have the murdering of me, Sally. What pleasure'll that be to you?"

Sally desisted, white and very angry.

"All right," she said. "Then you unclamp my hands, will you? And leave me be, Joe. I do no harm to you, and you do no harm to me. And so far as the Big Boy goes, how d'you know that I wouldn't make as good a wife for him as the next one?"

"Wife?" said the yegg, blinking at her. "Wife? My God, Sally, have a heart, will you?"

Sally endured this outbreak as well as she could, and then glared most evilly at Joe as he retreated to the storeroom. But it was plain that neither of them had uttered all that was within them.

Joe Christy had no sooner gotten inside the other room than he gasped and dodged backward.

"Who's held a gun on you now?" asked the girl sharply.

"There's the mean little runt in there!" breathed the yegg. "There's Sam Lee, the marshal, and I'd rather look at a rattler than look at him! He's talking with the Big Boy!"

"Sam Lee!" breathed the girl. "Sam Lee! What's he doing here?"

And seizing a polishing cloth and giving herself one glance in a little pocket mirror, she sallied out.

CHAPTER 16

EVEN in the midst of his home town, even in Fisher Falls itself, where the mantle of his position as Federal Marshal made him a person to be pointed out and wondered at, Sam Lee never abandoned his rôle of humility. Some people were prone to say that it was a false rôle, but others declared that what he acted was, in truth, what he most truly was. The heart of a lion had been combined with the soul of a mouse, and therefore when Sam Lee came into the gun-shop, he came in a hesitating, gentle, almost a deprecatory manner, as one who has no right to enter such an establishment.

As big Jim Pleasant saw the man of the law enter, he changed color a little, and he said to Lefty: "Go handle that fellow, Lefty! It's Sam Lee! I don't want to talk to him!"

Lefty did not so much as stir an eye, but he calmly advanced upon the little marshal, and soon he was deep in the explanation of an automatic, picked from the newest show case. The marshal was full of exclamations, but presently, he called upon Jim Pleasant, from the rear of the shop. His attitude was that of a man so filled with wonder that he cannot rest until he has a somewhat larger audience.

"Now, sir," said he to Pleasant, as the latter unwillingly came forward, "I'd like to have you tell me: why shouldn't everybody in the world that wants to use a gun have an automatic? Why should there be such a thing as the poor old single-action Colt? Can you tell me, sir?"

Pleasant was warmed by the thought in spite of himself.

He picked up the gun with his left hand. Always, he made sure that whatever he did was with the left hand, for that was a vital part of his disguise. It made it possible, for instance, for him to do his signing of letters in the broad, scrawling script which surely never could be recognized as the handwriting of Jim Pleasant, refugee and breaker of jail.

"Well, sir," he said, "for a person who doesn't want fine shooting, I suppose that you couldn't beat an automatic. If you had a wife to leave at home, and some danger that she might have trouble, an automatic would be just the thing. When she takes up this gun and pulls the trigger, she squirts a stream of lead like water coming out of a hose. And any roughneck or burglar who's tagged by a drop of the water from *this* nozzle, is pretty sure to drop and stay down. Or if he can run, he's likely to begin running and keep on."

"You don't say!" murmured the marshal. "Can you handle this gun?"

"A little, sir."

"There's a range right down the street," said the marshal with a sort of boyish eagerness. "Would you mind coming down and showing me what it can do?"

So Jim Pleasant was forced much against his will to accompany the other; Lefty found an excuse for joining in order to carry an extra case of guns and ammunition. And they went out past the little drudge, Sally, who had begun to polish slowly the door-glass of the store.

On the way, the marshal chatted in his semi-childish manner.

"You've been at this work for a long time, I suppose?" he said.

"What makes you think so?" asked Pleasant Jim, who was giving away nothing in his conversation, having learned the marshal's tactics long before.

"You got the professional air," said the marshal with admiration. "Now this other young man, here, this pale fellow, he knows his work. But he ain't got the same sort of a professional manner that you have. How long have you been at it, might I ask?"

"Three years," said Pleasant Jim.

"Only three years? Well, well! And here's the range. Suppose that we just step in here!"

They went into the little shop. A slatternly middle-aged woman ran the place; in the background, a red ball bobbed upon a steady stream of water, and against the steel-plated wall a procession of stately little white ducks constantly appeared and disappeared.

The woman offered them a rifle, throwing back the safety lock with a click, and with a familiar grin at the marshal.

"Not the rifles," said the marshal, nodding to her. "We've brought along some new-fangled guns, Mrs. Holstein. Now, let me see what that automatic can do, Mr. Holman."

Pleasant Jim took up the automatic.

It was a long-barreled, big-caliber type, and he directed it at the red ball. A shower of seven shots answered his pull on the trigger. The fountain was cut by three of the impacts, but the ball still floated.

"Well, well!" murmured the admiring marshal. "If that had been a man, he would be about cut in two, I reckon. What's wrong with the gun, Mr. Holman? I'd rather have it than a dozen of the old single-action Colts like this one!"

And he brought into his hand a long Colt and tapped it familiarly.

"Everybody to his own taste," answered Pleasant. "But the single-action gun has its points."

"What are they, then?"

"It shoots harder, and it shoots straighter."

"Ay, but even a single-action gun wouldn't be hitting that little red ball, hopping on top of the fountain, yonder."

"Wouldn't it?" said Pleasant Jim, setting his teeth as he squinted at the mark.

"No, sir," said the marshal. "Not even a gent like you, that's made it his profession—for three years, did you say?"

"Yes," said Pleasant Jim. "But I think that the red ball could be hit."

"Here's a gun," said the marshal. "Don't let that hold you back. And here's five dollars that says it can't be done say, in three shots."

A faint smile touched the bearded lips of Pleasant.

"Give me the Colt," said he. And taking it, he half-closed his eyes and balanced the weapon daintily in his hand. The balance was true, and the fit was perfect; never had he wielded a kinder gun.

"Here's my five," said Pleasant Jim, fastening his glance upon the target. "I'll have a couple of shots first, to see that the old gun shoots straight. Watch the ducks, if you please."

And tilting the weapon from the hip, he fired twice, not using the trigger, but raising the hammer with his thumb and letting it fall with sufficient force to detonate the caps. Two ducks in succession fell miserably over upon their sides!

"It's a good gun and a true one," admitted Pleasant Jim.

"And if I can't hit the ball with this, I can't hit it at all!"

"Neat work," said the marshal. "And from the hip! Turn on the other two fountains, Mrs. Holstein. There you are. There you are. Three targets, at five dollars a throw, if you can hit them! After all, a sliding duck ain't a bouncing ball! It's ten times the size, and it only moves straight!"

"We'll see," answered Pleasant Jim. "I couldn't hit the ball with an automatic. The first shot you throw is usually more to get the range than anything else in fine shooting. But the first shot of an automatic begins to throw the gun out of line. You might hit a man; you might cut a man in two. But again, you would miss a rabbit as it cut across the trail. Here goes! Now, Mr. Colt, stand by me!"

And laughing a little, he raised the gun, extended it to arm's length, and dropping it on the target he hit the water-column just below the ball.

He turned the weapon on the second little fountain; the red ball was knocked from sight; and from the third fountain the third shot blew the target.

"Hai!" cried Mrs. Holstein. "Who's shot like that in here since Jim Pleasant's day? Two out of three and with a revolver!"

"Wonderful!" said the marshal. "And left-handed, Mrs. Holstein! And a man who's handled guns only three years!"

"Aw, say," grinned that lady, "does he hand out that lingo? Quit the kidding, Mr. Holman, and admit that you was born with a gun in your hand!"

"Not at all," broke in the marshal. "Not at all! You take a fellow like that, with the right nerves and the patience, and he can teach himself pretty near anything inside of three years. Well, sir, I admire how you done it. Here's the other five, and I never was gladder to spend ten bucks in my life. When I ask for a posse the next time," he added, smiling, "I'm gunna call on you special, Holman. And I'll stick to the single-action Colt, thanks! No new-fangled ideas for an old-fangled man!"

So big Jim Pleasant got back to the store, and there he found waiting for him the anxious face of Long Tom, himself. He hurried and shook the hand of Pleasant.

"I thought you were gone, Jim," said he. "I thought that that damned marshal must have marched you away to the jail, and if you got inside of it the second time, I knew that we'd have our hands full to get you out."

Pleasant was extraordinarily cheerful.

"The old marshal ain't a bad sort," said he. "He came in asking about automatics. Well, I think I could have sold him one, but I couldn't advise even him to take what I figure is a bad steer. I told him to stick by the single-action Colt. And he asked me to come down the street and show him what the automatic could do at Mrs. Holstein's place."

"And you went?" exclaimed the leader.

"What else could I do?"

"Go on!" said the other, hoarsely.

"I couldn't hit the red ball on the fountain with the automatic. But I got two out of three with a single-action gun that the marshal handed me. And, Tom, I got ten dollars of his money along with 'em!"

Long Tom Rizdal bent his brows as though he had received a stroke of mortal danger.

"If you got ten dollars of his money," said he with a sudden decision, "he'll have ten years of your life!"

"You think that he's suspecting something?" asked the big man.

"Why should he be here asking for automatics when he's damned those guns every day of his life?" asked Long Tom Rizdal. "He wanted an excuse to get inside the shop and he's had his look around. He's had his look at you! God Almighty, Pleasant, I thought this bank was as good as in our hands, but I begin to think we're going to miss the richest haul that ever was inside of my fingers!"

In time of doubt, Jim Pleasant liked to be alone, and in time of danger he preferred his own meditations. Now he withdrew from the shop and into the pasture lot which lay at the rear of the place.

Long Tom remained behind to ask further questions of his lieutenants, and when he had gleaned from them every scruple of information which was to be had, he went with Joe Christy to find Pleasant again.

From the rear door of the shop they looked out on the pasture, and there was Mr. Pleasant seated upon the top rail of the pasture lot fence, and beside him sat the slender figure of Sally.

It was as innocent a tableau as one could wish to see, but at that moment the girl tilted her head and smiled up at Pleasant and he, bending a little over her, smiled back.

At this, Long Tom tapped the shoulder of Christy sharply.

"How long has that been going on?" he asked.

"I thought you'd spot it," said Christy, "but I'm here to tell you that it started on the first day and that it's been going on ever since! How does it look, Chief?"

"Like trouble," said the latter instantly. "My God, like what a lot of trouble it looks to me, and with a capital T."

CHAPTER 17

WHATEVER the concerns of Long Tom in the affairs of the girl and of Pleasant Jim, he was too much bent upon the work at hand to be greatly troubled by extrinsic matters. That Saturday night had been set for the date of cutting through the ceiling of the shop and so gaining admittance to the office of the bank president above them.

So, when that time came, Long Tom, the girl, Pleasant, Christy, and Lefty the yegg were gathered in the store silently. Behind the drawn curtains of the front windows, and the front door, they had hung heavy blankets, not only to make it impossible for light from within the store to reach the street but also to muffle any sounds of hammering which might be made within the shop. At the outer door was posted Sally, because her ears, as was said in the gang, were a trifle sharper than the ears of a cat. Jim Pleasant himself, as the strongest man in the crew, was to begin the cutting, to be relieved later by Long Tom, and then the others in turn.

They had to wait for a long time. The janitor sat at the door of his adjoining shop with his wife and it was well after ten before he and his better half retired to find their sleeping quarters. Then the cutting began, but when the deep plaster was removed from the ceiling and the slats above it cut through, they discovered that there remained a massive slab of cement and stone rubble to be pierced, and while they had plenty of tools for piercing wood or steel, they had nothing with which to attack such a barrier as this.

It was too late for them to secure what they wanted, and for that reason they decided to postpone the venture until the following evening.

They gathered once more at the appointed moment, Long

Tom never leaving the store, for he did not dare to venture away from the shop by night or day for fear of being recognized, since it was not the first time that he had operated in the vicinity of Fisher Falls and the price on his head now had mounted to the considerable sum of fifteen thousand dollars; a figure at which it was impossible for him to bribe men to hold their tongues. That is, unless he spent a fortune on each man.

They met in the store that evening determined to do or to die, for that same day an event had happened which frightened them all thoroughly and made them see that their time was short. Just before noon, it happened that Pleasant Jim had left the store and the marshal entered immediately afterwards and asked for the manager.

It was Lefty who met him and gave the information that "Holman" was out. "But maybe I can wait on you, Marshal Lee," said he.

"Maybe you could," answered Sam Lee with his cheerful smile, "but that Holman, he's got a way about him that I like, and from the shooting that I seen him do, I'd rather hear what he's got to say about guns. I ain't quite satisfied. I want to give the automatics another trial! Well, I'll drop in again!"

"Do," said Lefty.

At the door, the marshal turned again.

"When'll Holman be back?"

Lefty took wise thought before he answered.

"He's gone for a jaunt into the country, and he might not be back till Monday morning."

The marshal had raised his brows a trifle at this, and that trifle had been enough to make the heart of the yegg jump.

"Very well," said the marshal, "I'll try to see him when he comes back. He's a wise young man," he added. "All work and no play makes Jack a dull boy!"

And he went off, chuckling a little at his own remark, as though he had some secret reason for his mirth.

That secret reason was something which the rest of the gang could help Lefty to decipher. The suspicions of the marshal doubtless had fastened upon this man who had handled guns for three years only, and who yet was a dead shot even with the left hand. For that reason they determined to act at once. By Monday morning the place might be in the hands of the marshal!

Their suspicions received adequate confirmation the same

day, for it was observed that a new tenant had rented a long-vacant flat just across the street, and the man who had taken the new rooms seemed to spend most of his time at the window, smoking a pipe and looking down at the vacant street or across at the comings and goings through the door of the gunsmith's place.

They did not recognize the face as belonging to some man in the employ of the marshal; they did not have to shoot so close to the mark, for more than common sense was not needed to perceive that this man was a common spy. And it meant that their time was very short, indeed!

That night once more the janitor sat late in the door of his shop, chatting with his wife and with one of the two night watchmen, who paced up and down the block, meeting regularly at the bank corner to converse for a moment and then go off, twirling their sticks; but finally Sally gave word that the janitor and his wife had gone into their rooms, and the time to commence the work had come. Pleasant, striking hard and fast, bit rapidly into the strong, rocky concrete, and the thick flakes which he dislodged showered down upon the padding with which they previously had covered the floor. In this manner he soon was up to the flooring, which proved to be a double layer of hardwood and made difficult sawing, particularly since Long Tom insisted that the work should be done with such care that the carpet of the office should not be injured.

The planking, in turn, was cut through, and they climbed up, into the private office of President Lewis Fisher. When they were inside, it seemed as though every passer-by on the street could look straight in upon them, for the broad plate-glass windows were stretched all around the bank, showing the naked outlines of the safes, and there was a street lamp at the corner which cast a wide, glimmering light.

The two watchmen, approaching at that moment, seemed on the very verge of walking into the place, and the gang slipped to the floor and waited, breathless.

For long hours, so it seemed, the two watchmen maintained their conversation; then they sauntered slowly off, each casting glances which seemed to probe the dark bowels of the bank. Now Sally hurried to the door, and turning from that point, she squinted towards the safe, after which she came back to them: "Stand up and start work, Lefty," she said. "Everything seems bright looking out at the light, but looking in at the darkness even from the door one can't spot a thing. From outside the glass even an eagle couldn't see you!"

So said Sally, and Lefty obediently and willingly stood up. They dared not show a light, but he had a cigar going, and by the dim red illumination of its lighted end, he read the combination and fell on his knees beside the safe to listen.

No one stirred, no one whispered. It seemed to Jim Pleasant almost an amusing thing that this absent-minded dreamer, this stumbling, awkward, clumsy, useless bungler, should in the crisis be the cutting edge of the whole of Long Tom's machine. So not a breath was drawn, and a full quarter of an hour slipped away.

Then Lefty stood up and stretched.

"He's beaten!" said Long Tom fiercely, and through his teeth. "He's beaten, and the whole plan fails! No, by God! Christy, I'm going to blow the damned safe, and then we'll take our chances on getting what we can."

"We'd get jail, and that's all," declared Joe Christy calmly. "Are you done for, Lefty?"

In return, Lefty answered briefly, "Tell me the numbers. I can hear the tumblers fall, now. But one of you has squeaking shoes, and I wish that you'd stop shifting around on them. It drowns out everything!"

The others turned their head in the semi-darkness and smiled. To their less delicate ears, there had not been a single apparent sound.

Lefty now dropped to his knees again, and Joe Christy leaned beside him. From time to time, Lefty stopped, and when he stopped, Christy whispered the number which was indicated. Long Tom, dropping on one knee, wrote the quoted numbers on a broad pad he had taken from his pocket.

So the work went on; the silence grew more intense, and finally the soft whispers of Joe Christy seemed as loud as the shouting of a legion to the watchers with their wildly beating hearts.

Lefty paused again, and again stood up and stretched himself.

"Lefty?" gasped Long Tom, his usual stoical calm completely gone.

"I dunno," said Lefty in a very weary voice. "If I ain't got it now, I'll never get it. Now, Tom, come here and we'll check back that last set of numbers and see what happens!"

So Long Tom, reading the numbers by cigar-light, quoted them to his man, and Lefty worked the combination. There was a little click, and the wide door of the safe sagged open and fell slowly back. The ghost of light which fell from the street lamp of the corner touched upon the rows of boxes with which the inside of the big vault was lined, and where almost the total negotiable wealth of the banker was lodged.

They had a brighter light than this by which to look the situation in the face, for as the door of the safe reached its full width, there was another little click, and a broad electric light was shining down upon them, making the entire inside of the bank brilliant, and seeming to pour radiance out on to the street.

One gasp, one groan came from every throat, but Pleasant Jim acted as he groaned. He leaped for the steel fence of the cashier's cage, and sprang up to the second row of the bars. There he was able to reach the light that poured down bright ruin over their heads, and with a blow of his hand he quenched it; a little tinkling shower of glass fell back upon the floor, and after that the terrible, waiting silence began.

CHAPTER 18

AFTER the broadness of that light, it seemed most certain that the whole city must see and guess what was happening inside the bank. Lefty, his nerves quite gone, slipped down the hole into the shop below; and his teeth chattered audibly as he went.

He was in a blue funk, and would be good for little during the rest of that night when so much must still be done!

The rest, however, seemed steady enough; and now the two night watchmen came towards the corner, and it seemed like a blessing that they came without undue haste, swinging their clubs as calmly as ever. And yet that might be a cunning ruse, to pacify the criminals inside the bank, while sufficient forces to ensure their capture were brought together and pooled near by.

At the corner, as usual, the pair paused a moment in conversation, and then turning from the pavement, they pressed their faces at the same moment against the glass and peered inside. Their loud voices could be heard faintly, like far-off sounds in a mist.

"Can you see it?"

"Sure, I can see it."

"It's all right?"

"Sure, it is."

"I kind of thought that I saw something."

"You think too much. That's what comes of a high school education!"

And the two passed off, each on his separate beat.

Inside the bank there was a general stir, so terrible was the relief. And yet all danger was not gone, as the swift and eager voice of Long Tom assured the others at once. They had to make quick time, for the flare of light which had escaped the attention of the two night watchmen might well have attracted the attention of others above all, of that steadfast spy who observed matters from the building across the street from the bank. However, the light had not shone two seconds before the fist of Pleasant shattered it to bits, and there was a strong possibility that no one had marked its glare.

Now Joe Christy and Long Tom fell to work on the boxes within the safe. With wedges, with heavy hammers, with "can-openers" they struggled. Sally, from the door, peering down either side of the building through the big windows, gave warning by a lifting of her hand which told them when to stop all effort. And the signal was relayed by a whisper from Pleasant Jim.

The strength of that safe was in its walls of steel, and not in the individual boxes which it contained, for the banker had felt that it would be a needless expense to install units made of expensive tool-proof steel. They gave readily under the skillful handling of the two workers, and into a broad bit of canvas, which had been prepared, all the loot was dumped.

Every one of the boxes was opened; the safe doors were closed again and locked; the trifling débris was gathered up with care, and down through the hole in the floor they went, pushing the carpet back into place above the gap. Beneath, they had arranged a prop with a board on top so that no one stepping on the place where the hole had been cut would have any idea that robbers had come that way.

Pleasant Jim, by this time, was in a panic; he proposed that they start for their horses at once, in the spot at the edge of the town where Charlie Rizdal was to have the animals ready. Loot could be divided later on.

But Long Tom was adamant. He seemed to enjoy prolonging the suspense and, lighting a cigar, he sat down over the pile to sort it.

"Nobody has spotted us," he declared, "or they would have been at us long before this. Nobody is going to spot us, either, because we've covered up our traces. It will be about Monday at ten, when they open that safe, that they'll see what's happened, and after that it may be a time before they think to examine the floor of the office. This has been a neat job, boys, and neat jobs don't fall through. Before they start on our trail, we'll be more then twenty-four hours away, and with a start like that, who'll ever throw a scare into us? We've got to divide the stuff now, because if we don't, it will be too bulky and too easy to fall into the hands of some lucky guesser."

Swiftly they began the work, but it was not easily performed. All manner of odds and ends had been emptied from the drawers of the vault. There were old accounts, and ledgers, and even files of letters which that careful man of business had locked up beyond the reach of fire or of theft.

"There's stuff here," commented Long Tom, "that would make old Fisher yell if it were to be published. But blackmail isn't my line!"

It was a fixed business principle of Lewis Fisher's that ruined him now. The power of hard cash was what he worshiped, and his sense of power had only been fed by the knowledge that in the safe at the corner of his office there was a store of wealth which could be converted almost instantly into money. Money itself could not lie idle without sinful waste; but readily convertible securities were the same as cash and also they worked for the owner. He had broad holdings of real estate in the valley, as a matter of course, but the cream of them already had been sold and turned into his favorite form of investment, and in addition to that vault and its contents he had little indeed except his proprietary interest in the bank.

The wealth of Lewis Fisher, therefore, lay heaped upon that broad canvas strip, and the workers, busy and silent, checked the loot into even piles, eight in number. Three shares went to Long Tom, one for his brother, who had done much outside work in this affair, and two for the chief who had planned the work; there was a share apiece for Sally, for Joe Christy, and for Lefty; two shares also were reserved, according to promise, for Pleasant Jim.

The sum total was the magnificent amount of eight hundred and sixty-four thousand dollars; to Pleasant Jim, two hundred and sixteen thousand of the bulk was handed, and he stuffed it into a broad money-belt which he had provided for the occasion. It made a fat layer about his body, and he was smiling down at it when two sharp blows were struck at the front door of the gunshop.

Two terrible heart shocks were those strokes in the middle of the night! Who could be there?

Lefty, turning deathly pale, whirled to run for the rear exit, but Long Tom caught him with a hand of iron.

"You fool," he whispered, "they're giving us the scare from in front, but you can lay to it that they've spread the strongest net behind the shop. Out the front way, all of us. Pleasant, go beside me. It's Sam Lee. I'll swear to that! The rest of you come swarming behind. Soft foot it, now!"

Those directions he whispered swiftly, and added: "No shooting! Club your guns unless it's life or death. Then run straight down the street and double to the right down the narrow lane. Pleasant!"

With the last word, he glided towards the door, Jim Pleasant beside him. The heavy valance of the blankets which had shut all light into the store now acted to muffle the sound of their footsteps. Scarcely breathing, they stood behind the door just as two more thunderous knocks were leveled against it. A window screeched open, and the voice of the janitor called loudly: "Hey, you! What do you want down there? Don't you know the shop's closed, this hour of the night?"

There was no answer from the street; Long Tom, with stealthy, caution fingers, turned the key noiselessly in the lock and jerked the door suddenly open. At his side, Pleasant sprang through, his revolver raised, and he saw before him three men, grouped close together. Weapons glimmered in their hands; they were armed to the teeth, but doubtless they had felt, as Long Tom Rizdal guessed, that their summons would drive the herd through the rear entrance where they would be amply dealt with. One gun was fired; but it was merely a nervous contraction of a finger that sent a bullet into the pavement. Then Rizdal and Pleasant reached them, with Christy behind, and Lefty snarling like a furious panther. Down went the three as though a bolt from heaven had struck them, and while two lay crumpled and silent, stunned by the blows they had received, the third writhed blindly as the fugitives rushed on and began to scream in a dreadful voice:

"Help! Murder! Help! Help!"

That voice tore through the night, like light through darkness, and with each piercing syllable, a red pang of fear shot across the brain of Jim Pleasant.

He had fallen back towards the rear and now he half turned, his gun poised; but the girl, at whose side he had placed himself, tore at his arm.

"You fool! Do you want to hang?" she gasped.

And he went on beside her.

The others had drawn somewhat ahead, but not far. She ran like a deer, smoothly, with a springing stride, and so beside her, Pleasant dodged into the dark mouth of the alley.

A far Western town sleeps lightly; its nerves are too finely strung for heavy slumber; and a shot, a screaming voice, and then the heavy bawling of the frightened janitor from the window were enough to rouse more sluggish minds than theirs. Windows now began to be slammed up, and heads appeared, and beneath every head there was a gun.

Some had a glimpse of the fugitives; the others were told by the roaring voice of the janitor; and so trouble began to muster on the trail of the robbers, as wasps swarm forth to take vengeance upon an intruder.

Noise began to sweep over all of Fisher Falls; men shouted; dogs barked or howled wildly. But Long Tom, in the thick heart of the alley's darkness, halted his band. They stood close together, breathing hard.

"What's to do," asked Lefty, the most nervous of them all. "What's the plan, Chief?"

And the big man struck terror to every soul by saying swiftly: "We're cut off from Charlie and the horses; they're clean on the other edge of the town. Boys, God knows what we can do. I haven't a plan!"

CHAPTER 19

NEVER before had the Chief appeared so great to Jim Pleasant as on this occasion when he frankly confessed that his mind was at a loss and he himself in the utmost confusion. Silence held the rest, and Long Tom went on: "Whatever we do, we have to start for it soon. I say, let's go ahead for the railroad. The straightest way out of town would be along the ties; and perhaps when Charlie hears the noise, he may guess that we've gone on foot that way, and he'll come around to bring the horses to us along the track."

After despair, the faintest gleam of hope seemed bright and strong to them, and they followed willingly as the tall leader went on towards the railroad line, no longer running, but keeping a brisk walk. As for Jim Pleasant, he was in the rear, still, with the girl, and she panted as they went: "Now, don't you be a big sap, Jim. If the pinch comes, let me go. I could take care of myself. That's the agreement always when we're running for it. Every man for himself!"

Pleasant Jim looked down at her. He said nothing. And his silence spoke to her more than words. She wasted no more breath in protests, but as though realizing that he was beyond her influence, she kept on doggedly behind the others, breaking into a trot, now and again, to make up for lost distance. And Pleasant noticed that there was no hysteria or fear or of weakness in her. Alert, light-footed, she kept on her way with her head as high and her eyes as keen as though they were out for a pleasure stroll.

They reached the little railroad yard and got into the shadow of some heaps of ties as a small cavalcade of horsemen swept out of the body of the town and poured along the road towards the station. They were reading the minds of the fugitives, no doubt,

and guessing that they might head towards the iron trail. All the
town, now, was waking; lights gleamed from nearly every
window, and a gathering murmur showed that Fisher Falls was
rousing to its work. Five hundred mounted men, and every man
a good shot, might be sweeping over the countryside in the
search, before long.

And then, from a neighboring yard, they heard the piping
voice of a child saying: "That way! Towards the railroad yard!
They went that way!"

Crouched in the shadow of a pile of ties, the hunted looked
back and saw three men with rifles or shotguns in their hands
pause at the edge of the nearest fence. Hesitating there, they
seemed calling to the rear for help before they undertook the
dangerous search.

In that pause Lefty's nerve forsook him so far that he insisted
on thrusting his share of the loot under the pile of ties which
covered them with its shadow.

"Down the track a little, in that shed," said Long Tom softly
to his group, "is the hand-car. We haven't horses, but on the
downgrade we ought to make that car walk along faster than a
horse could run!"

So saying, he gave them a new touch of life. They had felt the
dangerous hand of the law reaching around them, and they
raced, now, to break from the circle before it should be
complete. Now that it was a matter of length of legs and power of
stroke, Jim Pleasant and Long Tom pushed ahead, side by side,
leaving the others well behind, and Pleasant was far ahead when
he reached the hand-car shanty and whirled around its corner
into the sight of two negroes playing a sedulous game of craps by
the aid of a railroad lantern.

"You Jack and Joe!" commanded Pleasant harshly. "Tumble
into the shed and help us roll out that car!"

Whatever fear they felt, the stimulus of the naked revolver
made them act. Pleasant had a glimpse of the rolling whites of
their eyes, and they rushed feverishly into the shed with him as
Long Tom came up. The doors were thrown open, and the
ponderous car started moving ah, with what sullen difficulty! out towards the track. Here were six men, however,
straining their muscles, and quickly the big truck was put aboard
the rails, and the party swarmed aboard it while Long Tom
tossed a handful of silver to the pair of negroes. They picked the

coins out of the air and then put their shoulders to the hand-car and gave it a flying start.

Hardly flying enough, indeed, for straight down the track came a mob of a dozen, bristling with guns, and gaining the fair view of the hand-car with the huddle of humanity aboard it, one of them called out loudly for the fugitives to surrender and the rest dropped on their knees to fire. What easier targets could they have wanted than this, with the straightness of the rails to guide their bullets home!

But Jim Pleasant, with careful gun, sent two bullets whistling about their ears. It would have been easy to drive every shot home, but his wide experience taught him that the sound of a bullet often will do more than the impact; the martial knot of heroes on the track melted away with yells of anger and fear; some random bullets they fired as they scattered, but not a soul on the moving car was touched. Now the pumping handles were beginning to pick up the speed; the hand-car shot out of view around the long, easy curve.

"Drop the car off the rails and take to the woods as soon as we're safely clear of the town," snorted Joe Christy, as he worked his turn. "They'll surely telephone to the Lower Falls and cut us off there!"

"We may beat the telephone message God knows!" said Long Tom. "But we have a ten times better chance if we get into the bigger country that lies beyond. Will you risk the Falls at this game, boys?"

They did not answer, except to pump at the handles more swiftly, until the hand-car was fairly reeling with speed. The grade was distinctly down; the power of their impetus sometimes threatened to jerk the handles from their grip, and a gale of wind was raised by their rate of progress.

On the front of the hand-car sat Sally. She kicked her feet and laughed as contentedly as a child on the back fence eating a piece of pie to the confusion of the neighbors. And in the meantime, despite the torrent of wind that poured into her face, she took down the masses of her hair, hitherto pinioned at the back of her head, and did it deftly into a great, luxurious knot at the nape of her neck. And with her handkerchief she scrubbed the red from her nose.

The moon rose untimely and showed the world an altogether altered Sally; and big Pleasant Jim had sight of her as he stepped to join the crew at the handles while the car approached the scattered hovels of the Lower Falls.

As they came, it seemed to them that they could see the fireflies of danger lighted before them, sparks gleaming from the windows of the cabins.

"Faster, for God's sake!" said Long Tom, and they began to saw up and down with all their might, until their arms went numb from wrist to shoulder and shooting pains settled in the small of the back.

Some one was running with a lantern, swinging it violently as he approached the track.

"Suppose that they've blocked the track!" cried Lefty the nervous. "We'll all be killed!"

"Suppose there is fire in hell!" answered Pleasant Jim. "We'll all have to wind up there some day!"

And fiercely they increased their speed and took the curve before the station, rocking with the violence of their impetus. The moon was well up, by this time, and under its light they saw men coming, some on horseback and some on foot, and three or four, in the lead, just scrambling up the bank.

"Drive 'em back or we're done!" said Long Tom.

And Pleasant Jim straightened his aching back, and stood against the wind with a gun in either hand. He was frightened. He was wonderfully and terribly frightened; but his brain was as clear as stars on a very cold winter night. He placed his shots with the nicest skill. He raked the ground with the first pair so that the cinders the bullets raised must have been dashed into the faces of those who were climbing the bank. Several fell back, shouting with fear, and only two men gained the upper level and ran on towards the track. Each was carrying a small timber and their purpose was plain. So much as a pebble placed on the rails would probably knock over the hand-car; and Pleasant Jim fired with a different purpose.

"Kill them!" thundered Long Tom. "Kill them, or we're done, Pleasant."

Something other than death was in the mind of Pleasant; and the words of the marshal drifted back through his mind. Sometimes, surely, it was valuable to be able to shoot so well that murder was not necessary in order to stop a man.

Just below the hips of the other man he drew his bead. It was not easy to fire from the rocking, rushing hand-car, thrust forward by the irregular motion of the handles, but after all, it was very much like firing from the back of a galloping horse only easier!

He fired   the man ran on and raised his timber to throw it on the tracks. He fired again, and man and timber fell in a heap. The companion lost all interest in the work he had undertaken, and dropping his piece, turned and fled wildly for safety beyond the bank.

A bullet singing near his ears gave him wings; and making a final leap he tripped and tumbled headlong to safety, while the hand-car shot past the danger point and the shriek of the wounded man ran up the scale into their ears and died down again as they shot on like a hurricane.

A scattering of rifle shots rang behind them, but then they drove on past the side of a line of freight cars back on to the siding, and so they had shelter until another curve of the tracks whipped them from the sight of the Lower Falls station.

Vague noises of guns and of human voices beat in the night behind them, but they were hurling on towards freedom, or at least towards a better chance of escape than had seemed possible since the moment the two knocks came on the door of the gun-shop.

CHAPTER 20

THEY rested from their work for a moment. The strong arms of Pleasant and Long Tom kept the hand-car rattling on at a good gait, but no longer was there the rushing wind of their speed about their ears, and the trees and telegraph poles beside the track no more were leaping wildly past them. Smoothly the wheels clicked along the rails, sweetly and easily it took the curves, for still the long down-grade favored them and its own weight was enough to keep the car rolling.

They discussed the best probabilities, then, and among the rest, whether it would not be wisest to ditch the car at once and take to their heels across country. For doubtless it would be expected that they would keep on the rails for many a mile, and all pursuit would tend headlong to a considerable point past this.

Long Tom, however, advised that they continue up the railroad as far as conveniently possible, for the tracks leaned well to the north, now, and soon would edge along the tall mountains in the heart of which, scattered here and there, he knew where they could find good and trusty friends, and horses to carry them on their way.

But even Long Tom was a little uncertain. In all the deeds of daring which he had committed the horse had been his means of approach and his means of escape, except for a few occasions when the blind baggage of a speeding express train had snatched him away from the reaching arms of the law. Cast now upon the resources of foot and hand power, he was a little bewildered, and although it was the coolness and surety of his advice which had carried them safely to this point, it was plain that he lacked any great self-confidence. That lack was reflected, now, in the spirit of criticism which was beginning to arise among his companions. And Lefty was the leader of the semi-revolt.

The nerves of Lefty were always on the hair-trigger variety. Good for a flash of fight, or a moment of heroism, his strength of body and mind was like the strength of a hunting cat. He could scheme patiently enough; he could spend his days and his weeks of planning, studying, preparing for a great adventure; and like a cat, he could strike brilliantly, swiftly, decisively. But afterwards he could not sustain his morale.

The force gave way; he began to disintegrate. A leopard can catch an antelope in a hundred yards and give the deer an ample handicap; but the antelope could beat the leopard over twice that distance, and fairly laugh if the course were a quarter of a mile. So it was with Lefty. The shocks and the strains of the robbery had worn him out; he was conscious, too, that in an early moment of stress he had abandoned his share of the loot, and a driving rain, or the removal of the pile of ties might snatch his fortune from him. Therefore, with only bitterness of spirit to sustain him, and with only gloom in his heart, Lefty's powers of mind and thought rapidly were giving way.

He curled up on the hand-car, blinking at the trees as they sailed by him, and shuddering now and again, as though the cold thought of past danger came home to him, or the dread of danger to come overwhelmed him.

He insisted, now, in an incisive, whining voice, that they should take the car from the rails at once and take to the woods.

Long Tom was the height of patience.

"And why, Lefty?" he asked gently. "What's the vital danger that we're in?"

"There could be a blockade of the rails," said Lefty eagerly. "They could wreck us as easily as I break this splinter!"

"How could they get word ahead?"

"Good God, man, by telephone or telegraph, of course! Ain't they done it before?"

"There's no station nearer than Wetherby."

"Something could happen something could happen!" insisted the querulous Lefty. "They might catch us up from behind!"

"Can horses run as fast as this hand-car?" said the calm chief. "I mean, on this downgrade?"

There was an interruption from another source.

"They got iron horses on this trail," said Joe Christy sullenly.

"You might as well think about that, Chief! Suppose that they get an engine out after us?"

"There was no engine in the yards at Fisher Falls!"

"Ay, but there might be one up or down the line!"

"There might be green cheese in the moon," said the cheerful leader.

"I tell you, you're closin' your eyes!" shouted Lefty, his nerves mastering him in a leap.

"Steady! Steady!" said Long Tom, but even as he spoke of steadiness his own impatience mastered him.

So he added in passion: "We need one head and one master in this business, and I suppose that that's my place. Lefty, keep still till I ask for advice, will you? They're not going to be able to chase us with an engine; and so we'll be able to run on the tracks close to the edge of the mountain."

Lefty was crushed to silence by this exhibition of authority, but now as the hand-car reached a long shoot where the rails were very smooth and straight and where the wheels made no sound other than a soft clicking, the fugitives heard a dull rumbling far behind them, then a blink of light like the glance of a great eye coming up from behind.

"What's that, if you know it all?" shouted Lefty, pointing in a frenzy of fear and excitement. "If that ain't an engine coming, I'm a fool and a sap!"

They should have brought the car instantly to a stop and heaved it from the rails so that they could get into the woods without being noticed, but Long Tom was too angry and stubborn to give the order at once and they remained under way, though with diminishing speed, until with a roaring and crashing and a singing like great strings under a resined bow, the pursuit engine came in full view around the next bend. It rocked with speed, and above it blew a cloud of steam through which the moonlight shone and made it whiter than any image of Parian marble from the Cyclades.

Now that the danger was so near, the crew of the hand-car fell to work instantly, stopped it, and heaved it from the track; it rolled down the bank, crashing among the brush, and the engine went by at the same moment that the gang took shelter in the shadows. The screaming brakes halted the big machine a short distance away, and Pleasant, lingering a little behind the others, saw streams of armed men descend. They seemed to have been packed in every inch of standing room on the engine and its capacious tender, and two-score fighting men were now running back to take up the hunt. Then he strode on in the direction of the sounds of crackling brush, far ahead.

Nothing could have been more foolish than to proceed so noisily, and it troubled Pleasant. Ordinarily these people were crafty enough, and that they should simply dash away like so many wild bulls amazed him. Apparently Long Tom's authority had received a fatal blow, for the time being.

He caught up with them as they struggled up an ascent, the girl not much in the rear of the others, but as he came striding by her he called after the men ahead: "Here's Sally pegging out. Are you going to let her go?"

"Every man for himself!" snarled Lefty, who was next in front of them. "And even if they caught her, she'd wheedle her way out of their fingers! Sally, if you have any sense, you give me your share to keep for you!"

Sally, breathing hard, said nothing, but worked steadily ahead, and Pleasant kept on beside her, beating back the brush to let her get through the thickets; sometimes he stalked ahead and broke trail for her. And so she managed to keep up with the weakest of the party.

They got to the top of the ascent, and found themselves on a low hill from whose bare head they could look about over the moon-misted woodland. Behind them the line of noise had spread out wide and thin as the hunters beat the forest for their game. The fugitives had flung themselves down on their backs to catch a fresh breath, and Pleasant kneeled beside the girl.

"Leave me alone, Jim," she gasped at him. "You'll throw yourself away. Take my slice of the coin and keep it for me. That's the best thing you can do. I haven't the strength to keep ahead of them!"

He said quietly: "You and I'll hide and let the rest go on, and afterwards we'll slip back to the engine; it can't be very heavily guarded. I'll get the drop on the engineer and make him take us on down the line. Would you have the nerve for that?"

Nerve for it? She sat up with gleaming eyes, her fatigue forgotten, but to mock them and beat down their hopes, at that moment they could hear the heavy, rhythmic puffs of the engine as it got up speed down the track, hurtling on, no doubt, to reach the next town and bring back a fresh supply of head-hunters.

The flight began again; but it was a little easier, now, for the ground sloped away before them, and the girl managed to keep up.

Dawn was beginning; the moon was turning dim; from white and black, the woods were turning to a dull gray when Long Tom called his band about him. Scouting well ahead he had found what promised to be a refuge to a certain degree.

On a sharp upslope behind a dense wall of brush, he had found the wide, shallow mouth of a cave. It was a damp, gloomy looking hole; only in the center could it be entered, but here they went in one by one and worked to either side. There was barely room for them to rest in the dark and the damp.

Day was coming, and with it the searchers pushed across the woods. They beat through the very thicket which lay in front of the cave, and finally some one dropped on his knees and peered into the shadows. He could have stretched out his hand and touched the motionless figures within; but he got up without a word and went on!

CHAPTER 21

"HE's gone for help to bag us!" said Lefty, even his whisper a sadly shaken sound. "He's gone on for help. Let's crawl out and make a fight of it—"

Long Tom did not argue, but he reached across and clamped his hand over the mouth of the safe-cracker.

So they lay in silence, a sick, long silence, waiting for the return of the spy with plenty of guns to back him up. But the other did not come back! The shadows through which those on the inside looked easily enough, had been too thick for that searcher to pierce.

The morning sun was high, now; it was a bright, hot day, and they could hear the oaths and stampings of the searchers, still beating wearily back and forth. Then a new terror came to the quiet fugitives, for feet trampled on the ground above their little cave, and a considerable amount of dirt and gravel fell on their backs; it seemed for a moment that they must risk burial alive or else crawl out and surrender, but no more fell, and presently they could hear, distinctly, the voices of two men in conversation; and one of them was the singular voice of Federal Marshal Sam Lee.

His companion was of the opinion that the whole group of fugitives had pressed straight on for the mountains; and in that direction he would throw forward the search-parties. But Sam Lee pointed out that already messages had been telegraphed and telephoned to all near-by towns in the mountains, so that a swarm of searchers surely must be out by this time to block all escape in that direction. Their duty must be to make sure that Long Tom and his gang did not manage to slip back down the valley to the railroad.

He pointed out, moreover, that the band could not have gone

very far, because a woman had kept with them. He himself had seen the print of her foot near the soft bank of a rivulet not a quarter of a mile back.

"And that," said the other, "I dunno that I understand I mean, Long Tom Rizdal keeping a woman along like this! He's in love with her, maybe!"

"He's in love with nothing," said Sam Lee. "He'd cut her throat if he thought it would really help them to get away. Lefty and Joe Christy would cut her throat, too. None of them would be bothered by her. It must be the other man Holman, he calls himself."

"If you knew 'em so well," said the other, complaining, "why didn't you clamp down on them before they got into the bank?"

"I only guessed; I sent for pictures and such things. I got them identified last evening. I was just a few hours too late. No, hardly more'n minutes. That's the luck of the law!"

He sighed a little. Then his voice came more loudly.

"There's a hole under this bank where a man or two could curl up!"

The hand of Lefty closed convulsively upon the arm of big Pleasant.

"Nothing in there," sang out the marshal's companion. "I got down on my knees and had a look at it, a few minutes ago."

Five hearts ceased thundering in the little cave!

"There'll be some fighting if we *do* snag them," suggested the posseman.

"Long Tom will die before he lets himself be caught," answered the marshal with perfect surety. "The other two might fire a couple of shots, but they'd rather be jailed for robbery than murder. Holman, as he calls himself I don't know about. I think he'll be a tougher job than Long Tom himself. What'll come of old Man Fisher after this?"

"He'll die of a broken heart."

"Ay, and maybe he will. Let's get on again and keep the boys busy. Mark me the five of them are not far from this very spot!"

So truly spoke Sam Lee, and they heard him walking away with his companions through the brush.

But that was hardly the middle of that dreary day. The sun still had to reach noon and then go slowly, slowly down the western sky, but still the five dared not leave their hiding place for all day long the sound of the hunters beat up and down through the woods, and twice they heard feet falling within a few yards of their screening thicket.

Darkness began to gather once more, but not until the blackness was complete would Long Tom crawl from the cave and allow his companions to do likewise. Then they stretched and beat their numb bodies into some sense of life; and after that they gathered in a close circle to consult.

The valley was like a loose sleeve, hiding them with its woods but also trapping them. The railroad was one margin for escape, but it would be securely watched; the mountains must now be honeycombed by the searching parties; and the upper and lower ends of the valley would be plugged by the care of Marshal Sam Lee. The decision of the leader was that they should hold straight across country, no matter how difficult, and point towards the mountains, as being the wall through which they could break with the greatest ease; but both Cristy and Lefty held strongly out against this course. They dreaded almost more than the certainty of imprisonment the necessity of having to face another march through the tearing underbrush. Moreover, they were desperately hungry. None of them had tasted a morsel for thirty hours, and during that time they had performed a great deal of physical labor.

So they headed back towards the railroad, taking a slanting course in that direction down the bank of a winding creek. To Pleasant, as a matter of course, was given the most dangerous post of rear guard, where he walked with the girl, keeping a keen lookout; Long Tom went ahead to spy out danger as they might approach it and break trail; and Joe Christy and Lefty were the main body, so to speak, and a very grumbling and discontented one.

Before they had gone very far, they heard the sound of a rooster crowing, and Lefty swore at once, and with vehemence, that he would have that rooster to eat before the night was an hour older. Long Tom vainly protested, declaring that they would be bringing down unnecessary dangers upon their heads if they lingered along the way or caused extra alarms to be sent out concerning their presence. However, Joe and Lefty outvoted him again, for Pleasant would deliver no opinion. He seemed to have fallen into a dream, striding along through the night, giving heed to all the sights and noises near him, but to no human being other than the girl. So the little column diverged to the right until, in a hollow before them, they saw the glimmering lights of a farmhouse. In the direction of that house, Lefty disappeared with stealthy haste. The rest waited breathlessly. They heard a dog begin to bark violently; the barking ceased with suddenness. Then a door crashed, and from an unhooded window a stream of light probed the dark; some one shouted sharp and high: "It's Lefty!" said Pleasant, and lurched forward, but the strong hand of Long Tom checked him.

"He's brought it on himself if he's snagged there!" said the Chief.

A gun exploded   not with the clang of a rifle but the roar of a shotgun, hoarse and sharp   a barking noise.

Then silence.

And out of the darkness a stealthy, hurrying form came back to them; Lefty, carrying beneath his arm a fat rooster whose head had been wrung off. And now that there was food offered, their raging appetites did the rest and there was no further criticism of Lefty immediately. They found a close cluster of trees where they risked a small fire and in the flames the chicken, having been cut into pieces, was roasted at the end of wooden splinters. But Pleasant, having cooked his portion with care, made only a pretense of eating it, but dropped back into the shadows and wrapped the meat in paper and put it away. Another notch of his belt drawn tight would take the place of food for him, for some time to come!

Lefty, in the meantime, explained the noises which had been heard from the house. When he drew near to it, he had been rushed by a dog, but he had clubbed the brute over the head with a billet of wood, and then gone on. But when he came to the entrance to the henhouse, he had touched a wire with his foot. Instantly a shaft of light came from the house and struck the henhouse and he knew that he had walked into a trap. Hunger, however, had made him desperate. A hasty reach secured him the rooster from the perch, and hurrying back again, he saw the farmer, shotgun in hand, come storming from the rear of the house. He tried to skulk away, unseen, but his shadow, moving against the white-painted chicken house, betrayed him, and the result was a two-barreled charge of shot that rattled all about him but left him luckily unhurt. The farmer waited to recharge his weapon, and before that was done Lefty was out of sight.

He was much cheered both by his exploit and by the food

which he had eaten, but as he finished he said: "Now admit that I was right, Tom! Admit that, will you? Because you've been talking pretty hard to me lately!"

There was no reply from Long Tom. They waited another quarter of an hour, but he did not come to them. This was his answer to the insubordination of his companions; he had gone off to try for escape by himself. A sudden and loud yell of hounds broke through the trees then, and Lefty and Joe Christy, thoroughly unnerved, leaped to their feet and dashed away. Sally would have followed them, but Pleasant held her back.

"They have put dogs on us!" she cried to him. "Jim, are you going to wait here to be pulled down?"

"Lefty and Joe are making trail," said Pleasant. "Maybe the dogs will take after them. At any rate, that's their business. How long could you keep ahead of a pack, Sally?"

And he drew her back into the shadow of the trees.

They were barely out of sight when half a dozen looming shadows of bloodhounds came through the trees. They circled, giving tongue loudly, near the remains of the fire; but then a cluster of men came panting up to them and cheered them on.

"It was the luck of God that quartered us in that shack!" one of them said. "Boys, we're gunna nab the whole gang. Get on, Faithful! Follow up, Grip! Go on! Yi! Yi!"

And the pack, after milling an instant later, picked up the trail of Lefty and Christy and plunged away through the trees.

CHAPTER 22

RAIN clouds had been piling in the sky, unnoticed by the wanderers. Now a volley crashed like musketry through the foliage, and other volleys followed, until the woodland was drowned in a roar of falling water. Even through the heaviest trees, fountains began to break, and the girl and Pleasant were drenched instantly. Thunder was beating in the south, and long arms of lightning reached hastily across the southern sky. In such a riot of noise and confusion, thought itself was difficult, and speech was almost impossible. So Pleasant put himself in front and made trail, pointing his course by the direction from which he first had spotted the storm.

The ground surface turned to slippery mud; every hole was filled with water; constantly he was plunging in, ankle or knee deep, and the going became tremendously difficult. Every moment or two he had glanced back towards the girl, but as he paused for breathing space, now, on the verge of a rapidly running little stream, she was no longer behind him. He waited; then he shouted in a great voice, but there was no answer, except the dashing of the branches under the wind and the rain, and the groaning of boughs against one another.

He turned and floundered back down the trail a few steps.

"Sally! Sally!" he boomed.

And then seeing a dense thicket, he lurched into it and nearly stumbled over a soft form which was curled up on the ground. He picked her up.

"Sally, what's wrong?" he asked. "Are you sick?"

She put her lips close to his ear, so that she could make him hear.

"I can't keep up. I'm numb and weak with the walking, Jim. Go on and save yourself," she said. "What good will it be for both of us to land in jail?"

He took off his coat and wrung it out, then wrapped her in it, in spite of her weakly protesting hands.

"I've let men lead me to-night," he said, "that had no more sense than a pack of jackrabbits. Now I'm gunna lead you   or carry you! You wanted to dodge me. Well, you wouldn't have dodged into a jail; you'd have dodged into a grave. You couldn't live through all of this water and hell, to-night."

He waited for a few moments longer, and then he forced her to get up and go on with him to the edge of the water. There she paused.

"I can't go on, Jim!" she said. "I can't get through that and you'll   "

He picked her up, lightly, and strode into the water. Midway, his feet sank into a sort of quicksand and the water rushed up more than waist high. For a moment he stood fast, struggling, and the shrill, eager, desperate voice cried at his ear: "Let me go! I'll manage   I'll swim! You're throwing yourself away!"

He merely gathered her closer and through the drenched cloth some faint warmth of her body came to him. It gave Pleasant an odd strength; the labor which had been overwhelming an instant before now became hardly more than child's play, and he stepped on through the water to the shelving bank.

There he put her down and rested his hand against a tree.

The wind and the rain had fallen away a little, just then; there was chiefly the wail of the storm in the upper branches, and the far-off pulse of the thunder to the south; they could speak now and be heard without shouting.

"Can you stand it a little longer?" he asked her.

She nodded.

"You're only weak, Sally? Not sick?"

"I'm strong enough."

"Gimme your word of honor that you won't try to duck away from me on the trail?"

She was silent. He caught her by both shoulders and shook her in anger.

"Damn it," cried Pleasant Jim, "you're chucking us both because I wouldn't try to win through without you! Do you hear? I'll carry you into the first house and give us both up!"

"I'll go on," said the girl in a broken voice. "I'll try to go on. Ah, God, Jim, but you're a terrible man!"

"Curse me, and it'll do you good!" he directed. "Set your

teeth and damn me. It'll buck you up a lot. Now, come on!"

And he started on through the woods, still slipping and sliding, and wondering at the ease and the grace with which the girl kept beside him. Twice they forced through great thickets through which it required all his strength and skill to break a passage for her, and she kept close behind, never crying out when the branches lashed her as he was forced to release them and let them fly back. But when they came to a stretch of farm fields with the blocky outline of a dark barn and house standing in the midst, she was staggering with fatigue.

Here, perforce, must be their harborage for the night.

They found cattle on one side of the big barn, and several horses on the other, and had she been in better condition, he would have insisted on saddling a pair of the mustangs and riding on with them towards the mountains in the north. But she was far too spent, and he made her climb up the ladder to the loft.

There, lost in the pitchy darkness, with the warmth and sweetness of the newly mowed hay, he told her to take off her clothes and throw them to him. He wrung them as dry as his powerful hands could twist and tossed them back with directions that she should put them on again and then burrow into the hay. He himself did the same, and sleep leaped in a benumbing wave upon his brain.

He dreamed of wandering through a vast and starry universe on wings, with the light of a distant goal before him, and with him Sally flying also, but her pinions flagging. He took her in his arms and flew on, but her weight was dragging them both down and down—even with the light of their goal close before them. And he heard her voice, protesting bitterly, telling him that it was better for one to be saved than both lost.

And then he wakened suddenly and found himself in the warm hayloft with the warm mid-morning sun streaming through the cracks; and leaning above him in this golden-streaked gloom was Sally!

He sat up and stared at her.

"I thought that you'd never wake up," said Sally.

"How did you do it?" asked he. "How did you manage it, Sally?"

"To wake you up? By tickling your face with this straw."

"You look as fresh as a daisy."

"I combed out the seeds and the chaff from my hair; I always keep a comb with me, and you'd better use it, Jim."

He could do nothing but wonder at her, for she was by no means the white-faced, pinched, and hollow-eyed ghost of his dream. She seemed to be blooming as he never had seen her bloom before. Sally the blank-eyed drudge was gone, and Sally the hard-headed, sharp-tongued thief was gone also. It was not all in the way she had combed her hair, knotting it gracefully at the nape of her neck. Her jacket and blouse and dress were streaked and stained and covered with a network of fine wrinkles, but still there seemed a bloom upon her. It was more than the color in her cheeks. A sort of light was breaking out from her as though her body were translucent and something of the spirit came through. A continual smile was on her lips, and yet there was no mockery about it; and her eyes were like a luminous mist as they gazed down at Pleasant Jim.

He stood up and regarded her again.

"You look changed, Sally," he declared in all honesty. "And you look wonderful, too. You look as if—you look as if   "

He paused for a word, but he found none, only adding in some confusion: "As, if you'd turned into another woman! But look here," he added, "you got to have something to eat; I'm going to forage."

"There's no use," answered the girl. "There are two or three men working in the field near the house and the barn. You couldn't dare to go out. But we have a decent chance. We can saddle a couple of the horses that are still in the stalls down below us, and then we could make a break for it, through the door. The foothills aren't half a mile away."

"We'll have breakfast before we start," said he. "You'll have it, I mean." And he went on, as he drew from his coat pocket the rather bedraggled bits of roast chicken: "It don't look good, Sally, but it'll give you strength. As for me, I got a quicker way. I just pull up my belt a couple of notches. And there I am. I'm used to it, you see."

She looked at the food in amazement; and then broke into hushed laughter.

"I might have known," said she. "This is like you! Try the other pocket, Jim!"

Astonished, he dipped into it, and brought out a parcel like his own, wrapped in a handkerchief. She, too, had saved her rations of the night before. And she had dropped them into his coat.

He handed the meat to her without a word; without a word he devoured his own share, always gloomily contemplating the golden light that sifted through the cracks in the side of the barn, with a host of sparkling motes dancing in each narrow shaft. He frowned because otherwise he felt that he should break into hysterical, foolish laughter. A sort of warm joy was dissolving his self-control and his heart leaped like a bird on the wing. Moreover, he dared not look at her, for when he saw her picking the bones with perfect daintiness and composure, and smiling at him continually with that new-born spirit, he knew that he could not trust himself or his speeches.

"We'd better be starting on," said Pleasant Jim at last. "I'll look over the ground first."

With that, he crawled to the edge of the hay and looked down. There were only four horses remaining on that side of the barn, and his eye was gladdened by the sight of saddles on the pegs behind them; no other living thing was in sight. So he and the girl climbed down the ladder, he first and she following, and while he was still a step or two from the ground he heard a quiet voice say: "Just freeze right in that place, Mr. Holman, will you?"

He jerked his head around and saw the steady barrel of a rifle covering him!

CHAPTER 23

ONE may take chances with a revolver, which is a careless and sometimes a foolish weapon; but there is a sort of philosophical calm about a rifle which discourages questions and sudden starts, and brave attempts. Behind the rifle was a face like the face of a bull terrier that is to say, there was a long, down-bending nose, and a narrow forehead which hastily hid itself in short-cropped hair, and two eyes very small and black, crowded close under the shadow of the nose. There was a thin-lipped broad mouth cut in a straight line and under this a chin which receded, without giving token of weakness. It was a face which, in a photograph, would have looked extremely simple, but the brightness and the animal intensity of the eyes, in actual life, gave it meaning. There was no touch of grayness about this man, and there was no trace of a wrinkle even around the eyes, and yet something in the ruddy, weathered skin made one understand that he must be at least fifty.

Above all, he was not the sort of man who would miss with a rifle!

He said in rather a sharp and boyish voice which had little or no excitement in it: "You put your hands over your head, Holman, and come down the ladder that way. The lady, she better stay where she is, up the ladder!"

Pleasant Jim had been in many narrow corners, and it was very nearly impossible for him to think of a predicament in which he would not be able to strike back; but here he knew that he was helpless. He put his hands above his head and climbed down the ladder to the ground, where he faced the farmer.

From the distance a woman's voice wailed: "Jo-el-l-l! Oh, Joel! Jo-el-l-l!"

"Coming in a minute, wife," said the farmer with a grin. "I'm just hung up here a minute!"

"Joel Peet," cried the shrill voice, "where are you?"

"Be still," said the farmer softly, with a shrug of his shoulders. And he added to Pleasant: "Here's four of you caught already! If I had the robbing of a bank and got the stuff in my hand, I'd aim to make a better getaway than that!"

"Four?" echoed the girl from the ladder.

"Are you chimin' in, honey?" asked the farmer. "Four, I said. Lefty and Christy are in jail, now, at Fisher Falls, where you two will be before very long. And here's the pair of you added!"

"Hold on!" said Pleasant. "I've a bargain to make with you, Peet, if that's your name."

"Go on," said the farmer. "You have my name right. Now let's hear the bargain."

"You take me and the money that's on both of us and call it square. What good will it do you to drag a girl through the dirt and put her in a common jail?"

"I dunno," said the other, "that it makes any particular difference, except about ten thousand dollars. But I'm a kind of a close-fisted man, and ten thousand is a sum that I could use to sort of put up some new fences and even repair the old ones, maybe!"

He grinned with a deep delight as he spoke, and added: "No, old son, I see that you're kind of sweet on the girl, though by the sassy look of her I'd guess that she ain't sweet on nothing but herself. But I'll tell you what; neither of you is going to slip through the fingers of Joel Peet!"

"Look here, Mr. Peet," said the girl, "suppose that we make another proposition to you. You turn us in; you get twenty thousand for the job. Well, that's a pretty nice piece of money. But suppose you don't turn us in. How much money would you have then?"

"Tell me!"

"A hundred thousand, Mr. Peet. You'd be a rich man!"

"Thanks," said Peet. "That's a doggone kind suggestion, but lemme tell you something. For a gent like me, twenty thousand is enough. More'n that would be enough to make my wife put on airs. Besides, I ain't a crook, I never been one, and I ain't gunna start. Holman, how many guns you got on you?"

"If I had one," said Pleasant with apparent bitterness, "do

you think that I would have held up my hands for any one man in the world?"

Mr. Peet looked into the blazing eyes of his captive and smiled broadly. There seemed something delicious, to him, in the pain which he was inflicting, and Pleasant Jim thought of the smile of the bull terrier, as it fixes its hold deeper in the throat of a victim.

"I got no doubt that you mean what you say," said he. "They say that you're the cool one that run the gunshop right under the nose of the bank all that time, and cut through the floor. That took nerve, eh?"

Pleasant Jim said nothing.

"But," continued the farmer, "how come you to be such a fool as to lose your guns? Doggone me if I can imagine doing that, no matter what happened!"

"I got a weakness for old things," said Pleasant. "I hate to chuck an old coat, say."

"Me too," agreed Peet. "Go on."

"And that damn gunbelt, I'd packed it ever since I was a kid. It was cracked and weak, but I thought it was my luck. And when I was hot-footing it through the woods with the marshal's men behind me, it caught on the edge of a broken branch and ripped clean away. I was twenty feet on through the brush before I could stop myself, and then I seen the head and shoulders of a gent coming after me, and closer to my stuff than I was."

Mr. Peet groaned.

"Mean luck!" said he. "Well—here you are. And you got a second belt, I see?"

"Yes."

"What's that for?"

"Money."

"It seems pretty fat and bulging."

"There's nearly a quarter of a million in it," said Pleasant Jim, honestly enough.

"A quarter of a million!"

"A shade less, for a fact, but not much."

"Peel it off," said Mr. Peet huskily. "And you was gunna offer me a hundred thousand for a clean pair of heels, ma'am?" he grinned at the girl.

"Jo-el-l-l!" shrilled the impatient wife.

"Wait a minute, sweetie," said the farmer, with his repulsive smile.

And he added: "I ain't exactly wasting my time. Peel off that there belt, Holman! Peel it quick!"

"Friend," said Pleasant Jim, "you got no more right to that belt than I have. You'd be robbing me as much as I robbed the bank!"

"We'll see," said the farmer. "There's a difference between us—the difference of a rifle, say, coverin' the mark and damn ready to go off any minute. Will you peel off that belt and quit your talkin'?"

"You bully and coward!" cried Sally from the ladder, swinging around and facing the farmer. "You got a helpless unarmed man and you—"

"Shut your face, will you?" said the farmer in his strange, squeaking tones. "You got some of the loot on you, too, I suppose?"

"Whether I have or not, you'll never get it."

"We'll see. That's right, stranger," he added, as Pleasant Jim obediently undid the buckles of his money belt. "Let it drop and—"

"Peet! Stick up your hands!" cried the girl suddenly.

The muzzle of the rifle jerked away from Pleasant towards the girl on the ladder, at that alarming cry; there was a bright glint of metal in her extended hand that well might have drawn a shot from him, but with a grunt he pulled his gun back to cover Pleasant Jim. And all in the smallest split part of a second.

However, in a still smaller space, the hand of Pleasant Jim had leaped up under his coat and snatched out a revolver from a spring holster beneath his arm-pit. Rifle and Colt exploded at well-nigh the same instant, but the smaller gun spat fire first. A bullet hissed at the ear of Jim Pleasant; a sting of smoke cut into his face and eyes, half blinding him, but there stood Joel Peet, his rifle fallen to the barn floor, and his bleeding right arm grasped by his left hand. All his face was pale, except for a purple splotch in the center of either cheek.

And he said, above the trampling of the frightened horses: "Thanks, Holman. You might of aimed for the heart, just as well!"

"You're a cool devil," answered Pleasant. "Stand where you are—Sally, keep him covered!"

She had sprung down from the ladder instantly and picked up the rifle, and Pleasant Jim turned to the horses. Of the four, any amateur could have selected the better pair. They stood side by side, a roan and a bay mustang, now dancing and shaking their heads. From the pegs along the wall, he snatched the saddle and bridles; never was a pair more rapidly accoutered than this.

Footsteps, in the meantime, and anxious voices approached the barn: "Jo-ell!" screamed the woman, coming rapidly nearer.

"Tell her you're all right. Your gun went off by accident!" commanded Sally.

"Mary, you fool!" shouted Joel Peet obediently, "can't I take a shot at a rat without bringin' you running?"

"Joel, you fool!" said the better half of the farmer. "Are you wastin' rifle ammunition on game like that? You come into the house right quick. I got something for you to do. And you boys," she added, apparently to the laborers who had come running up after her, "you get back into the fields. There's nothing happened."

"I heard two shots," said one in protest.

"You heard an echo. Don't stand there arguin'. You just want a middlin' excuse for layin' and wastin' time!"

The footsteps retreated, and Pleasant Jim led the two horses towards the door. There he picked up and opened the money belt.

"Here's five hundred dollars, Peet," said he. "I suppose that's the price of the pair—and the cost of healin' your arm?"

The other was silent, his eyes as keen and glittering as ever as he regarded the bulky contents which remained in the belt.

"Can you pull back the door for us?" asked Sally, as she and Pleasant mounted.

"Easy," nodded Joel Peet.

And he drew open the creaking, groaning sliding door of the barn; outside, they saw the gleam of the open country, and the glitter of the sun in the distant trees, and beyond the brown mountains and the blue.

"Go it!" said Peet. "It's cost me a good deal to stay honest, but maybe it'll be worth the price."

And his eyes were still smiling as they went by him, and the smile was not without a tinge of honest mirth.

Straight through the doorway they cantered, their heads high, alert for any sign of danger; but the two laborers already were deep in the field, at work; and Joel Peet's wife did not so much as turn her head on her way to the farmhouse. There might be some chance of a rear attack even from the wounded Peet, however, so they pulled their galloping horses to the side and presently a shroud of trees had rolled a green cloud between them and that narrowest of escapes.

Then Pleasant drew the horses back to an easy gait. He turned to the girl, and she laughed back at him, an electric laugh of joyous excitement.

"What did you use for that bluff, Sally?"

"The comb," she answered, still laughing.

"That trick might have brought a bullet through your head," he suggested gravely.

"But it didn't. It brought us three hundred thousand, and freedom, and everything."

"Until Sam Lee gets on our trail."

"He'll never be near us again. I've forgotten him; he's behind me!"

"Sally," said he, "take it from me, he'll be bringin' himself back into your mind, one of these days!"

CHAPTER 24

THEY were in the hills, but still all was not ended in the way of anxiety, for as far as they knew the most difficult wall to break through might be the swarm of posses which, beyond doubt, now moved through the whole face of the mountains looking down towards Fisher Valley. And if, as they gathered from Joel Peet, the banker had offered a ten thousand dollar reward for each and every man of the posse, then it would be strange if every man in the district were not out on horseback, or slipping in small parties through the woods and up and down the creeks looking for the fugitives. And men who had in view such prospects of reward would be very hard to bribe—even old friends of the Rizdal gang might not easily maintain their alliance under such a strain as this.

In a scattered grove of scrub-oak they made a halt just before noon. The mountains now rose sheer before them and soon they would have to commit themselves to one or another of the difficult trails where often it was impossible to leave the narrow limits of the bridle path because of precipices of a broken ground.

They took stock of the ground that lay before them and Sally proved that she was worthy of high place on that occasion, for she took a peg and sketched on the ground the main features of the mountains just before them and spotted on this rough map the exact position of every friend of the outlaw. They were some twenty miles apart, scattered in a loosely connected chain through the range, and showing like a well-established system of forwarding posts when they had been spotted down. By means of those posts, the outlaw and his men were able to plunge into the highlands and be swept away at dizzy speed from the possible pursuit of a posse. For as the outlaw passed, he gave word that pursuit was behind, and every small farmer made sure that his horses should be scattered to the most hidden corners of his range, lest they should be requisitioned for the merciless hard-riding of a posse which was not inclined to pay for wear and tear except at a most nominal rate afterwards. So the law was thwarted and crime received a helping hand partly because there was more money in that end of the business, but more largely, even, because there was sure to be a sort of happy game in the feats of the bandits, in their talk, and in their trail. Who can love the hunter so much as the hunted, whether it be beast or man?

To such a man as Sam Lee, some manner of vague knowledge about that "underground" and "overland" route must have come, and he was sure to maintain such an outlook as he was able along the way; again, he might have succeeded in outbidding Long Tom Rizdal for the services of a portion of the chain of small farmers, so that they would only pretend to welcome the long-riders, but really would betray them to their pursuers. But those chances would have to be taken. There seemed no other possible way of whisking themselves out of the reach of Sam Lee and his forces than by committing their fortunes to the "underground." Next, they had to decide in what manner they would get at the line. They could go straight ahead to one house, or travel a slightly greater distance to either side in order to strike either of two other stations. But by this time, Peet must have sent out an alarm as fast as he could send a galloping horse; doubtless that news would be relayed towards the mountains, and the straightway ahead was very apt to be closed. They determined, therefore, to turn to the left and try to make the twenty-five-mile march to the next "station."

In the meantime, they let the ponies graze, and since it seemed impossible that any one could be within hearing distance, Pleasant went for squirrels and returned with a half dozen. The fire was a more dangerous thing to try, but he knew the system of making a blaze with little or no smoke, and soon the meat was grilling. There was no salt, but no salt was needed. There was no coffee, but water from the next brook was better than wine or coffee either.

Then they mounted, and all during their halt they had spoken not a word to one another of anything except the labor before them and the risks through which they must pass; and it seemed to Pleasant Jim that he dared not meet the eyes of this girl when he spoke to her.

They were headed for the Truman Denby farm, Denby being an old "lineman" of the Rizdal forces who had turned "straight" and thereby become a more efficient helper than if he had remained in active service as a rider. Once started, they urged their mustangs on to a brisk gait, uphill and down. There were not three possible variations from the single line during the entire twenty-five miles, but the narrow trail jagged up and down through the wilderness, climbing out of the lower forests and gaining presently the shrubbery, the grass lands, and the stunted trees of the upper plateau. On the edge of the wall, they turned and looked back into the valley and far off they could see the town of Fisher Falls laid out in the district like a map rather than an actual city; below it stretched the railroad, perfectly visible as it went through the Lower Falls, where they so nearly were blocked in their flight, and then down to the dark shadows of the forest where they had thrown the hand-car from the rails and taken to the woods and all the perils and doubts that waited for them there. It seemed to them fairly miraculous that they had been able to get up the mountain wall without being intercepted or marked down, for they could look down on the trail itself as it looped back and forth and climbed rugged towards the height. A watcher posted at this place could have seen them far off and either waited to pick them off himself or else gone for help if he had not the courage for such single-handed work.

"And that's exactly what may have happened!" suggested Sally. "Suppose that we pull well off the trail, here, and wait in cover to see what may come!"

It appeared an excellent idea, so they turned the mustangs from the bridle path and wormed to the left. A knoll a mile away was the point of vantage towards which they aimed, and as they came to it Pleasant dropped from his horse as if he had been struck by a bullet. Sally imitated that good example without need of a word spoken. He merely pointed ahead with an eloquent gesture, and leaving her to hold the horses, he crept ahead through the rocks which fringed the head of the hill.

There he had clear view of what had first alarmed him. In a pocket beneath the crest were half a dozen men and horses who waited in the saddle of the hill and keenly watched the trail which the two had left not long before. They were so close that even their voices came clearly up to the waiter.

Sam Lee was with them! The ubiquitous marshal sat on a rock and fanned himself with his hat while he smiled at his companions and chatted cheerfully, describing how word had come to him by telephone and then by messenger on horseback, telling what reason men had for thinking that the two fugitives had come this way. It was Mrs. Peet who had sent in the alarm, and when her husband was hastily questioned, he refused to talk. At last they had pressed him too closely and he simply answered: "All I know is that a gent came up and asked me for a couple of horses that he wanted to buy. He paid me five hundred dollars; which was more than they was worth. Then he went off. That's all I know!"

"Did five hundred dollars shoot you through the arm, Peet?" he had been asked, to which he replied that he had taken a shot at a rat—and shot himself instead. Nothing could budge him from this statement, even when it was pointed out that the bullet had gone through his forearm the reverse way. He was asked if he had seen a woman, but he said that he had not. Both of the laborers in the field, however, plainly had seen a man and a woman galloping towards the trees.

"And Joe, there," went on the marshal, "has spotted them again. As sure as the devil, boys, that fool of a Holman, as he calls himself, is trying to get free himself and take the woman with him! And if he can manage that—if he can break through and take a girl with him, why, it will make us the laughing stock of the entire country. The range will never stop hooting. And remember—in a pinch there's as big a reward for her as for him. Ten thousand apiece!"

It was a speech which, for some reason, made the blood curdle in the veins of Jim Pleasant, but he had heard enough. He slipped back to the girl, and leading their horses, one hand always ready to stifle any snort or neigh, they worked their way through the rocks for another quarter of a mile before they ventured to take to the saddle. Then they slanted down towards the trail, reached it safely, and headed on towards the farm of Truman Denby.

CHAPTER 25

THE way had been roundabout, the labor hard over the rough country, and the twenty-five miles were not completed until dusk was beginning to settle over the range, thick in the hollows and rosy on the heights. Then they came in sight of Truman Denby's shanty ruling a little fertile hollow where the roughest of the mountain winds never would shake it too severely, where water ran freshly near by, where the low woods tangled on the upper slope, giving him constant assurance of fuel and building material, and where, at least, he could be certain of sufficient elbow-room. He was a hard and keen man. By dint of crime, to begin with, and then through constant labor as a farmer, a trapper, a hunter, and even a little mining now and again, he was said to have built up on considerable fortune, and yet he lived on like a miser, constantly casting about him for means to recruit his substance.

Sally and Pleasant, from a little knot of trees, observed the shanty anxiously. But it was a veritable picture of peace and content, with its front door standing open, and from the sagging chimney a thin twist of smoke rose in the windless air, gradually melted against the evening sky. Truman Denby himself, stalwart of outline even in the distance, was putting in the latest hours of the day chopping wood near his shack, and the powerful blows of his ax sent out ringing reports, like the explosions of a distant rifle.

Halfway down the slope rode the two and then called and signaled. Truman Denby instantly waved back a signal for them to approach, and they raised a weary gallop from the mustangs to get to this welcome hostelry.

Denby came a few strides to meet them and welcomed them

heartily enough. He lifted his hat to Sally; he gave Pleasant a strong grip of his hand.

"You busted through after all," grinned Denby. "And they all swore that you'd never have a chance."

"All who swore it?" asked Sally sharply.

"Sam Lee and his crowd. They been here. They suspect me of bein' one of the underground," said Truman Denby, grinning more broadly than ever. "Come in. Sally, you rustle the grub. You'll find plenty of it in the shelf behind the stove. I'll fix your horses."

"And what else have you for this pair?" asked Sally.

"As soon as I get the harness off this pair, I'll ride down and bring in another couple. Don't worry about that, Sally. I'll put you on horses so fast that they'll never smell the dust they raise!"

And he went off with a reassuring wave of his hand. Sally, however, wore an anxious look as she entered the house. There were bacon, cold pone, and a can of fruit jam on the shelf, together with a stock of coffee, and that made provision enough for them. Yet still she was moody as she went about the cookery. Pleasant helped her, carrying water, building up the fire, and keeping constant watch through the door and down the plateau towards the trail.

"What's wrong, Sally?" he asked at length.

She looked quickly and darkly up to him, pausing with the knife in mid-stroke through an ample loaf of pone.

"I don't like Denby's carryings on," said she.

"What's wrong? He seemed mighty cheerful."

"Sure he did. Just that!"

"Too cheerful, you mean?"

"Do you know him?"

"I only met him once at a rodeo."

"I know him like a book," said the girl. "He was one of the crowd three years ago. He's always been a gloomy devil. Devil and gloomy, and both the words are true words. And now he meets us to-day and acts like a fox when it meets a goose. What do I think? I think that he has something up his sleeve!"

She turned to watch the coffee, as it came hissing towards a boil. Big Jim Pleasant, from the doorway, stared after Denby, as the latter cantered across the table-land and disappeared through a gap between two high-backed hummocks.

"We've had our share of the bad luck," said Pleasant, "and the good luck is bound to begin breaking."

"That's what the boys say when they're bucking faro," said the girl in answer. "But I tell you, there's no mercy in cards, and there's no mercy in men. They're tigers, mostly, and this Denby is one of the worst. Did you see the way he eyed your money-belt?"

"I saw," said Pleasant. "But why not? Every dog will eye a bone even if he don't mean to try to steal it!"

"Stuff!" said Sally, who could be short enough.

And still she was gloomy with thought as they sat down at the table. Pleasant ate with some difficulty, it appeared, and suddenly she grew solicitous.

"You've lost your appetite, Jim," she exclaimed. "You ought to be a wolf, and you're not. What's wrong with you? Are you sick?"

"I am kind of," said Pleasant, growing thoughtful in turn.

She dropped her knife with a clatter and sat up stiffly in her chair, her eyes very big.

"What's wrong?" she asked hoarsely. "Is it a touch of fever, Jim? Lemme have your wrist, and "

He brushed her solicitations away.

"It's not that," he said. "I dunno just what's wrong. I never had anything happen to me before, like this. I've had the fever, and I've had the sick insides that you get after a bullet has bored through your innards. But never anything like this."

She waited, hushed and expectant.

"I feel weak around the heart and fluttery, sort of," said Pleasant. "My head spins, pretty easy, as though it was a sort of a top, y'understand?"

She nodded as though she dared not interrupt for fear of cutting off the remainder of his coming remarks about his condition.

Pleasant threw back his head and struck the table so that there was a jangle of tinware.

"Sally," he said, "I ain't a fool and I'm not a coward; and I've never met man, woman or child that I couldn't look square in the eyes but here I am starin' at the ceilin' instead of facing you!"

A heavy silence fell between them. Sally had commenced to frown, piercing him with her sharp watchfulness.

"What are you driving at Jim?" she asked at length. "What have I to do with you feelin' sick?

"Ah," she added suddenly, "but I understand, now! You been draggin' me through so much trouble that the sight of me brings you into a sort of prison horror. Is that the way of it, Jim, old fellow?"

"Horror? No, not that. But I'll tell you, I was sitting here watching you after you'd rolled up your sleeves and taking note of the way of your hands, and the confounded dimple in your elbows   "

He paused, and bringing down his wretched eyes from the ceiling, he looked her fairly in the face. But only for a moment. Then his glance fell to the floor.

"I'm like a four flusher that has been called in front of a gang of men," grumbled Pleasant Jim. "I'm all shakes, Sally. I couldn't hold a gun steady enough to hit the side of that wall, just now!"

Sally was silent for another moment, before she returned: "It sounds like dope, to me. But you wouldn't be fool enough to use anything like that. I'll tell you what   how long has it been since you rode up out of the valley?"

"Not many days. The trail to Black Mountain was high enough."

"It's not mountain sickness, then," said Sally. "Stomach, most likely."

"It feels sort of like something wrong with the stomach   sort of a hollowness."

"It'll pass," said Sally with wise decision. "You'll see that it'll pass away, right enough. Worry   and having to drag a girl through what you dragged me   and no food half the time   and the boys welching on you the way that they did   that's pretty near enough to make you sick!"

He shook his head, first faintly and then with surety.

"That's not it. Now that we're through the hole in the wall I wouldn't have any of the rest of 'em along with us   except the Leinster Gray, of course. I'd give a pound of blood for him!"

"We're not through the hole in the wall," the girl assured him, as they began to finish their meal. "We won't be through till we're out of this shack with two good horses under us   and by the way, it's about time for Denby to be coming back with the pair that he promised us. He's had time to go to the farther end of his place, by this. Is there any sign of him?"

Pleasant stood at the door.

"Not a trace of him anywhere."

"It's queer," said the girl. "It's mighty queer!"

She hurried from the house, and through the dimness of the

mountain evening, faintly lighted by the afterglow from the west, she stared, but there was nothing before them. Then from behind the house, they heard the snort and stamping of a horse.

They started as though a gun had been leveled on them. Then Pleasant, grim of face, a Colt balanced in either hand, slipped around the rear corner of the house. There was nothing in sight. The empty horse shed was at their right. Behind the shack was the dense tangle of small trees.

"I'm going in there," said Pleasant Jim. "Stay here and "

"I'll go where you go," she said staunchly. And she followed straight behind him as he glided through the darkness of the woods.

Not two minutes of such work brought them to a small gap in the trees, and before them, hobbled short, and grazing on a scattering of bunch grass they saw three tall horses, and one of them a glimmering gray which seemed to show itself by its own light. Jim Pleasant groaned with wonder and joy:

"Sally, it's the Leinster Gray!"

CHAPTER 26

STILL with a heavy Colt gripped in either hand, he pushed forward, for it seemed impossible that they could have found these horses waiting at such a place and at such a time unless there were waiting guns ready to open fire upon them. But it seemed that the three fine animals were not the bait of a trap. Swiftly they cut the hobbles, while Sally, quivering with excitement, interpreted.

"I knew that Denby was going crooked, and this proves it. Sam Lee got these horses from Charlie Rizdal. Perhaps Charlie's in the can now. Lee came up here and cached the horses with Denby and bought him off to his side, in case we came this way. Quick, Jim! Get 'em to the horse shed and we'll have saddles on 'em! Oh, the dog! He had to ride out to get mounts for us? He had to ride out to get the signal to Sam Lee!"

Pleasant Jim said nothing. He was too busy urging the horses through the woods and back to the shed, where they picked up their lately discarded saddles and threw them on the backs of the horses. And as they worked at the cinches and the bridles, they kept an ear open for the sound of approaching horsemen. No such noise came to them. In the thickening darkness, they led the three new mounts towards the door of the shed and as they went, they heard what they dreaded—the volleying of hoofbeats across the plateau, and then the cheerful voice of Denby ringing from the distance: "Here you are, Jim Pleasant!"

Out of the dusk they saw Denby coming, leading two riderless horses. No others were in sight; and Pleasant stepped out from the horse shed, leaving the girl behind to hold the three thoroughbreds in the dark of the interior.

"Over here, Denby," he called. And Denby swung from the direction of the shack towards the shed.

As he came to a halt and swung down to the ground, he continued as gayly as ever: "Here's a tough pair of brutes, Pleasant. They'll take you through safely. Where's the girl? Where's Sally?"

"Waiting inside," said Pleasant, and pushed a gun into the stomach of his host. "Keep your hands away," he added savagely. "Because I'm hankering and hungering to send you to hell, Denby, you double-crossing dog!"

He reached for the buckle of the other's belt, and drawing it, allowed the belt and its dependent guns to fall to the ground. Denby groaned as they fell.

"Are you nutty, Pleasant?" he asked. "What's wrong? What's biting you? What's happened, in God's name?"

"Sally!" called Pleasant. "Bring 'em out!"

And Sally obediently led the three fine horses from the shed. Denby saw them coming and exclaimed in amazement: "Where'd you get 'em, Pleasant? Fine lookers, too, as much as I can see of 'em!"

"You dunno where they come from," muttered Pleasant savagely. "Sam Lee didn't leave 'em with you, of course. He didn't cache 'em behind the trees, yonder, and bribe you to give him word if we came this way?"

"Pleasant," said the other, "so help me God, I—"

"Shut up!" commanded Pleasant. "I hate to even listen to your yapping. Denby, I've never killed a white man!"

There was so much hidden eloquence in this remark that Denby refrained from any attempt at speech. He obediently mounted his horse again, and turned towards the upper trail in haste, Sally in the rear, leading the spare horse, and Pleasant riding in front, gun in hand, beside Truman Denby.

They had not gone a quarter of a mile up the trail when Denby broke his enforced silence.

"Pleasant," he said in a rather stifled voice, "I wouldn't go on this way, if I was you."

"Why wouldn't you?"

"Because I got an idea that trouble is waiting for you, pretty pronto."

"You sent 'em up the trail, did you?" suggested Pleasant. "You didn't want the killing done in your own shack, I guess? Oh, Denby, damned if I know what keeps me from blowing you to hell! Which way'll we go, then, to be safe!"

"Back to the valley, Pleasant. And I want to tell you that—"

"We'll not go back to the valley. There's some trail ahead of us through the hills. Which is it?"

"There's only a small, rough one   a damn bad one for night-travel, Pleasant!"

"Lead us that way, and only talk when you have to!"

Truman Denby obeyed explicitly, like a man whose head is in the lion's mouth, and turning to the right, he soon brought them to an irregular cattle trail which wound up the side of a dome-shaped hill, and then on the other side turned here and there through the bad-lands beyond. At length the trail came on to a small road, along which they could travel with greater ease and security. Then Pleasant halted.

"Denby," he said, "I know the way, from here. Now tell me what reason there is why I should let you live?"

Denby was sullenly silent.

"There's no reason," declared Pleasant Jim. "I'll let you do two things   pray if you got a prayer in you, and send some message, if you got a message to send to anybody on earth.

"I got no praying to do," answered Denby, "and what message should I be sending?"

"Then God have pity on you, because I'm not going to!" said Pleasant, and raised his Colt.

But Sally exclaimed: "You won't do it, Jim! You won't shoot him down!"

"He would have trapped us like rabbits," declared Pleasant Jim. "He sold us, Sally!"

"But our luck's kept with us," said the girl earnestly. "Let him go back to his home."

"Go back, then," said Pleasant Jim. "But don't stay there, because when this here is known, I won't be the only man that'll come gunning for you. You understand me, Denby?"

Denby said nothing, but cautiously he reined back his horse, and since no word or bullet stopped him, he turned suddenly, and dashing his spurs into his mustang, raced into the shelter of the brush and then was gone, riding like mad down the hillside. Pleasant listened vindictively, and then turned with a sigh to the girl.

"He ought to be a dead man," said he. "But two things saved him. One was you, and one was the Leinster Gray   I was so confoundedly glad to see him again!"

To this Sally said nothing, and slowly they went up the trail; the way improved; they could manage a canter here and there, and at worst they could maintain a trot, and so they voyaged through the mountains until the moon rose at last and showed Pleasant the face of the girl.

Her lips were set tight, and though her head had not fallen forward, he saw that she was half-dead with fatigue. He himself was weary enough, iron as he was; but the work of the last two days and particularly this long, long trail had taken toll of her strength. He dared not sympathize, for fear that sympathy might unnerve her more. And so they kept on doggedly. Twice lights gleamed before them, but they went on past the farmhouses, for these were not proved places of refuge. A third time they saw the distant glimmer of lights, and now they quickened their horses to a strong gallop. Neither spoke, but both knew that this should prove a harborage, unless Sam Lee had been able to reach the "underground" even at such a distance as this.

They were too exhausted to use caution but rode straight up to the door of the shack, and Pleasant leaned from the saddle and beat against it with the butt of a Colt. It was opened at once by a man in shirt-sleeves with a shotgun thrown into the crook of his left arm.

"What's up?" he asked.

"Who knows Long Tom Rizdal here?" asked Pleasant bluntly.

The other stepped out further into the night and peered up into the face of the rider; then a smile came on his lips.

"It's Pleasant!" he exclaimed. "And he broke through in spite of 'em! Hey, Maggie! It's Pleasant and the girl, and they've come through in spite of Sam Lee and his hired men. Step down, folks; gimme your horses; Chuck, come grab these nags, will you? And shake out some barley for them and give 'em the wheat hay. Come in here, Pleasant, and you, ma'am! Doggone me, if I ain't glad to see you both; though I never expected that you'd be able to come through!"

It was impossible to doubt his genuine nature. If he had sold himself to the long riders of Tom Rizdal, he had sold only a portion of his nature, and the rest remained bold and bluntly free. Maggie, Herculean, red of face and hand, was nonetheless cheerfully excited, and all in a moment they were seated before food at a rough pine table. Slabs of ham, biscuits, and steaming black coffee made up the bill of fare, but never had they tasted a more delicious meal.

Their hosts, in the meantime, ran over with questions which

they hardly allowed to be answered. They were full of the great adventure. The impossible had been achieved, and Marshal Sam Lee had received the first black mark against his name and record. With five hundred manhunters he had been unable to capture a fugitive who was burdened with the care of a woman, and surely the heart of Sam Lee must be breaking with grief.

"He hasn't got a heart that'll break," said Pleasant. "He'll be booming up this trail as fast as hired horses can bring him. Friend, get your boy Chuck to wait at the head of the trail, yonder, where it dips over the hill, and fire two shots if strangers come riding up that way tonight, and get your wife to put this lady to bed. Sally, can you wake up?"

"Yes," said Sally.

But she did not open her eyes as she spoke. She had slumped back on the stool, resting against the wall, and her head had fallen over her shoulder.

"Take a lamp and show me the way!" said Pleasant, and raising her in his arms, a loose and unconscious weight, he carried her up the narrow stairway and into the coolness and the peace of the bedroom that waited for her.

CHAPTER 27

As for Pleasant himself, once stretched on a bunk in the room beneath, he slept heavily and with many a troubled dream, such as come to exhausted men; but he felt that he had broken down the last great barrier and that he was safe, now. Then a nightmare seized him, and he thought that the gray stallion had been stolen and that he saw a familiar form galloping the big horse away, and the laughter of Long Tom Rizdal came floating back to him as he vainly ran in pursuit.

He opened his eyes to find that a broad shaft of sunlight was striking in through the open doorway towards him, and in the shaft was the black silhouette of Long Tom, himself, and he was laughing indeed.

"Suppose that it had been Sam Lee that walked through that door?" said the chief. "Where would you be, Pleasant?"

"Here's a man I could trust to warn me," said Pleasant. "Or besides that, I could have trusted to sort of smell Sam Lee if he came within a mile of me! Tom, how did you break through them?"

"Partly by luck and partly by nerve," said Long Tom, "but the main thing is: Did you think I was welching by running by myself?"

"Every man for himself is the rule," said Pleasant, rather bitterly. "And I knew the country as well as you did."

"When I saw that you wouldn't leave the girl," said Long Tom, "and Lefty and Joe were making a snarling match of it, then I knew that it was better to split up. It stopped argument, for one thing. I headed straight for the railroad, grabbed a freight on the grade, and mixed in with a fresh gang of possemen who'd come down from Fisher Mills. They didn't recognize me in the night. I dropped off before we hit the next station and cut

38

for the hills. And so I landed here, as you see. But if I'd had a girl on my hands—why, I couldn't have gone a mile, old man, and God knows how you managed it. They'll talk of nothing else, in these mountains, for ten years to come!"

"What happened to Charlie?"

"He was waiting with eight horses on the edge of the town, but Sam Lee, the old devil, had a patrol watching. They discovered the bunch in the trees and opened fire. Charlie's horse was shot from under him. He managed to get on another, but the rest of the band were caught. He got away with nothing but his skin, and barely that. Sam Lee appropriated the Leinster Gray for himself and got to Denby's house. Then he cached his horses in the woods back of the shack and arranged with Denby to sell you out if you or I came that way. Lee and the rest took some mustangs from Denby's place and went to block the trail. But you know that better than I do! It was a grand play that Lee made, take it all in all, but all he got was two out of six, and one-quarter of the loot."

"They caught Joe with his share on him?"

"They did, and they found Lefty's part where he'd stowed it in the pile of ties. More than two hundred thousand goes back to Fisher, after all!"

"And how does Fisher take on?"

"He went nearly mad. Got on a horse and went down the valley to find the robbers, knocked his head on a branch of a tree as he was riding past, and had to be carried back to the town. A run started on the bank, of course, but he paid everything on the nail, and take it all in all, I think he's stronger than ever. People think that a fellow who can lose nearly a cold million without going bankrupt is a genius and a great man. And I suppose he is—but a crook, too, as you know! However, now he's campaigning for our scalps and he'll have them if money can buy us, and already he has some tidy information. Lefty broke down the minute he was caught and they got a full confession from him. He named Jim Pleasant, so Holman is now out of the picture and you can shave whenever you're ready. Now tell me about yourself. I'm hungry to hear!"

"We had a couple of tight squeezes," said Pleasant, shrugging his shoulders, "but Sally got us out of the worst of them by using a metal-backed comb as though it were a gun. That's the only reason that we managed to get this far! Hey, Charlie!"

For Charlie Rizdal had come, broadly smiling, into the

room; and a moment later Sally came down the stairs, her wrinkled clothes laid aside for a gingham dress borrowed from their hostess; and though it fitted her most loosely, yet she wore it with a sort of trailing grace, set it off with a wisp of yellow wildflowers at the breast, and looked to the dazzled eyes of Pleasant Jim, on the whole, more like a queen than an ordinary woman. The Rizdals surrounded her with a cheer; and then there was breakfast; and such a joyous gayety filled the air that Pleasant Jim felt he was nearer to heaven than ever before in all his days. Certainly, he told himself, there was one angel at that table, and he grew more and more unnerved as he watched the clumsy tin coffee cup supported by her slim fingers, or all her motions, as dainty and graceful as a bird's upon the wing. He felt himself growing dizzy; all that was around him seemed unreal; and finally he left the table and went outdoors where the cool, wide arms of the mountains received him and his thoughts. But even there was a touch of the ideal—and that was the shimmering form of the Leinster Gray, galloping across the meadow like a white cloud blown over the face of the sky. Pleasant Jim felt that he had walked into a new world.

In the meantime, the talk of the three who remained inside the shanty had turned upon Pleasant as a theme.

"You got him groggy," said Charlie Rizdal, with his broadest smile. "He's wild about you, Sally! Have a cigarette and tell us about him."

"I've cut out smoking," said Sally. "He doesn't like it, very well!"

"You can duck it, if he comes back. Besides, you're not married to him."

"Married to him?" said Long Tom with a sudden sharp lift of his voice. "Not quite, I guess!"

Sally lighted her cigarette and said nothing.

"But look here," went on Charlie, not unwilling to annoy his older and more famous brother, "you call Sally your girl and say you're going to marry her, and all that. But you let another man take the hard job of bringing her out of hell, so to speak."

"What if I did?" said the big man angrily, seeing nothing to smile at in this. "She's been caught before, hasn't she? And I've always got her out again, haven't I?"

"Three times," said Sally, in a grave, emotionless voice.

But Charlie Rizdal insisted on making his point, and insisted the more because he saw that his brother was wincing.

"You've let her be nabbed three times," he said, "and three times she's had to live in jail and eat jail food, and talk to the crooks and the thugs there! A fine life you've given her to lead!"

For a moment it appeared that Long Tom would strike his brother, for his hard fist balled; but he controlled himself with a sudden effort and turning to the girl, he laid a hand over hers.

"It would have been the spoiling of any other girl, and I know it," he declared. "But Sally's a cut above the ordinary run of 'em, I hope. Water won't hurt a duck; and trouble don't hurt Sally, she slips under it or floats over it, and tar can't stick to her. Dear old Sally!"

Sally, in reply to this eloquent praise, lifted her wide, steady eyes and looked her lover fully in the face. But she said nothing. There was never a time when Sally's tongue was not under full control.

Long Tom grew alarmed.

He said hastily and eagerly: "Does it look as if I've given you a hard row to hoe, old girl? Perhaps I have. But it was your own choice. You remember three years ago, when I found you, I said: 'We'll settle down on what I can make doing some clerk's tinhorn job, or else we can fly wide and high and try for the big stake.' You made your choice then, Sally! Is that right?"

"Have I ever complained?" asked the girl steadily.

"No, not you. You're the true little thoroughbred, the clean-bred one, old dear. But from the way Charlie has been talking, I was almost afraid."

He paused and hastily wiped his forehead. Plainly he was much excited.

"When do we start?" asked Sally suddenly.

"Whenever you're ready."

"I'll go get on a hat."

And she went hurriedly up the stairs. The two brothers looked after her, Long Tom frowning darkly.

"What in hell made you start that line of talk?'" he asked.

"Because I wanted to tip you off," said Charlie. "I tell you, Pleasant Jim is mad about her, and he's done enough to make her think a good deal about him. He has a way of blinking when he looks at her, and she has a way of not looking at him at all. Well, Tom, they don't *hate* each other, I suppose, and if it's not hate, what is it?"

Long Tom Rizdal drew in his breath sharply and glared.

"I understand," he said at last, with much venom. "Of course you can smile, but you've never forgiven Pleasant for hunting you down and beating you in the fight. You can't get even with him using guns; so you're going to try to use me to square him. Confess up, Charlie! That's your game. You want to make me jealous for that reason!"

"Figure it out your own way," answered Charlie Rizdal, pushing back his chair. "But while you're waiting, Sam Lee will come up the trail and grab you."

Long Tom reached out for his brother and caught his sleeve.

He said in a low, troubled voice: "She's so out in the open and square that if she was thinking about turning me down, she'd come straight to me and tell me that she wanted Pleasant more than she wanted me!"

"Would she?" sneered Charlie. "If she loved Pleasant, would she arrange for you to cut his throat? Is that logical? Why, you talk like a sap, Tom!"

CHAPTER 28

THE last to be ready for the trail was Pleasant Jim.

They found him busily grooming the Leinster Gray, standing back from his work, now and again, and looking at the polished body of the thoroughbred very much as an artist stands back to admire the effects of his latest brush strokes on a canvas. And by the time the others were in the saddle, he was still carefully arranging the padding blankets on the back of the big horse.

"Hurry up!" said Charlie Rizdal impatiently. "Anyway, you'll have to chuck him for a fresh pony at the end of the next march!"

But when at length he was ready to join them, he acted as though the stallion must carry him to the end of his journey, no matter how far. On sharp down-pitches he refused to risk the forelegs and shoulders of the fine fellow by going at any speed; and whereas the other three were willing to spur cruelly on the steepest up-slope, Pleasant Jim would even dismount and do the bitter grade on foot, the Leinster Gray idly comfortable with lightened saddle behind him. And yet, for all their hurry, they did not gain, for now and again came a free sweep of road neither too steep in rise or fall, and over such distances the stallion went with a stride so powerful and easy that he soon was up with the scampering horses of the others. Indeed, he would have passed them well before the day was ended had not Pleasant reined him in to keep even with the others. Particularly through chopped and broken ground, of which there was much to pass, the Gray went like a cat until Charlie Rizdal cried in admiration: "He's got a special eye in each foot!"

But as the result of the careful manner in which he was rated through the work of the day, whereas the other three horses were hanging their heads and needed to be twice-spurred before they would lurch ahead, in the evening of the work the Gray still carried on daintily and gayly, and scarcely seemed to know that he had been employed or that he carried in the saddle a more ponderous burden than any of the others.

"How does he manage it?" grumbled Long Tom, looking rather sourly at their companion. "It looks as though he'd had the brute on a feather bed all day, instead of keeping up with us through the whole day's work!"

"I'll tell you how it is," answered the girl, who had spoken very little during the whole day's ride. "It's because he loves his horse, and love can manage miracles!"

Charlie Rizdal put in, with his ever-present, quiet malice: "That's how he was able to bring you through the lines of Sam Lee, maybe. What do you say, Sally?"

Sally said nothing, resorting to one of her frequent silences, but Long Tom was greatly irritated, and his under-hung jaw thrust out even more than usual as he replied: "You talk like an absolute ass, Charlie. You hear?"

However, the speech had sunk home, and for some time after that, he stole glances at the girl, as though he hoped to surprise in her expression, at an unguarded moment, a secret which he would have been very glad to know.

And as they went on towards the dusk of the day, urging the tired horses, he let big Jim Pleasant and Charlie take the lead, while he fell back with the girl a trifle behind them. He felt that he should have waited until another time; he felt sure that this was no topic to be discussed in the middle of a weary march; and yet an imp of the perverse drove him on and forced him to break out the disagreeable subject.

"Sally!" he said.

"All right," said Sally. "Now let's have it all out."

"Have what out?" he asked.

"The thing that's bothering you."

He stared at her almost angrily. It was his pride that he wore a gambler's mask and that no one could read his state of mind.

"I don't know that anything's bothering me," he declared, steering his horse with a sort of absent-minded cunning down a twisted part of the cattle trail which they were following.

"There is, though."

"Well, guess at it then."

"It's the Big Boy," replied the girl, pointing with her quirt. Long Tom sighed. Her calm, the smallness of her gloved hand on the butt of the whip, and the green steady eyes with which she watched him, all of these small matters joined together to disturb him. She seemed more desirable than ever a thousand times more so.

"Go on," said Rizdal. "Let's hear some more of what you think."

"It had better come from you," she answered.

Always, since the beginning, he had reserved a sort of right to command, and he used it now, in the height of his vexation.

"Damn it, Sally, do what I tell you to!"

She turned her head, and for the thousandth time he felt in those sea-green eyes that a nature as deep and cunning as the nature of a hunting cat was taking stock of him.

"All right," she submitted at last. "I'll tell you, but it comes awkwardly from me. You've noticed that Pleasant Jim is fond of me."

"A fool—a blind and deaf fool could guess that!" said he, fiercely. "Well, go ahead. Is that what's bothering me?"

"Partly that. Because you think, to cut a long story short, that I may be half as fond of him as he is of me."

He began to breathe hard, it angered him so thoroughly to have his mind read in this fashion.

"I don't really worry about it," said Long Tom, at length. "I know that you have too many brains to make a mistake like that. If I listen to my reason, my reason tells me that you couldn't be stupid enough to make such a blunder. You know he's a good fellow. So do I. You know in this affair, he's got sentimental, and made a hero of himself for your sake. Of course that would impress a girl. And even you, Sally, can be impressed! But in spite of all that, I don't think that you'd balance him against me and prefer him. Am I right?"

"It wouldn't be reasonable," she agreed, nodding.

"Let the color in the West go," said Rizdal roughly, "and look at me. I want to know something."

"Fire ahead."

"Has he been telling you how much he loves you?"

"No. I don't even think that he knows he cares for me."

"What you mean by that?"

"There've been more horses than girls in his life. He doesn't even recognize the symptoms of—of caring for a woman."

"I never heard of such a thing," said Rizdal, darkly suspicious.

"Neither had I," she said. "But in lots of ways, he's only a baby."

"I don't like that baby talk," said Rizdal, "concerning a fighting man like Jim Pleasant. I tell you, the killings that that man has—"

"You don't know him," she insisted. "He's simply in a tangle about me. He's like a colt with a touch of colic. He feels wrong in his stomach, so to speak. Poor Jimmy!"

"Poor hell," said Rizdal. "The man's playing a part with you!"

She shrugged her shoulders.

"Don't ask me to tell you, then," she said.

"If you were another girl," said he, "I'd say that your head could be turned by the size and the strength and the courage of that fellow; but you're yourself, the hardest-headed youngster that ever—"

"Cracked a bank," she suggested without emotion.

"Well," said he, "you know black from white, and you can see this fellow for yourself. He's done something, here, because it was shoved in his way, and he can do other things, so long as he has me to think for him, but without me, where would he be? He's fit for nothing but to run a horse-farm. Well, he's stepped over the dead-line, and he'll never run a horse-farm, and you can be sure of that! He'll never be allowed to go straight. The police would see to that, and he's made himself too famous. He has to live as a crook, then. But you have too much sense to think that he can make a success at that unless he follows the leader. Am I right?"

"I think you are," she said thoughtfully, after a pause.

"He isn't made of the same stuff that you and I are made of," went on the criminal. "He hasn't the same freedom and the strength of—"

"Conscience—or the lack of it, you might say," suggested the girl.

"I don't like that," he answered briskly.

"I'm sorry. But it's the truth. However, you're right. He's not like us. I tell you, Tom, that I saw him stand to a fighting man, with his hands over his head, and the rifle of that farmer at his breast—and yet when he had a chance to shoot, he didn't shoot to kill. The farmer knew it, too. And that's why he tried to cover our trail. But you—or I, Tom—we never would have taken such a chance! He's different. White men mean something to him."

There was a trace of bitterness in her tone that made him study her once more, but he learned nothing.

"He's new in a new game," said Rizdal. "He'll learn to shoot straight, after they've put a few murders on his shoulders—things he wasn't within a thousand miles of—as they did with me. He won't care! However, to get back to our subject, I was saying that an ordinary girl might have her head turned by such a chap as Pleasant, but you see the difference between him and me."

She answered instantly: "Yes, you could build an empire where he could hardly be more than—cowpuncher, say, to the royal herd. I understand the difference between you. You have the brains, Tom. I've always known that; every one knows it."

"You say that you know it," said he, pressing his horse a little closer. "And there was a time, Sally, three years ago, when we started this game, there was a time when you thought you cared a little about me, because you felt that one day we'd do some great things together, and be rich! Isn't that a fact?"

"Yes," said she. "That's a fact."

"But now you've changed."

"How?"

"You treat me as if I were a stranger!"

"Do you want me to hang on your neck?" she said, rather curiously than with emotion. "If I did, it would be sending you off to be killed."

"Just explain that, will you?"

"I don't have to work hard to explain it. If Pleasant Jim saw me so much as pat your hand, Tom, he'd take you to one side and kill you as sure as that sun is turned red in the west."

Long Tom swore softly.

"No man—" he began with heat.

"Tush, Tommy," said the girl, and he felt that the green of her eyes enlarged and glowed as she said it. "You know it as well as I do. You're a grand fighting man, Tom dear. You're a fearless and strong man. But you're just not like Pleasant Jim. He feeds on danger. He loves it. And if ever he had what he felt to be a fair reason for killing a man, not you and not Charlie, not hardly you and Charlie together could stop him. You don't need to be ashamed to admit it. It's simply true, isn't it?"

Long Tom started to make a swift and bitter answer. But he checked himself, for she was not, as he himself had pointed out so many times, like other women. She was capable of judging dispassionately, keenly, accurately. And he knew that she was correct.

"Perhaps you're right," said he, his brow very dark. "But the fact is, Sally, that right now we're riding here together behind their backs, and yet your eye never softens when you look at me."

"Did I ever gush over you? Did I ever play calf?" asked the girl.

"You have a sweet way of putting it," growled Rizdal.

"You found me starved and sick and done for," said the girl in explanation. "You gave me a chance to do something—to be a sort of power—to handle men, you know, and money. Well, I loved it. I've always loved it, and the danger and the excitement, as well. I'm a crook. I'm a natural crook, and I admit it. Well, Tom, I said that I wanted to learn the game and you've been teaching me. I said that I like you. I do. I said that I would marry you some day. I suppose that I shall. But in the meantime, don't ask me to fondle you and pet you. I can't and I won't. It isn't in me."

"There's no possibility of love being in you!" exclaimed he in bitterness.

"Maybe there isn't," she answered with composure. "But if you ever find me a bad bargain, chuck me quick. I'll never blame you, you know! Only—I've got to let you know the truth!"

This straightforward reply seemed to take his breath. Actually, with one hand he gripped the pommel of his saddle and stared down the trail before him with eyes that saw nothing.

"You take what I said too hard, Sally," he replied. "I don't mean you to go after me like this. Be reasonable! God knows I'd like to have you a little softer—to me! But perhaps if you were, I wouldn't be so mad about you! It's just because you're different from the rest that I'm wild about you. You're full of differences and contrasts. The other girls, if they go wrong in one way, go wrong in all ways. But you've robbed banks—and remained as straight as a string as a woman. Of course I want you straight and clean. And if I've got to take the hardness with it—why, I'll do it. Besides, when we have a chance to make a home, Sally, I think I'll find ways to warm your heart!"

She did not avoid his glance, but looked fairly at him, and smiled with a sort of good humored appreciation of his enthusiasm.

"And, Sally, when we settle down, it'll be a real place. No

sneak's resort. The Riviera would about fit us. Something near Nice. Cannes, maybe. A swell villa in the hills. About a million servants. A yacht tipping at anchor in the harbor for us. A car as long as a snake and as strong as a train. Jewels, kid. You know. The pigeon-egg, hundred per cent red ruby and emeralds to match your eyes, honey. Why, Sally, we'll be like a queen and a king, I say!"

She listened to him. She canted her head a little to one side, and sighed as the beauty of this proposed life grew before her mind's eye.

Then his tone changed.

"But what about Pleasant?" he asked suddenly. "What are we going to do with him? What you feel about him?"

She answered without the slightest hesitation: "I can't let him down, Tom. You know that. Not after what he's done. I have to string the poor simpleton along and try to break the news to him gently. What else could I do? Tell him he ought to go back to his farm? The poor devil hasn't one any more!"

CHAPTER 29

THERE was no sign of the pursuit of wise Sam Lee behind them all that day, but that did not mean that the veteran had decided to throw up the trail. It simply meant that he knew he had lost his first trick, and that he was determined to win the second.

Two tricks in such a game as Tom Rizdal played might come far apart, and therefore Sam Lee determined to act as though he had half the world and all of the future years in which to win his battle with the criminal. He did not blindly persist on the trail. He had laid one excellent trap for the capture of Pleasant Jim, and when that trail failed, while the criminals feared him every instant behind them and pushed their tired horses by relays across the mountains, Sam Lee went straight back to Fisher Falls.

He could have pleaded that he lacked authority to act, now that the pursued were over the state line, for he had been acting, in this, merely as deputy, and not in his federal capacity. Counterfeiters were his quarry. But bank robbers, after all, should fall to the lot of the regular state police.

However, such a plea never for a moment entered his thoughts. He was here to enforce the law, and enforce it he would, and in all of its phases; for in many ways, a more ideal officer of the law never strapped on gun, or stepped into creaking saddle-leather. He went back to Fisher Falls to be at the center of action, to collect new clews, to discover, if he could, to what extent, if any, this had been an inside job, to lay his plans for the future, and to gather around him a few most efficient helpers to be used on the long trail which he foresaw lay before him.

When he rode into Fisher Falls, he was received in a manner which was a novelty for him. All his days he had been the great, the rising warrior of the frontier, the faultless, unfailing destroyer of crime and criminals; but now he found men's eyes fixed coldly upon him, and he could hear their whispers and their derision behind his back.

It hurt him, of course, as it hurts all men, but it did not cause him to back water or to change his good resolutions. He never had turned his back on guns; he would not turn his back and run away from gossip. So he let them talk, listened with the ears of a fox, but showed not the slightest dismay or concern. And that took more courage and more iron nerve than anything he ever had done before.

The last man another would have wanted to face was the first one he went to interview.

He went to the bank and saw Fisher.

The banker had turned from rusty gray to white. Hair and face both were without color, but instead, his eyes were shot with red, and his nostrils flared, and a smile could not come on his lips.

"Have you come back to ask me to thank you for your work?" said the banker, rising and striding to meet his famous caller. "I say, it's the existence of fools like you, blind men, weaklings, half-wits, that encourages bank robbery! By the eternal God, you suspected them the day before the robbery and you didn't act!"

The marshal stood under the shower of fire and did not wince.

"I did not," he confessed.

"Have you got the brazen nerve to stand there and admit such a thing to me?" roared Fisher, some of his color at last entering his face.

"I have to admit it when I make a mistake," said the little marshal.

"Mistake? Ruin! You could have done half a dozen murders and done less harm than you've allowed to come to me and my bank! The future of the valley—tied up here—advancement— progression—irrigation—better stock—new railroad—every- thing—all tied up in my bank—and you've let them cut the throat of my bank—you've let them bleed me dry—you've put the country back a hundred years—maybe you've ruined it! Maybe you've ruined the whole valley—maybe forever!"

There was a cub reporter of the *Evening Democrat* sitting outside the office, hoping for an interview which for two days had been denied him. And now he heard this thundering voice as every one in the bank must hear it, and as even those who passed in the street were sure to make out its flooding torrent of noise. The pad and the nervous pencil were snatched up, and he began to make notes. He saw a headline forming, in the back of his mind. He saw an article which would be copied by the biggest newspapers in the state. He felt the congratulating hand of the editor upon his shoulder. He saw fame. And he wrote shorthand like mad and crowded his brain with additional notes.

If the marshal standing under that shower of verbal stones, saw headlines also, they were of a nature to scourge him, like the fabled scorpion whips. But still he did not wince.

"I made a mistake," he repeated earnestly. "I should have acted sooner, but I hoped to make a clean scoop and gather in more of the tribe. I should have struck in the evening, when there was a chance to block their escape, but I waited until the later night because I was sure that I had arranged a complete and perfect net   "

"Net, hell!" screamed Lewis Fisher. "The rotten trap that you put up any child could have broken through! A ridiculous, damned, idiotic fool's affair that even a—"

"Excuse me," drawled the marshal, setting his teeth to keep back his temper, "but as a matter of fact it wasn't such a doggone bad idea that I had. Only I missed out on one thing. I knew that this gent Holman who has turned out to be Pleasant I knew that he was a strong one and a dangerous man. But I didn't know that Long Tom Rizdal would be mixed up in the affair. If I had, I'd have armed every man in town and blocked every street before I went to break open that gun-shop!"

"Second thoughts! Second thoughts!" cried Fisher. "Who can't have good second thoughts?"

"I haven't done so badly," said the marshal. "At least, I've handed back to you a quarter of the loot—"

"Twenty-five per cent. My God, I think you're actually proud of it!"

"I am," said the marshal.

Mr. Fisher recoiled. He thought this quiet little man had come in to humble himself. He discovered that he was mistaken, and softness of voice did not necessarily mean weakness of spirit. It chagrined the banker that he could not bully the marshal at will, but nevertheless he felt much better because he had had a chance to blow off steam, as it were, on the subject of the wrongs which he had endured.

"I am proud of it," said Sam Lee, repeating the idea. "Even as it was, I should have caught all of them, with the possible exception of Tom Rizdal. Pleasant and the woman were in the hollow of my hand."

"Were they? Were they?" shouted the banker, growing more furious again. "Then why didn't you close your fingers and catch them? Will you tell me that?"

"Because Pleasant performed a miracle. You think he made a fool of me. No, I don't feel that way about it. He beat me, I admit, but it took wonderful work for him to get away."

"You dropped in to tell me how pleased you are with yourself, I see," said Fisher.

"No," said the marshal, "I dropped in to tell you that in spite of the failure I've made, I'm going to keep after them and I hope I'll land them. And the higher you can boost the price for their capture, by making some arrangement with the governor, the easier my work will be and the bigger your opportunity of   "

"Of getting back the rest of the money?" exclaimed Fisher.

"No," said the marshal, "probably you'll never see another penny of it, unless we should catch a couple of them and let them ransom themselves. And that's a low business."

"The regaining of half a million dollars," shouted Fisher, "is a high business no matter how you look at it! You've been talking like a fool, Lee!"

Sam Lee stood up, and he smiled at the other.

"You think about boosting the price," said he. "I have to go to find men."

"Find men?" cried the astonished and irate banker. "Ain't Fisher Falls full of men?"

"Of course it is," replied Marshal Sam Lee, "but when I said men, I meant *men*. Good-by!"

With that, he left the bank, while Lewis Fisher sank back into his chair with a renewed interest in life. For, even if he had to lose half a million—six hundred and odd thousand dollars, to be exact—he seemed to have an excellent chance, now, of at least getting some revenge upon the criminals. And he hardly knew which would please him most—to have the money back in his vaults and the matter called square, or to see the scoundrels condemned to spend the rest of their miserable lives in prison.

Certainly there was no justice in the law if they were given sentences any smaller!

On the whole, he felt decidedly better, and all that irritated him was that Sam Lee appeared to have come through the interview with flying colors; accordingly, when the editor of the *Evening Democrat* sent him an article purporting to describe the meeting of the marshal and the banker, and saying in a note that accompanied it that it made things rather hot for the marshal, Mr. Fisher did not so much as glance at the manuscript.

He simply scratched on the margin: "OK. Give him hell!"

And so the document went on to its destiny in the printing press; and Mr. Fisher turned to consider a proposal for the sale of the farm of Jim Pleasant and the stock upon it. The details were laid carefully before him.

There were five hundred acres, nearly all land of the finest quality; they were close enough to the town and the ground rich enough to make a truck garden out of a part of the place. Indeed, Jim Pleasant already had started one. Then there were fine fields where grain crops could be rotated, and strips by the river where alfalfa grew like mad and offered four large cuttings in a single year. Money had been loaned upon that farm as upon mere grazing land; as a matter of fact, here was a purchaser who was willing to pay a hundred and fifty dollars an acre for the ground alone. Seventy-five thousand dollars! And nothing thrown in— he would pay extra for the buildings, and he would pay for every tool, wagon, and animal on the ground. Particularly he wanted to carry on with the horses. There were seventy-five head of near-thoroughbreds or actual clean-bred ones. And that famous stock was worth close to five hundred a head. Add that on, and the price offered for the Jim Pleasant place by this prospective purchaser was pushed up to close to a hundred and twenty-five thousand dollars!

Spot cash, too! This was a millionaire from the East.

But the banker beat his fist upon his desk.

"If that little valley is worth a hundred and twenty-five thousand dollars to an Easterner, it's worth two hundred thousand to me. I'll make that land worth three hundred an acre, and I'll raise the cost of one of those Pleasant horses to a thousand dollars. Why, every young rancher and every miner who strikes it rich, and every one who wants to make a splurge has got to have a Pleasant horse under him why, hell, my friend, that farm is going to be one of the jewels in my crown! It'll pay me back nearly for the money that I lost in the robbery   by Heaven   yes, there is a Heaven, after all! And I'll have my recompense!"

You will have observed that there was something of the spirit of the booster about Mr. Fisher, but at the same time he rarely embarked on such flights of fancy as this one. Then, sitting back in his chair, he set his teeth and his eyes puckered almost shut and glittered with pleasure. For what had he paid for this handsome property, this farm which promised to be a treasure trove?

Mr. Fisher rubbed his hands together. He began to laugh. After all, so long as God spared him his brain, he would be sure to be able to make money!

CHAPTER 30

In the meantime, trouble was pouring upon the marshal. For when he wakened the next morning, he found that Fisher Falls was up in arms against him, and the reason was printed in headlines across the *Evening Democrat* of the preceding afternoon.

The marshal was held up as a most doubly-damned traitor to the community. According to that stinging article, Sam Lee had declared that there were no men in Fisher Falls. And the news article was not without lengthy and withering reference to the marshal's recent failure in his office.

In conclusion, on the editorial page the editor with grinding teeth had attempted to make cooler comment upon the marshal's lack of respect for the Fisher Falls population, and in his final paragraph he announced that one no longer could expect real service from the marshal—the years were taking their toll not only of his body but of his brain, and it was high time that Washington should know the status of its representative in this section of the country!

Sam Lee read all of these remarks from the first to the last, and as he consumed his breakfast, he pored over the paper as though he were studying it. Others in the diningroom looked askance at him and frowned darkly, and muttered behind their fists to one another. However, no one addressed him until a young man sauntered cheerfully across the room and tucked his hat under his arm.

"Good morning, Marshal Lee," said he. "I come from the *Evening Democrat!*"

He waited to let this announcement sink in, but Sam Lee was blandly stirring sugar into his coffee, and he merely nodded cheerfully at the youth.

"Well, sir," said the other, "the *Evening Democrat*, it always aims at giving everybody a chance. It doesn't want to stab anybody in the back without giving him a chance to hit back."

"Dear me," murmured Sam Lee, "how interestin' you are! Will you sit down here?"

"Thank you," said the reporter, and he sat down briskly and put his straw hat across his knees. The top of it made an admirable table on which to rest his notebook. He took from an inner pocket a little sheaf of pencils and smiled aggressively at the marshal.

"I'd call that a fair policy," said the marshal. "Your paper would never hit without letting the other fellow hit back?"

"That's exactly it, sir. Our editor says that   "

"I've seen your editor," said Sam Lee thoughtfully. "He has a scar under his right eye, I think?"

"Exactly! And—"

"I'll have to try to remember him," murmured Sam Lee. "Man with policies like that, he ought to be looked up to. For instance, he wouldn't print anything that he wasn't sure was correct?"

"Certainly not!"

"My, how glad I am to hear it! And the editor, he wouldn't even think about doin' such a thing as rollin' over a man whose back was turned to him, would he?"

"Certainly not!" said the reporter.

The soft voice of Sam Lee continued: "Or, if he did, he'd be mighty sure to turn around after he'd driven his steam roller over the man, and ask him if he wanted to get up and fight it out, fair and square?"

The reporter started to answer, but suddenly he saw that there was no answer to make. Also, he began to notice other details, for he was a youth well suited to his profession, and possessing admirable eyes for small things. He observed that the marshal had been stirring his coffee with a spoon held in his left hand, and that he was now sipping the coffee, holding the cup in the same hand.

Most remarkable of all, when that cup was raised and the smiling lips of old Sam Lee were hidden from view, it was extraordinary to the last degree to notice a change; for it could be seen then that the eyes were not smiling at all. They were as straight and hard and gleaming as the eyes of a wild animal about to spring!

Sam Lee put down his cup. He was still smiling, gently, affably; but the young reporter had seen enough. The right hand of Sam Lee did not appear at all. What devilishness was going on in the mind of this man-killer?

He started to his feet.

"Hold on! You ain't going to run along, young man?"

"I—I just remembered something—I forgot—I'll be back later, if I may! Only—Mr. Lee—I got to ask you one question did you mean what you said about there being no men in Fisher Falls?"

Said the marshal: "It's a statement I never made."

Suddenly his voice had grown louder, so that it was clearly audible throughout the dining-room.

"It's a statement I never made," repeated the marshal distinctly, "but since it was made for me, perhaps it may as well stand. And if your editor wants fair play—"

"Yes, yes, yes!" stammered the youngster.

"Then tell him that he may as well put into his paper to-day that I'm waiting around, for a little while, to see what Fisher Falls is going to do about what I'm supposed to have said!"

The reporter backed towards the door, much shaken by this badinage. But the calm, clear voice of Sam Lee followed him: "You may as well say to your editor, too, that I'll drop right in on him and find out where he got his idea for that story!"

The reporter turned and fairly fled, and Sam Lee mildly asked for another cup of coffee and sat for a long time over it, always stirring in the sugar with his left hand, using his left hand, also, to raise the cup. The right was free and it was continually fumbling or stroking his cravat—a position which makes it very easy for one to get a revolver from a holster beneath the arm-pit!

There was no need for him to use it, however. Fisher Falls seemed pacified strangely and suddenly, in part by the enormous reputation of this man of the law, and in part by the vast distinction between his quiet self and his famous deeds. He sat in the hotel at Fisher Falls and quietly bearded the entire body of that rough population, and you may be sure that he enjoyed his stay.

In the meantime, he had sent out many telegrams, and as a result, after two days, he began to receive visitors at the hotel. Almost without exception they were slender men burned almost black, and with cheeks so hollow that it seemed that they had been seared by the fire in which they lived. They were all as alike as so many wild-cats; and they possessed much the same characteristics of manner. That is to say, they could sit for hours and hours doing nothing but look at the sky with dreamy eyes, and if the sun moved onto their faces, it made little difference; for still they could sit and dream. They rolled Bull Durham cigarettes, leisurely, continuously, so that around each man's chair there was sure to be a little golden circle of dust. And that was all they cared to do—to sit, never to speak, to stare at nothingness, to smoke thin cigarettes of their own manufacture. When they rose, it was only because of the dinner bell, and then they seemed almost too weak to stand. They went into the dining-room with stilted steps, and their legs bent much at the knees, as though their strength were giving out. Indeed, as this little collection of the marshal's "friends" grew, they looked not a little like a row of corpses sitting on the veranda of the hotel at Fisher Falls, their hands in their laps, naught about them moving except the pale-blue clouds of cigarette smoke.

There were six of them and no one knew anything about them until the editor managed to get a glimpse of them.

It was difficult for him to get that glimpse because, shortly after the reporter returned to him from the hotel, the editor of the *Evening Democrat* had thrown himself upon his fastest horse and fled for his life. Thereafter, he lived a skulking existence on the borders of Fisher Falls, waiting for the terrible little marshal to leave the town, and in the meantime running his newspaper from afar. Curiosity almost maddened him when he heard about Sam Lee's odd group of visitors. So he desperately adventured into the city and from the roof of a house across the street, he peered at the line of smokers. After he had looked at them for a long time, a pang seized the editor. He sat straight up and began to run his hands through his hair. His lips worked and finally he slipped away and rushed for his place of retirement on the edges of the town.

There he sat down before a typewriter and plunged into his labors, merely pausing now and again to rummage through a vast and well-sorted collection of photographs which always were at hand. It was not chance that had made Mr. Robert Ezekiel the editor of this growing evening paper; it was labor, keenness, and the inventiveness and good memory of a devil. So, before he had finished his work at the typewriter, he had poured out full three thousand words narrating what he knew about the men who sat with the marshal on the veranda of the hotel.

"Five slayers of men sitting in a row," said the fearless editor, "with Marshal Sam Lee at their head. For what are they waiting? Who is about to die? How many are to be slaughtered by this army of ghostly killers? Gunmen, professional, cunning, dauntless, cruel as eagles and as sure of their prey, how has Sam Lee been enabled to gather them?"

The editor began in this strain.

And then he answered his own question with a good deal of acumen. The marshal had gathered these fighters for the sake of wiping out the blot on his own fair fame. He had brought them together for the sake of capturing or killing the great Tom Rizdal and his lately famous partner, Pleasant Jim.

That article was read and instantly it was believed, and people began to hold their breaths, for they felt that they were sitting in the presence of a new Iliad, a new battle of the giants.

And then, on a day, six magnificent horses were brought before the hotel, and the little marshal and his five bland and terrible companions mounted the saddles and rode out of Fisher Falls.

CHAPTER 31

LEWIS FISHER was the gladdest man in the whole range of the mountains when he saw those men ride by. There was no spirit in them; they slumped sadly in the saddle; they appeared all round-shouldered weaklings; and in listless fashion they went, Sam Lee at the head, and the rest trailing out in single file, as though already they were riding some narrow mountain way.

They were armed to the teeth, with rifles, revolvers, and long, cruel knives; and the packs behind their saddles were significantly small; it was plain that they meant to live on the country, like veritable Indians, and only grossest idiots would have doubted their ability to do so. Such men as these could enter a thousand miles of desert with a rifle and some salt, and come out on the farther side fatter than when he entered the sea of heat. And if they did not pour out of Fisher Falls with ringing cheers and much swinging of their hats, all the more token that they would stick to the trail with the patience of wolves. It did not occur to people to doubt that they would win their victory, even with Long Tom Rizdal and Pleasant Jim staked against them. So Lewis Fisher stood at the window of his bank and grinned a great grin, and seemed to drink in the air of a cruel satisfaction.

There was a stir beside him.

"Uncle Lewis, I'd like to be riding out with them!"

"Don't be a damn young fool," said the uncle. "Lee would laugh himself almost to death if he was to hear you say that!"

"I don't think he would. I'd like to try!"

"You lie!" said Lewis Fisher. He always rather scorned to hunt for pretty words, but had preferred since he gathered his first million, to speak his thoughts in an outright fashion. Let the chips fall where they might! "You lie," said the banker. "You're

161

trying to throw a bluff and impress me. You'd be scared to death if you were riding on their errand. You know it; so let's stop arguin' about it. Go back to your desk! Or else live up to your talk, get on a horse, and ask Marshal Lee to take you along!"

This terrible and disgusted speech was hurled fairly in the face of the nephew. He was a pale and hollow-chested young man who looked habitually upon the ground, only raising his eyes in flashes and those flashes usually not of a pleasant sort.

He was not very industrious and he was not overly intelligent, but for the banker he had two overwhelming recommendations. On the one hand, he carried what the rich man felt to be among the best first names in the world: Lewis. On the other hand he fortunately possessed the final family name of Fisher!

In other words, there was a second Lewis Fisher, and often the banker, dreaming through cigar smoke, probing the vast future, fingering the outlines of the future, told himself that fate had given this youth that name of Lewis, foreknowing that the banker would have no son of his own. However, by fortune both father and mother of the lad were gone; there was no fence between Lewis Fisher the First, and his assured successor to the bank presidency and all the far-flung fortunes of the originator of the bank. In a word, the boy was, in the eyes of Lewis Fisher the First, the one priceless jewel in the world, for he was the one jewel without which life for the rich man would be converted into very much of a joke   all purpose and final point would be removed, in short!

As he delivered this volley to put his heir in his proper place, Mr. Fisher Senior strode on past him. It was characteristic of the banker that, having made his point, he never dreamed of looking again to make sure that his auditor had accepted his remark at its pretended value.

Now he failed to see the face of his jewel wither into shame and fury.

Five minutes later, young Lewis Fisher had jumped into a saddle and was riding furiously out of the town. A slowly moving wisp of dust hung in the air, as he passed through an avenue of trees; a little further and he saw the long and slender line of six riders winding up a hill-face.

He plunged for them and came at once to Sam Lee. He was no longer in the van but in the rear—where the dust was sure to be the thickest, but his bandanna was serving its greatest purpose and through it as a sieve he sifted the dust from the pure air.

Even this short canter had powdered the clothes of Lewis with white. But he was regardless of his appearance as he drew up beside the marshal.

"Hello!" said the latter. "What's the news, son?"

"Do you know my name?" asked the boy.

"I dunno that I do."

Young Lewis nearly fell from his saddle. He felt that hardly a blind man could be able to ride into Fisher Valley without being informed about the great double star which reigned over the district the Fisher Stars, in other words. But now he was disclaimed.

"No," he answered, however, "my uncle, he crowds into the limelight all the time and takes all the credit for everything. Why should anybody know what I look like? My name's Lewis Fisher," he finished.

And he waited with a vain smile broadening upon his lips.

"How are you, Fisher," said the marshal. "Any trouble back there in the town that brought you out here to me?"

"There's trouble," replied the boy, "but it's trouble that bothers me, and not most people."

"Go on."

"Marshal Lee, I got to make a name for myself!"

"Every young man does. Go on."

"The old man, he plugged away and got famous making money. Well, I hate to sit at a desk all my life. And, besides, I want to do something quick. The old man thinks that I'm a worm. By God, I'll show him that I'm not!"

Thick as the dust was, it had not settled upon his face thickly enough to disguise the strange green of his complexion as he said this. Malice and hate and envy fairly choked him.

The marshal waited, not amused, very attentive.

"Lee, I want to go with you!" said the boy huskily. "Will you let me come?"

Sam Lee shook his head.

"I got enough," he said. "These are all hand-picked. Besides, you know I ain't hunting black bears that'll take to the trees!"

"Don't I know it? Of course I know it! Marshal, you give me a chance to fly with you in this hunt, and I'll play my hand as well as the next one."

"Can you shoot, Fisher?" asked Sam Lee, with the air of one who does not wish to be blunt and rude in a refusal.

"I can, and I will, what's more," said Lewis Fisher the Second.

"Of course you will," said Marshal Lee. "Of course you'll shoot, and I can see that you're a game young feller. And one of these days I'd be glad to have you along with me, but you know what they used to say in the silly old stories about the dead shots, son?"

"I know a lot of nonsense about people that never missed. Well?"

"Well, Lew, that's what these old boys are. They can miss their targets, sometimes, but they never miss their men. They're what the old books used to talk about. They're dead shots. They ain't a one of them that hasn't averaged three hours a day for thirty years working with rifles and revolvers, drawing 'em, shooting 'em, cleaning 'em, taking 'em apart, putting 'em together, loving their Colts like their children. You understand what I mean? They're the kind that never miss!"

Young Lewis Fisher, breathing very hard, looked full into the face of his companion and then his lower jaw thrust out a little, which is apt to be the sign of a man with a fighting spirit.

"Gimme a try, will you, Lee?" he asked suddenly. "I haven't had thirty years, or even twenty. But since I was fifteen   that's eight years ago, I've fairly lived with a gun and waited for a chance to use it! Does that sound a little more to you?"

"There's a tree, and there's a blaze on the side of that branch. Don't let that hold you back, none, if it looks like a proper target to you. Just blaze away."

"Thanks," said the boy, and instantly he whipped out a Colt and fired.

It was a thin little branch with a white notch in it, and the bullet passed cleanly through the mark, at which the branch sagged slowly downwards.

"All right," said the boy, "gimme something else to hit. Give me something moving, Lee. That's what I can do pretty well."

"You've done enough," said the marshal rather dryly, "and if you want to go along with us, you're damn welcome, my son. But you can't travel in those togs that you got on."

"Can't I?" cried the boy, joy ringing in his throat suddenly as he heard the decision. "Lee, you've promised me that I can go, and you can't go back on your promise, y'understand? I'll be damned before I go back to get other togs. You'd be too far away to catch before I could start again, and if these clothes aren't too good for a bank they're not too good for the funeral of Long Tom and Pleasant Jim. My gad, what a trip it's gunna be, Sam Lee!"

The marshal himself had been very young, and though that was a good many years ago, he never had forgotten. Now an actual sympathy gleamed in his eyes as he regarded the boy.

"I think that you're going to do some good for us, Lew," said he. "What about your uncle, though? What will he have to say when he hears that I've kidnaped you?"

"He'll have to say," declared the boy, "that I have something better to do than waste my time in a damned bank. My God, Lee, I'm the happiest man in the world!"

"Good," smiled the marshal, "but just you watch your work every day on this trail, because if you don't, you might change from the happiest man in the world into the deadest!"

So spoke the marshal, almost prophetically!

CHAPTER 32

THERE were three great matters for Jim Pleasant. One was how he was to return to a peaceful and hard-working life to raise horses; the second and most important concerned his peculiar emotions concerning Sally, which he felt would wear away were he once back at his familiar tasks; the third was that which had to do with the danger from the long arm of the law, and to this he paid the least attention, because for one thing he trusted himself, for another he trusted his companions, and in the third place he was enormously sure that no horse in the world could bring danger near him so long as he had the four strong legs of the stallion, the Leinster Gray, beneath him.

The working point was the matter of his return to his old concerns, and in this he felt that he made no progress. He began to distrust the big man, Long Tom, and his good-natured assurances that everything would be well in the end.

So his discontent grew.

They were domiciled, for the moment, in a small mountain shack, waiting for the dust of their latest exploit to settle. The farmer and the farmer's wife and son were their servants, cooking for them, waiting on them in every conceivable manner. And life should have been easy enough had not divine discontent continually stirred in the breast of Pleasant Jim.

He began to press Long Tom. When was his return to the ways of peace to be arranged? Where and how would he go back to normal life? Long Tom, with a really touching patience, assured him that in the end he would be able to arrange everything. But what was to be done in the interim except to retain his patience. He had schemes on foot, said Long Tom, which would give his companion everything that he wanted.

So Pleasant Jim continued to wait, and his temper grew more

sullenly restless every moment. He was up early and he was awake late. He found on the place half a dozen unbroken mustangs and it was his diversion for a little while to handle them; but they were intelligent enough to understand when they had met a master, and after a few sessions with them, he could not raise an interesting session with them even when he worked his spurs overtime. They became so tame that they even lifted their ears cheerfully when they saw him coming, and he could catch them in the pasture without a rope.

The farmer was charmed and amazed by this performance, which he declared bordered upon the miraculous, but Pleasant Jim was disgusted. He wanted occupation to fill those big hands of his, and he was dismayed by the prospect of quiet.

He hunted, too. But hunting could not be carried on at any great distance, for always he must be close to signal-sight of the shack in case of an alarm. He managed to get a few rabbits and squirrels every day; two deer walked unluckily within the range of his rifle; and one strong black bear, a nervous and inquisitive fellow, came to the end of both nerves and curiosity when he stepped into the charmed circle and received a steel-jacketed bullet.

The skinning and the curing of the hide occupied Pleasant Jim a little, also. And, indeed, the story of his life in the hills would have been an eventful chapter in the careers of most men. It was not enough for him. Eagerly, hungrily, he sought more occupation. A set of boxing gloves were snapped up. Long Tom would not pay any attention to many invitations to put them on, but Charlie Rizdal tried twice or thrice. He could not stand to the fast handwork and the terrible shoulder power of Pleasant Jim, and no matter if the latter tried to strike softly, he could not control his strength when he saw an opening any more than a bear can control the power of its forepaws. So ennui began to settle upon Pleasant Jim, and he concentrated upon his last means for diversion, which was Sally.

There was never a moment when he was not besetting her for a walk, a talk, a ride together, and though she dodged him on one pretext after another, he managed to spend a great many hours with her and so to increase his peculiar feeling of joy and sorrow when she was near.

Sally had changed a great deal. She was not so full of slang and fire; she was more reserved, gentle, quiet, and there was about her smile and her voice something out of a new world.

Pleasant Jim sensed it. But he could not tell whether she actually had altered or whether he simply was beginning to know her better.

In his present humor, however, all his senses were sharpened, and two things he very clearly made out: the first was that she really liked to be with him and the second was that she was filled with terror every instant she was in his company. Of course that did not help to clear away the mystery; and finally all other employments were dropped for the sake of Sally. The family on the farm laughed openly; even an infant could have seen what was wrong with this big man who dogged the steps of a girl day and night, waited for her in the morning, teased her to stay up later at night, and brought to her the head and skin of the deer he killed, and the mask and pelt of the bear.

Pleasant Jim was aware that the other two men felt he was paying too much attention to the girl. It made Charlie restless, and Long Tom's brow often was clouded. But as for the opinion of any one in the world, Pleasant had not the slightest care. Nothing is so desperate as ennui.

He was explained to himself by sheerest chance. They started for a ride in the early morning, the two of them, and as he helped the girl up into the saddle, her horse moved and she slipped back into his arms. It seemed to Pleasant that she fitted into them with miraculous neatness and at the touch of her body a wave of dizzy joy passed over his brain. He held Sally close to him and kissed her twice upon the lips before she thrust herself away from him.

She was actually pale with fear; but it was not Pleasant alone that seemed to frighten her. Instead, her glance wandered towards the house and the barn anxiously.

He came after her, only acutely aware of his great discovery.

"Sally, I want you!" said he. "That's what's wrong. I love you, Sally. Do you hear? Look at me! Tell me what you think! I love you, Sally!"

Sally shrank away from him, found her horse, and acted as though she would have mounted, if not in fear that he would catch her the instant her back was turned.

"Don't come near me—don't touch me!" she stammered. "Don't!"

"I won't poison you!" said Pleasant, frowning. "And if you take it that way, I won't trouble you none. Hell and fire, Sally, you just despise me, don't you!"

Still she looked not at him, but towards the house and then

towards the barn and the horse shed near it.

"Of course I don't despise you. Only, there's danger. Dear Jim, do have sense. Don't come an inch nearer!"

She was whiter than ever, but she began to laugh; and the laughter was a sadly staggering sound. The excitement of Pleasant Jim shook him from head to foot.

"What's wrong, Sally?" said he.

"Will you let me get on my horse—and not come any nearer?"

"Well, yes. Will you tell me then?"

"Yes!"

He stood frowning while she mounted, but once in the saddle she forgot her promise and fled with whip and spur across the valley and into the trees on the farther side. Her horse was very swift and she rode like a jockey, but for all of that, she had something almost as quick as fate behind her, and that was the Leinster Gray. The big stallion was mounted at one bound by Pleasant, and went like an arrow in pursuit.

Through the trees he sped and Sally's bay was seen dodging out of sight in a thicket.

Through the thicket crashed the Gray, mad with the excitement that quivered down from the hands of his rider, and in a clearing beyond, the iron hand of Pleasant caught the reins of the bay and brought it to a halt.

Sally, panting and wild of eye, dropped the reins and raised her hands rather blindly in self-defense.

"My God, Sally," cried Jim Pleasant, "what's wrong? Why d'you act like this? Am I poison to you, maybe?"

She lowered her hands, and stared at him with a desperate appeal in her eyes.

"I won't hurt you," he said hastily. "Now tell me what's the matter. I only chased you to find out what's wrong!"

"I'm afraid!" stammered Sally.

"Afraid of what? God A'mighty, we been through enough together. Can't you trust me?"

"I—" she began.

And then, sighing as though she had taken a great resolution: "Jim, you see, I'm going to marry Long Tom!"

She had spoken very much as though he had drawn a gun, and the effect upon Pleasant Jim was almost as decisive. He stiffened, and the Leinster Gray, on edge from this burst of running, sprang sideways a stride.

"You're gunna marry Long Tom!" muttered Pleasant. "Well,

I been a damn fool and a swine. But I didn't guess. I didn't aim to say such a thing as I've said, never guessing that you loved Long Tom."

"I didn't say that I love—" she began. And then checked herself. "I mean," she added, "that it's all right. Only you understand."

"I don't understand nothing," he assured her. "Why didn't you blat out the minute that I touched you: 'I belong to Tom Rizdal'? That would of stopped me, and you ought to of known it. And then you turn around and tell me that you're going to marry him, but you don't love him. Sally, what's the meaning of that? Why should you marry him if you don't love him? What hold has he got on you?"

Sally looked at him as at a creature who cannot be persuaded.

"I do care for him. I can't explain anything. Only you must never touch me again. Will you promise that?"

"Right quick I'll promise it," said he sourly. "I don't force myself on nobody, I hope!"

And he rode suddenly through the brush and back towards the house.

CHAPTER 33

IF his humor had been dark and restless before, it became settled and black as night thereafter.

That evening he was asked by Long Tom and Charlie to play a hand of poker, but for an answer he rose and strode silently from the house. The two men looked blankly at one another.

"What's happened to the Big Boy?" asked Charlie Rizdal.

"Why do you ask me?" said Sally, strangely on fire. "I can't read his mind!"

And she slammed out of the room and went to bed.

Long Tom continued to shuffle the cards, looking down to them with an evil smile.

"Something has got to happen," he said at length, "speaking personal. Something has got to happen, and pretty damned pronto."

"Not to Pleasant?" asked Charlie Rizdal.

"That'd hurt you a lot, wouldn't it?" exclaimed Long Tom. "You aren't aching to see him done for, are you?"

"His killing would be worth about a quarter of a million," responded Charlie, full of thought.

"By God," breathed Long Tom, "sometimes I think that you got the soul of a rat, Charlie! D'you think that I'd shoot him for his money? No, if he has to go down, his money goes to charity! And in his name. Something for the world to remember him by, because he's worth remembering, I'd say. I've never met a man like him!"

"I see that you're fond of him," said Charlie, with cunning malice touching upon the right string. "I see that you're pretty fond of him, but for all of that, I guess that you ain't as fond of him as Sally is! There's something between them. They're acting like a pair of lovers that have had a falling out."

Long Tom said nothing, but continued to shuffle the cards, and then with a fluent skill he began to deal them so rapidly that they fell in a brightly glinting shower upon the table. Three hands he dealt. And Charlie picked them up and turned them.

"I see," said he, chuckling softly. "I do the bucking. *He* makes the high bet, and you win the pot!"

Long Tom answered nothing, but swept up the cards once more and began to deal again. It was said that he could have made an excellent living as a gambler if he had not gone in for a greater game. At any rate, once more he ran up the pack, and once more he dealt with his accustomed speed and sureness.

Charlie did not turn the cards over. He was too interested in what he had in mind.

"I'll tell you what, Tom," said he, "there's only one way out of this for us. Sally is out of her head about him."

"She likes him. She's got reason to," said the chief. "But that's all right."

"Sure it is, if you say so. Otherwise, I would of thought that she was sort of   well, let it go! Pleasant will ride off with her, one of these days, pretty quick!"

Long Tom flicked the hands over, read their faces with a glance, and swept them into a firm pack again. He worked with the very tips of his fingers, apparently, and one hardly would have asked for a more open shuffler.

"Charlie," said his older brother, "you're fine, and I'm damn fond of you. But you live small; you think small; and you can't figure what's gunna happen to big people. The girl likes Jim. She ought to; he was a man when they were adrift together."

"Maybe, maybe!" said Charlie. "But on the other hand, you got to see that perhaps she didn't tell you everything. Pleasant ain't a saint!"

At this, Long Tom instinctively reached for a gun, but after a black moment he drew his empty hand from beneath his coat. Slowly he mopped his forehead with a handkerchief.

"You're a poisonous devil, Charlie," he said at length. "Hating him the way that you do, it's a wonder to me that you can keep on smiling at him every day!"

"I'm waiting," said Charlie Rizdal. "I don't commit suicide, that's all."

"But he's got to die, so far as you're concerned?"

"Sure he does, and so far as you're concerned, too; if you're what I think you are."

Suddenly Long Tom crossed the room and struck on the door of the girl.

A complaining, weary voice answered him.

"It's Tom," he said. "Come here a minute, Sally."

She came to the door and opened it a little and stood a dim glimmer of whiteness in the black of the room.

"What's happened between you and the Big Boy?"

"Who said anything had happened?"

"We have eyes, old girl."

"I had to tell him that I—belong—to—you!"

And she closed the door softly. Long Tom remained before it as though he were about to call to her once more, but thinking better of that idea, he turned and went back with his noiseless step to the table, and sat down there.

"Well?" said Charlie.

Long Tom cast at him a withering glance.

"You're right," he said at length. "Something's got to be done."

"Sure it has," went on Charlie, smoothly expanding the thought. "She's heading off Pleasant because she's afraid that you'll see how much she loves him and then—"

Long Tom started up and cast down the cards. They slipped from the edge of the table and cascaded to the floor.

"Oh, damn your rotten heart!" said he softly, and went from the room into the outer night.

Charlie remained alone, and with an absent air, he collected the fallen cards. He was smiling a little with a fox-like content.

"It seemed to be about my turn," said he to himself, "to take a little hand in the game."

And he began to shuffle with hardly less skill than his older and more talented brother had shown.

In the meantime, Long Tom, striding through the dark, was confronted suddenly by a form as tall as and a little more powerful than his own.

"Well, Jim," said he, "you're in the dumps to-night. Still thinking about the farm?"

"I'm thinking about the girl," said Pleasant, speaking instantly from his heart. "How come that you're to have her, Tom, when as a matter of fact she don't love you?"

Long Tom considered this remark for a long moment; as a truth, he dared not trust his voice, at once.

"Did she tell you that?" he asked, finally.

"No, I guessed it," said Pleasant in haste, feeling that he must not betray her. "Anybody can see by watching her when she's with you!"

"You think you know her, but wait awhile and you'll see that there's more to her than you guess," suggested the bandit. "You can't read Sally in one minute, and you can't read her in two. But now, I've got an idea. If I send you down to Kentucky, I know where you can pick up and start again, Jim. You can have your horse farm, and I'll steer you to it. You want the details?"

"Horse farm?" said Pleasant. "I pretty near forgot that there was such a thing in the world. What's important to me—well, it ain't horses!"

"What is it?" asked Rizdal.

"Excitement is what we live for," said Jim Pleasant. "And I want my share. I'm going to stick with you fellows, Tom. I've made up my mind to it."

"Ah?" said Long Tom.

"I've had my taste of high life, and I like it pretty well. You understand?"

"Of course," said Long Tom. "Of course I understand. You want to see a few more banks crack open. Well—you'll have it your own way. Of course I've always wanted you with us permanent, right from the first. Are you going back to the house?"

"Yes. Are you?"

"No, I'm walking on for a while!"

So Pleasant went back to the house. He felt that he had come out fairly well from his talk with Long Tom. At least he had brought their relations out into the open, and that was a great point, for he hated to work in the dark. Now Tom knew that he wanted the girl, and from that moment, let each man take his own advantage.

And as for Sally? Well, he still hoped. She was an odd person, and it was hard to understand her, but the hardest trail usually can be solved by time and patience spent on it!

In his room at the shack, he saw that Charlie Rizdal already was in bed and breathing regularly, so he turned in at once. For a moment he stared at the darkness, then sleep formed over his brain; dusky forms in imitation of life passed across his mind, and his eyes closed.

The moment his breathing changed, there was a rustle in the window; and that instant his scattered consciousness returned to him. He was wide awake, every sense on the alert and the gun which never left him, day or night, gripped in his hand.

Yet he did not stir, and instead of letting his breathing alter, he began to snore a little, rhythmically and regularly.

And all the while the bright shadow of danger was growing in the room. Trifle by trifle he turned his head until he saw the dim silhouette of a man's head and shoulders against the stars beyond the window, and the glitter of steel in his hand

His own gun he snatched over his head and fired; the answering shot boomed heavily and the slug tore at the wall beside him.

He was out of the bed with a bound, but the window was empty, and when he reached it, he had only a fleeting impression of some one running around the corner of the house.

Another man would have stood a moment to curse, or else turned and hurried down to the door. Pleasant Jim slipped through the window and dropped like a cat to the ground, gun in hand, and then sprang in pursuit.

CHAPTER 34

"WHO fired that shot!" shouted the familiar voice of Long Tom, and as Pleasant turned the corner of the shack, he encountered the latter running from the door of the house.

Into the stomach of Tom Rizdal he thrust the muzzle of his Colt.

"Rizdal," he said savagely, "you tried that on me yourself!"

"You're a fool, Jim," said the other without excitement. "Think it over, and you'll see that you'll have to admit that you're a fool. Look at my guns. Have either of 'em had a shot fired out of 'em?"

"Then where's the man?" asked Pleasant.

"Yonder!" said Tom Rizdal, and nodded.

Across the valley swept a shadow with the speed of a bird on the wing. It was a horseman riding at full gallop and heading away as fast as his mount could leg it.

"You're right," said Jim Pleasant, "and I'm a worse fool than you said. Excuse me, Tom."

"Forget about it," replied the gunman. "What's happened?"

The house was in confusion.

"Some one started to take a shot at me while I was in bed. But I got a hunch, spied him, and beat him to it by a shade."

"Did you nick him?"

"I dunno. It was a snap shot over my head. But I may have touched him."

"He rides like it!"

The sharp voice of Sally came bursting from her room: "Jim! Jim Pleasant! Where are you?"

"Here!"

"You're not hurt, Jim?"

"Me? Not a bit. What made you think that I might be?"

"I heard the noise in your room. I— What happened?"

"I dunno," said Pleasant Jim, "except that somebody may of spotted us and come down here to clean up a big reward and get a reputation by doing some midnight murders. That's about the caliber of some gents. But as soon as there was a little gun-talk, he changed his mind."

"It was that sneak of a boy, Pete!" said Sally, speaking of the farmer's son.

"There's Pete now," answered Pleasant. "And him that tried this snap shot at me was twice bigger in the shoulders than Pete. Besides, he cut away across the valley. I never seen a faster move in my life!"

"What'll we do?" asked Charlie Rizdal, hurrying down the stairs. "How'll we get Emmet, for this?"

"Emmet?" cried Sally. "Do you mean Dick Emmet?"

"That's who I mean."

"How could you tell?"

"I seen the side of his face against the stars, and I recognized him, too, in the flash of his own gun. It ain't hard to recognize Dick Emmet's broken nose."

"He'd never do it!" said the girl.

"Wouldn't he? Men'll do a lot for ten thousand dollars!"

"What'll we do? Trail him?" asked Charlie.

"We'll go to bed and get our sleep out," said Pleasant Jim, and straightway he went up the stairs.

The others followed him with their eyes; and when he had disappeared, they presently heard the creak of the bed as he threw himself down on it, and then a faint sound of whistling of an old tune.

"He's happy!" said Sally. "He—he liked it!"

"Sure," answered Charlie Rizdal. "That's just a nightcap, sort of, for Pleasant!"

"Are you going to bed, Sally?"

"Yes. Good night."

"You ain't upset?"

"No, I'm all right."

She disappeared, and the Rizdals stepped out into the darkness.

"Did you see what he did?" asked Tom Rizdal.

"Aw, I was only faking sleep. I was watching every trick. I had an idea that something would happen to-night."

"I thought I had him for a dead man," said Tom. "I was about to pick him off while he snored. The snoring was a sort of a light, you might say, to guide my shot. And then he twitched a gun over his head before I could wink right in the middle of a snore, as you might say."

"He's a snake," said Charlie Rizdal. "Of course he was faking, too."

"Naturally. He suspected something."

"How did you have the nerve to meet him when he came down?"

"I ran out the door asking who'd fired the shot. He came around the corner on the jump and shoved a gun into my stomach before I could draw. How did *he* get down so quick?"

"He jumped through the window. Speaking of fighting men, he's a breed all off by himself."

"He accused me. I think he would have murdered me, too. But then I saw somebody streaking down the valley. Must have been some rustler who thought that the shots were meant for him and hit the high spots getting out. That lucky chance was what saved my life!"

"Of course it was. He ain't pleasant to have a run in with, is he?"

"No, old son. And we both know it, now!"

"Sally took it hard."

"She suspects something," agreed Tom Rizdal. "But she'll get over it."

"Only," said Charlie, "God knows how you ever came to think of such a thing."

"Meaning what?"

"That it's not your style."

"Anything's my style. Fair and free fighting, if that will serve. If not then anything to get the wrong man out of the way. You don't know me, Charlie! Nobody does. But the flash of my gun gave you your first real glimpse of me to-night. Don't fool yourself, though. I can go straight and be faithful. You know that. Play my game and you'll never stop thanking God that you have me for a brother!"

So, frankly, without shame, they discussed the matter.

"Emmet won't thank you," said Tom.

"He won't have a chance either for thinking or for thanking," said Charlie Rizdal. "He'll die so fast when Pleasant comes up to him!"

And the older brother chuckled.

"What did you do with the gun you'd used?" asked Charlie.

"Chucked it into the brush as I slipped down the side of the house. Of course I figured on every chance and was carrying three guns instead of two. Now, let's go to bed."

"Listen," said Charlie, as they stepped back into the house.

They heard a faint snoring from the story above them. All the rest of the house was already quiet, for the poor farmer's family, in terror of its dreadful guests, had slipped away to their own beds as soon as they could. The air of the night was heavy in the house, and the stale scent of cookery hung in the room.

"Is he really asleep or simply faking again?" asked Charlie thoughtfully.

"I dunno," answered Long Tom. "But this I do know: I'm not going to go investigating!"

And he went off to bed.

Of course there was much talk during the next day about the strange happenings of the previous evening, and all joined in with conjectures and surmises; but the idea of a head-hunter having made the attempt was the idea which was most convincing to every one, apparently.

Long Tom, finding himself later beneath a scrub-oak with Sally near by brooding over a brook, said: "You haven't turned a page in half an hour, Sally. What are you doing?"

"Standing at the window with the head-hunter," said Sally slowly, without lifting her eyes. "If I wanted to kill only one man, I'd have done just that—stood at the window and taken a careful shot, but if I'd been out for a big handsome reward, I should have slipped softly in through the window—and tried to bag two men!"

"Of course," nodded Long Tom. "But the scoundrel didn't have the nerve, you see. He was a coward."

"No real coward," replied the girl, "stalks a house where Long Tom and Jim Pleasant are living. No, there's something very odd about this whole affair!"

"What do you make of it, then?"

She raised her head and watched the monotonous faint shifting of the upper branches and the odd patterning of the light as it slipped through.

"I don't know," she said softly.

She added after a moment: "Tom, if anything should happen to him—"

"To whom?"

"To Pleasant Jim."

"Well?"

"I think that you and I would have to say good-by!"

He started up and glared down at her.

"Are you tying me up with that bit of dirty work that was tried last night?" he asked.

She did not answer. She merely closed her eyes and her brow still was wrinkled with the effort of thought. However, when she looked up again she did not speak, and suddenly the tongue of Long Tom clove against the roof of his mouth and he felt himself growing paler.

"Well?" he asked huskily again.

"I'm not going to talk to Jim," said the girl. "I'm just telling you!"

CHAPTER 35

Up through the mountains, softly and steadily, never rushing their horses, and yet never favoring them, went the procession of Sam Lee, Federal Marshal.

It mattered not a whit to these veterans that he recently had been balked in a public and signal manner. On the contrary, they valued him rather for what he was than for what he had done, and they knew that his shot was as straight and his draw was as swift as that of any of his followers. They knew that he had planned this campaign with a sufficient cunning, and they were therefore, considering their ample pay, quite ready to serve under him.

Sometimes, at first, they looked a little askance upon their youngest and most lately added companion, until a deer flicked through the brush two hundred yards ahead of them and the man who stopped it with a brilliant snapshot was no other than young Lewis Fisher.

After that, they asked no more questions. If he were a little green and raw about camp and hardly knew what to do with himself or his blankets, they were perfectly willing to show him and, in a measure, to take care of him. For such a shot was worth having along, and might help to enrich them all.

Besides, they pointed out rightly that he was the seventh member of the party, and therefore good luck must be in him! All, therefore, was going well with the party, whether it were considered spiritually or physically.

In the meantime, it was apparent that the marshal was not proceeding to make a blind cast. On the contrary, he was constantly receiving reports from people who rode suddenly into the camp or came up with them on the day's march. He had set out not before the telegraph and the telephone had prepared the way before him as nearly as possible.

Therefore, no one was disturbed when a rough mountaineer rode freely up to them just as they were scattering for an evening halt and gave a letter to the marshal.

He read it as the stranger disappeared again down the gorge. It ran thus:

"My dear Sam Lee,

"If you can't have all of the men you want to get, at least you ought to be glad enough to get one of the three   and given to you for nothing.

"They have heard how you're passing through the mountains, and they feel that you can do them and yourself a good turn by showing up at the Newberg shack just after sunset Thursday night   which will make easy marching for you.

"If you come up to the place, you'll find no resistance. The two Rizdals will be out of the way, and young Pleasant will be there alone. You couldn't ask for anything better than that!"

There was no signature to this strange epistle.

But the marshal remained studying it for a long time, by the last of the daylight and then by the fire. He had in his pocket a number of letters and other documents, wrapped in a section of oiled silk, and these he now began to compare with the letter which had newly arrived.

The latter was printed out roughly in sprawling characters, as if by one who desired to disguise his handwriting, but the worthy marshal had deciphered handwriting before and taken a prolonged and special course in that intricate and uncertain science. He was, indeed, an expert, quite capable of having run a department in a magazine and analyzing the characters of his correspondents.

When he had finished his survey, which meant the free use of a magnifying glass from time to time, he next took out his writing materials and wrote a letter in turn. He composed it with care and with deliberation, and when he had finished, he called young Lew Fisher to one side.

"Lew," said he, "you've showed up well on this trip, and on the whole I think you have in you the makin' of a mountaineer!"

Lewis Fisher, prospective millionaire, half closed his eyes and blinked with joy at the most delightful words he ever had heard.

"But now," went on the chief, "I'm gunna give you a trial, and

a real trial. I want you to take this letter and ride on ahead
through the mountains to King's Gap and through the gap and
on to the lower plateau beyond. There you'll come to a fork in
the trail and one part of the trail will run to the right down hill
and the other part will go straight ahead and climb a little. The
right fork is well-traveled, and the left fork is most likely pretty
blind. But be sure to take the left fork. Then you'll come to lava
rocks, and the trail will go out altogether. You'll go five or ten
miles through the rocks, and when you get on the farther side,
you'll have to cut for sign again, and when you've found the path
again, you follow on until you've reached a narrow valley, and
there be on the watch because when you come to it you've come
to enemy's country, where bullets will be fired before questions
will be asked. Follow that ravine up until it broadens a little, and
in the center of the broadest part, with a spottings of brush and
trees all around it, you'll find a shack called the Newberg shack.
Now, son, I want you to get close to that shack and find young
Jim Pleasant—"

"And kill him! And, by God, I'll do it!" exclaimed Lewis
Fisher. "Wouldn't Uncle Lewis go nearly wild if I were to kill
Pleasant?"

"Hold on!" said the marshal. "You can kill a man from a
distance, if you can catch a sight of him, but you've got a much
harder job than that to tackle. You've got to get to Pleasant and
stand up and pass that letter into his hand, without getting a
bullet passed into your body first. You understand?"

The boy listened to this proposal with a gray face.

"I understand," he said with stiff lips.

The marshal studied him intently.

"You're scared," he said frankly, "but that sort of a scare
doesn't paralyze a man, and I think that you're going to do
pretty well, Lew. When can you start?"

"When I've finished saddling my horse."

"Wait a minute. You like that black mare that I've been
riding, don't you?"

"She's the finest thing I've ever seen in horseflesh. I think
she's finer than the Leinster Gray!"

"She ain't, though," said the marshal with a sigh. "I've rode
them both and I know the differences between them. However,
she'll run true and straight till she drops, and she'll never let you
down on a long or a hard trail. Take her along with you. She's
your horse!"

Lew Fisher had received many and handsomer presents from his rich uncle. He had received houses, land, blocks of stock, but never had he received a gift such as this—on the field of battle, so to speak. And he grew whiter with joy than he had been with fear.

"Yes!" said Lew Fisher huskily.

"Mind you," said the marshal quietly in parting from his young recruit, "you might be able to get up close enough to kill Jim Pleasant, but that's not the trick. I want him to have this letter. It's more than twice as important as his death. Do you understand?"

"Yes."

"Then saddle the black and go as fast as you can!"

Lew Fisher did exactly as he had been told to do. He saddled the black and went as fast as he could.

It was a hard and a lonely expedition; never before had he been alone among the dusty gray faces of the mountains, or ridden through the dreary, pine-covered uplands. In a hundred glades he could have dropped dead and never his body been found till the end of time.

And a funereal sense of failure to come oppressed young Lew Fisher. He began to think fondly about Fisher Falls, in the far distance, and suppose that he should turn to the side down one of the long, easy valleys, and start to return—afterwards he could manage some excuse—he could say that he had fallen sick—he could say anything! But not to ride on into this certain failure where failure was death!

But somehow he kept going, and it was very much as though that brave-headed black mare had taken the matter into her own possession and decided with her brightly pricking ears to carry her new master straight on to his destiny.

He grew more afraid of her. Once he pulled her deliberately away from the trail and rode for half a mile among the pines, but when he gave her her own head she wound straight ahead among the trees—and eventually came out on the correct trail once more.

Perspiration burst out on the forehead of Lew Fisher—a sadly sunburned forehead it was, now—and he felt that destiny had taken bodily possession of him.

However, there was one advantage. He would surrender to the inevitable and let her do as she chose, since after all she could not be opposed.

In this manner he completed the journey, and crossed the pass and took the left fork at the trail, and then he entered the narrow and dangerous ravine, but he rode on boldly, without forethought—for God or the devil must handle this matter of his fate, not he!

And in due time, the trees before him scattered more and more widely.

Suddenly he saw before him a tall man riding on a great gray horse—and young Fisher snatched his rifle from its long scabbard beneath his leg and covered the stranger.

Right into the sights rode the big fellow and the great gray. Now the man alone was in the sights, and now his head—

A dead bead! Ten thousand dollars and fame as well for a single touch on the trigger! And Lew Fisher trembled with desire to shoot.

What held him back was not altogether shame to take advantage of an unsuspecting man, and neither was it altogether the behest of the marshal; it was rather a sense that Fate had brought him purposely and swiftly to Jim Pleasant.

So, still drawing his bead, he called: "Pleasant!"

And Jim Pleasant stopped his horse with a jerk of the reins.

CHAPTER 36

THEN, when mentally he twice had put a bullet through the head of the famous warrior, Lew Fisher lowered his rifle regretfully into the hollow of his left arm.

"I had you, Pleasant!" he exclaimed, in the raucous voice of triumph.

His nerves were wonderfully soothed by the steady and instant retort.

"You had me, kid, and you had me dead to rights. I must have been riding blind. I walked right into that gun!"

The malice of one who could have killed, had he so chosen, diminished suddenly in the breast of Lew Fisher. The voice was so deep, so gentle, so manly, that it touched the best and most hidden chords in his breast.

"All right," said Fisher, "but there was ten thousand and a good deal of reputation right there under my trigger finger!"

"There was ten thousand dollars, all right," admitted Pleasant Jim with his perfect good nature. "Maybe some reputation, too. Why didn't you shoot, stranger?"

And the answer started unbidden from the lips of Fisher: "My God, man, it would have been murder, you having no warning at all!"

It thrilled him when he heard his own voice. And all at once he felt a rush of good feeling, directed towards this man.

"Maybe you're right," said Pleasant. "But not so many would have stopped to think of that. And not so many," he added with a little touch of grimness, "would have taken a rifle off its bead against a pair of Colts!"

There was just a hint of a threat about that last speech, and it sent a chill through the blood of Fisher. Had he done rashly? Was this to be his last moment on earth? For he had heard much about the uncanny speed of this man with weapons, and before he could jerk the rifle back into position, perhaps a pair of leaden balls would crash through his brain!

No, Pleasant Jim, guiding his great gray horse with a touch of the knee alone, rode straight on and stretched out a hand.

"I want to know your name," said he.

How tall, how magnificent, how free he seemed as he came closer. And the stallion was hardly gray   it was silver, pointed with black, glorious beyond belief! No wonder that the marshal had said there was a difference between the mare and the horse. So a shadow of true awe for the first time in his life fell upon the heart of Lew Fisher.

"My name is Lew Fisher," he said, hardly finding his voice.

"You?" cried the other heartily. "You the nephew of Lewis Fisher? Well   I'm damned glad to know you!"

Much, much was implied in that statement. Lew could feel it, and the unspoken inference: "I know your uncle to be a rascal but you're a cut above him!"

How dearly he wished that his self-satisfied uncle could have been at hand to hear that voice speaking!

"I brought up a letter for you from the marshal," said Lew Fisher. "Here it is."

He handed it over, and Pleasant remarked as he took it: "This here is friendly and neighborly of the marshal. Instead of sending men to shoot me, he sends men with letters." And he added rather warmly: "Tell the marshal, no matter what's in this letter, no matter whatever comes out of this manhunt, that I know that I got to be a crook, now, to the end of my days, but tell him that it's him that drove me into it. No, not his fault, and I understand that. But I wasn't trying to push any of the queer! I did a job for Long Tom. Well, that was wrong. But it was only carrying a message and the pay I got for it was counterfeit. All right, and while I'm in prison waiting a trial, I lose my farm." He set his teeth hard. "You can ask your uncle, Lew, how I happened to lose my farm! And after that I had to go wrong because there was no chance for me to go right! Say that to the marshal, will you?"

"I'll say that," replied Fisher. "But about you and your farm and my uncle—what's that?"

"I don't accuse no man behind his back," said Pleasant. "But you ask him, will you? And he'll put you right, maybe!"

They said good-by, for it obviously was not healthy soil for young Fisher to linger on.

Away he rode down the narrow cañon, and big Jim Pleasant opened the letter.

He read:

"Dear Pleasant,

"This is to let you know that I've just had a letter from some one printed large and rough, but I think that the hand that printed it belonged to Tom Rizdal. The letter tells me that on Thursday night I'll have a chance to find you alone in the house of Newberg. Because he and his brother will make it a point to be away from the place.

"Well, Pleasant, it's my job to get you if I can, and I'm surely going to try hard, but on the other hand I don't want to cut a man's throat in the dark. Take a look around you and see how you stand with the fellows who are calling themselves your friends. For my part, I hate a traitor worse than I do the devil.

"Yours with as much friendship as the law allows:

"SAM LEE."

He read this epistle back and forth twice, and then he dismounted in haste from his horse and touched a match to it. It reduced to a wisp of gray ash which rose like a bird and dissolved in the wind. When it was gone, he felt rather incredulous; it seemed utterly impossible that the Rizdals could wish to betray him; but far more impossible than that was it to believe that such a man as Sam Lee would descend to trickery.

He had a vague impulse to ride after young Fisher and tell him to carry the marshal his thanks, but he controlled that impulse, realizing that his work was strictly confined, for that moment, to the valley.

Then he remembered. The marshal had not asserted, definitely, that the hand which had offered to betray Pleasant was that of Tom Rizdal. He merely had thought so; though Pleasant shrewdly suspected that the "thought" of the marshal was apt to be more accurate than the "certainty" of most men. At any rate, it had led the man of the law to send this difficult warning, risking the life of the messenger in no uncertain manner.

The heart of Pleasant grew hot with a sort of stern gratitude. There was Fisher, too, who had carried the letter and had him helpless under the sights of his rifle. Well, that act was almost enough to wipe out his sense of grudge concerning the uncle. It appeared that honesty and the world of honest men were worth something; and for the first time since his outlawry, Jim Pleasant felt as though he were living within a high and terrible wall.

What was the seeming freedom of the outlaw? It was rather an actual prison in which he lived, shut out from most of the good things of life and above all from the companionship of unexceptional men!

In that mood he rode back to the shack. Thursday was the next day in the week. More than twenty-four hours remained during which he could discover whether or not Rizdal actually was false to him. And, at any rate, the marshal had given a sort of indefinite promise that the trap which was offered would not be used on him!

Cheered by that reflection, determined to key himself to the highest point, and make every shadow tell, he came in view of the Newburg house, and there was Sally walking moodily beside the creek.

She hardly looked up when he reined the horse beside her.

"Sally," he said, without dismounting, "if you'll do me a mighty big favor, tell me how wrapped up you are in Tom Rizdal?"

She did not answer, simply poking aimlessly at a stone with a walking stick which she had cut in the woods.

"I mean," went on he with some guile, "suppose that I heard that Rizdal was sick—could I hope that maybe supposing he should not get better, you'd be willing to look at me, afterwards?"

He thought that he was very subtle, but she merely raised her head and looked him in the eye.

"Jim," said she, "are you asking me what I'd think if you were to shoot Tom?"

It fairly made him blink, that direct assault.

"All right," said he, "I'm not talking murder, but if you're going to take it that way—"

He rode on, and knew that she was looking after him.

In a way, she was like the others. At least, he never quite could understand her. Men like Sam Lee were complicated enough, but in their honesty he could touch the bedrock of their natures time and again. But Sally was different from other women, almost as Tom Rizdal was different from other men. He could not get her under the full finger of his comprehension, so to speak.

Doubly troubled and embittered, therefore, he put up the Leinster Gray in the corral, tossed in to it a forkful of hay to browse at if it chose, and then went slowly back towards the house.

The door was open; the wind had fallen to the softest breeze; and therefore, while he still was at a distance he could hear the voices inside.

Charlie Rizdal was saying: "I'll roll you for the guns, then!"

"Take you!" answered Long Tom.

And even the clinking and chipping of the dice were audible.

"They're yours," said Charlie Rizdal, with an oath. "Damn me if you don't have all the luck, and you need fine guns a lot less than I do."

"It ain't the gun that makes the dead shot. It's the talent, Charlie," said the older brother. "You wouldn't inherit his shooting even if you had his guns to work with!"

"Well, maybe not."

And it suddenly occurred to Pleasant Jim that this conversation had to do with him. They were shaking dice for the guns of a superior marksman—well, how many men in the world shot straighter than the Rizdals?

There was one he could think of, and that was himself!

So, softly, he slipped a little closer to the door and listened, standing still as a stone.

CHAPTER 37

THE two gamblers talked of other things. Sometimes there was only the rattle of the dice, for minutes at a time. They were inveterate gamblers, and their luck and skill were so very evenly matched that neither could be a very great loser to the other, in the long run.

"We've shaken for the other stuff," said Charlie. "Now how about the horse?"

"Hell, man," said Long Tom, "you might as well shake for his boots! He ain't dead yet, you know!"

Interesting conversation was this, under any circumstances, though doubtless he would not have paid any attention to it if it had not been for the warning letter of the sheriff which had served effectually to focus his suspicions. How many shadows float by us unnoticed in the ordinary course of events.

Now, his teeth set, Jim Pleasant felt that he was close to words which would betray the facts to him at last. He waited, his heart beating fast.

"I say, for the horse now. We'd fight about the gray afterwards!"

The gray!

"Shake them up, then. Poker horses, eh? Let it go!"

"There's only a pair of fives, Tom, but watch 'em grow!"

"I watch. Shake again."

"There you are. Beat three fives, old son."

"Easy! Here you are at one roll! A full house will about be enough, old kid."

"You got God Almighty's luck tucked up your sleeve, but the devil'll help me now. Come on, Tom. Pass me the box. Here's deuces and aces. Well, I'll fill. It ain't a thing to me to fill out two pairs. And *there* you are, son. A deuce full on aces, my lad. Talk to it, will you?"

"A horse on me. Here you go, then. Follow your hand. If I can't beat a measley pair of sixes I'm a goat. One flop is all that I needed, you see! And here's the third hand. Four little deuces standing in a row! I'm going to have the pony, Charlie, my boy."

"You yell when you got him in your pocket. Now, babies, hear your daddy talking. Be good—and—three fours give me a flying start, Tom. Turn cold, you sucker, because that horse is mine. Here it is—four fours. I'll ride the Leinster Gray, Tom, after all!"

There was all the proof that big Jim Pleasant could ask for. Certainly they considered him no better than a dead man, so that already they were gambling for his guns and his horse. He thought of the proud back of the Leinster Gray carrying one of them, and straightway his blood was boiling, so that a red mist covered his brain, and he could not think calmly.

He went to the door of the house and looked in on them, and though he cast no shadow, Long Tom suddenly sat erect in his chair; and then Charlie looked quickly askance and started violently.

"Hello, Jim," said he. "I thought—I thought that you were hunting to-day?"

"I am," said Pleasant grimly, and he walked across the room.

He felt the guilty, alarmed glances of the robbers crossing like swords behind his back as he went through the hall door and then up the stairs to his room. There he made his pack quickly, still hot with rage and disgust.

He had barely finished it when he glanced out of the window. From the barn he saw Sally galloping off on her long-legged bay, and there was something about her handling of the horse as she went up the creek that made him certain that she would not come back at once.

After that, he threw his pack across his shoulders and hurried down the steps again, but halfway to the bottom, his brain cleared with a sudden touch of thoughtfulness.

If he came down into that room again, what would the two brothers do? If he walked across the room, with his pack on his back, would they let him go, unscathed? They had made up their minds to compass his death, and no doubt they would achieve their end if they could.

Half a dozen alternatives came to him. He might turn about

and go back to his room—but if he did, they were sure to suspect something and be on the watch for his descent through the outer window. What could be better and easier than to spit a man with a bullet as he climbed down the wall of a house?

With that in mind, he went on.

Suppose that he stopped on the stairs to think things over? The instant that he paused, the pair would be prepared for him, knowing that there was suspicion in his mind.

In fact, he could see that through his blind anger he had walked into a quite efficient trap; and all he could imagine doing was to attempt to cut his way out of it, in spite of the expert guns of those two fighters.

As he came to the little hall at the foot of the steps, he saw that the door to the room was a trifle ajar. Was he being spied upon through the crack?

He unslung his pack and hurled it with all his might; it dashed the door open and flew on into the room and all the questions of Jim Pleasant were answered instantly by the crash of two guns.

He himself pitched to his face at the verge of the door, a revolver stretched out in either hand, and he could see the two Charlie near the kitchen door, pale, his lips curled away from set teeth, a repeating rifle in his hands; Long Tom by the table, his feet spread a little and his head thrown back, like a true fighting man enjoying battle.

Pleasant tried two snap-shots in rapid succession. The first hit Charlie in the breast and he dropped the rifle, clutched the wound with both hands, and began to sink slowly to the floor. The second was aimed well enough, but it found the edge of the table and plowed a furrow straight across its top.

Long Tom, like a duelist of an older day, standing straight, high-headed, one arm behind him and the other extended stiffly with his Colt, was dropping bullet after bullet.

His first was aimed too high, almost as a matter of course, for a man lying on a floor presents an awkward target. His second clipped through the long hair on the back of Pleasant's head.

A swirl of smoke had formed before him, and having fired twice, he leaped to the side and shot again, but his own movement disturbed his aim. The third shot from Jim Pleasant toppled him to the floor.

Still he was not done; for as Pleasant scrambled to his feet, Long Tom spun himself over like a cat at play and caught up a revolver for a final shot.

Once more Pleasant fired, reluctantly, for this man was already down. He saw the head of Tom Rizdal jerk back as though struck heavily by a fist, and then the famous outlaw lay still. He would never rise again!

Charlie was groaning by the kitchen door, crawling slowly towards it. When he heard the step of the conqueror, he turned himself with a face made hideous by fear and stretched out his hands.

"Don't kill me, Jim," he moaned. "I'm a skunk. I know it. But don't kill me, Jim, for the sake of all the camps we've made together! I'm gunna die anyway! Lemme take my own time about it. Don't murder me, in the name of Jesus, Jim!"

"Lie down and stretch out," said Pleasant Jim. "I'm not going to murder you, though God knows what you've deserved. Lemme have a look at you!"

He slashed open the coat and shirt. It was a small purple-rimmed hole oozing blood and well down in the body below the heart. There was hardly one chance in five that it had not found a fatal spot; the terrible, spasmodic groans of the injured man seemed each one to be giving flight to his soul.

Pleasant Jim stepped into the kitchen and there he found the three members of the family cowering. He told them there was no danger, but to come back into the other room and take care of a badly hurt man.

Dumbly they came, and the woman screamed as she reached the door. Her husband, however, was made of sterner stuff and was instantly on his knees beside Charlie Rizdal, barking orders for bandages and hot water.

Then, stooping and fumbling in the coat pocket of the wounded man, Pleasant pulled out the wallet, fat and hard with treasure. Charlie Rizdal opened his glazing eyes and acknowledged the transfer with a ghastly smile.

"It'll do me no good in hell, where I'm going," said he. "Take it and welcome! Ride hard, Pleasant, and I wish you luck. You been squarer to me than I've deserved."

Upon the table, Pleasant counted two thousand dollars.

He said to the busy family:

"I'm leaving. And here's two thousand. One thousand for you for taking care of Rizdal. The second thousand is for Charlie if he gets well enough to ride, ever. Mind you, if ever I hear that you've short-changed him, I'm coming back here to settle with you for it."

He stepped to Long Tom and from his pockets he took the two big shares which the chief had apportioned to himself. Then he picked up his pack and waved good-by from the door. The room was still streaked with pungent smoke from the burned powder. The dead eyes of Long Tom smiled horribly and vacantly up to him near by. And yonder was a group working frantically over Charlie Rizdal to the accompaniment of his groans.

It was very easy to paint a different scene—his own dead body lying at the foot of the stairs, and the two brothers, gun in hand, touching him to make sure that life was gone.

So he backed from the house, a gun still hanging naked in his hand. For who could tell what wild thought might come to the man or the boy who remained in the place? One well-placed shot would make them the masters of more than half a million dollars!

However, they had seen enough of his handiwork on that day and required to see no more.

He reached the corral unhindered, and saddled the gray in haste, suddenly frantic to get away from that neighborhood of death. But, for all his haste, he could not help noticing how his pack was punctured by two holes—

The first shots of the Rizdals had been well-aimed indeed.

CHAPTER 38

HE had no thought of working out a trail problem behind him to baffle pursuit, when the marshal and his men came up; his mind was too busy with other matters, and he simply drifted straight on towards the higher mountains.

He had no sense of victory or of elation. For the treasure which was now in his hands he had no more regard than for a handful of dead leaves. Over eight hundred thousand dollars had been taken from the bank and divided among six persons. Of the six, two were in prison and probably would spend the rest of their better years behind the bars. Two lay dead, or dying, stripped of their loot. One was a woman. And she never would forgive him for the slaying of her accepted lover.

No, Sally was taken out of his life forever!

What utter loneliness came to Pleasant Jim then as he worked his way up a narrow ravine and listened to the distant, booming voice of a waterfall, no man could guess. He would have given much, he thought, even to have the Rizdals, with murder in their hearts, riding one on either side of him. But he was left alone.

All had been stripped from him in these last few months. He had given up his farm and the horses whose blood was almost as dear to him as his own. He had given up the friendship of all law-abiding men and women. He had given up the protection of his country. He had given up all the old ambitions which had ruled his life. And, above all, he had given up Sally.

A grim man was Jim Pleasant on this day, thinking of all that had chanced. And a dreadful sense of guilt oppressed him, seeing that with his own hand he had shot down two members of the band which had worked so long with him!

For all that he had sacrificed, he had gained what? Money,

money, money! And what could he do with the money? It would not buy him friends, or home, or the old hopes, or the woman he loved. It was less than nothing, in fact.

Moreover, it was a deadly danger. Of six, four were gone to death or prison or long sickness. One was a girl wandering through the hills.

And now what would he do?

Well, he could ride on until the dusk, and then camp and shoot a supper for himself and cook it. Each day must be sufficient unto itself!

He resigned himself as well as he could. Henceforth, who could tell for how long, he must live as the beasts live! So he worked on until dusk, and then he made camp.

He left the gray in a small bit of grazing land, enclosed by brush. He himself ate freshly shot rabbit, broiled over a small fire, and he slept in a thicket, also, made miserable by mosquitoes and small flies which bit with the strength of snakes.

In the morning, early, he was on his way to take advantage of the fresh time of the day; all through the middle watch of the day he camped again and let the horse graze, and in the evening he came with the Leinster Gray down into a small hollow.

It was dimly starred with many lights, and Pleasant Jim rode hungrily towards them, for his very heart was empty and aching for the sound of the voices of honest men, freed from the catlike purr or the doglike snarl of the criminal's talk. Boldly he rode, knowing that danger was thickening around him, but caring not at all.

Screened behind a hedge of poplars, he saw the faintly illumined forms of four children playing before a house and on the lighted veranda of the house the parents sat. It was a weary, gray woman, and a man with shirt open at the throat, bared, hairy arms, smoking a pipe. He was some common laborer. And yet his lot seemed to Pleasant Jim a vastly enviable one.

He went on a little farther and came to a shack in which the light seemed as small as the house in which it glowed. One small, bent old man sat in the doorway; and Pleasant Jim rode boldly up to him.

"I smell ham, father," said he. "Got any left to fry for me?"

"Sure, I have," said the other. "Get down and rest your feet, son. I suppose that you ain't got a regular hotel price on you, eh?"

And he laughed with a sort of feeble good nature. But the

sound was delicious to Pleasant Jim. After this one evening, how far and long he might have to ride before he would be allowed to mingle with human beings again except such as he persuaded at the end of a revolver!

"Take your pony around to the shed," said the host, "and chuck him in a feed of barley. You'll find some at the bottom of the box, I reckon!"

Gladly Pleasant obeyed, and by the time he had finished grooming the Leinster Gray, a smoking supper was waiting for him in the little house.

The old man sat near by, squinting through his heavy glasses.

"You look sort of familiar to me," he said. "You ain't Dean Tucker's boy come home, are you?"

"No. I'm just riding through. I hear that there's work up the valley."

"At the Y Bar, maybe you mean?"

"Yes, that's what I was told."

"Sure, you can find work there."

"What's in the paper, father?"

"Why, there ain't much except about Pleasant."

Pleasant Jim gritted his teeth on his fork.

"Ye-ah?" he queried. "What's he done now?"

"Him? Why, you wouldn't believe it."

"Go on and tell me. He's the bank robber, ain't he?"

"Yep. Jim Pleasant. Gunman and robber and what not. Counterfeiter. All-around bad one. Nacheral crook. Used to pick up coin hunting heads. Well, what good would you expect in that sort of a chap?"

"I dunno," said Pleasant thoughtfully. "I dunno! I sort of thought that that game wasn't the best in the world. Still, a man has to work for what he gets in it!"

"It takes a thief to catch a thief," said the old man with much positiveness, "and it takes a murderer to kill a murderer. I got no use for no gunfighter, no matter whether he's holding up the law or breaking it down. The same tar is on all of 'em, I tell you!"

"Maybe. But what's Pleasant done now? Escaped again?"

"He's made fools of 'em all. He's made fools of 'em, complete! I laughed when I heard what he done to Sam Lee. Sam is a wise man and a tolerable good one, but he was made a fool of by Pleasant. It'll be some time before they catch that lad. Well, you ask me what he's done lately?"

"Yes."

"You guess, will you?"

"Busted open another bank?"

"It's all in the paper, here," said the old fellow; "here you are: 'The celebrated desperado, James Pleasant, either in a drunken brawl, or else determined to rob his partners in crime, yesterday according to recent report shot down in single battle both of the Rizdal brothers. Thomas Rizdal, known as Long Tom, is dead, with two bullets through his body; and Charles Rizdal is now lying, dangerously wounded, in the hands of Marshal Sam Lee, who arrived at the scene of bloodshed with his posse shortly after the shooting affair. Pleasant has fled towards the mountains; the woman who was with the outlaws also has disappeared and is believed to have gone with Pleasant.

"'According to a statement made by Charles Rizdal, he and his brother were playing a friendly game of cards when Pleasant treacherously attacked them—'"

"He lied!" cried Jim Pleasant.

"Hello! What makes you think so?"

"I know something about that man. He wouldn't take an unfair advantage!"

"Maybe you're right," said the old man. "There's folks that have a mighty fine sense of honor, and they're mighty particular how they do their murders! Lemme give you some more coffee!"

"I've had enough," exclaimed Pleasant, starting to his feet. "I have to be going on. Thanks for the feed—and how much is it?"

"Aw, nothing," said the other. "It's a pleasure to fill a hungry man's belly, and it done me good to see you eating."

"Take this, then," said Pleasant, and he held out a ten dollar bill.

The other took it, scrutinized it carefully on either side and then passed it back.

"Thanks," said he, and shook his head.

"Why not?" asked Pleasant.

"I don't want your money, stranger."

"You don't! Dad, you can't afford to be throwing away your chuck on every stranger that comes along. You take that and shove it into your jeans!"

"Well," replied the old fellow, "I'd sort of like to do it, at that. I ain't the richest man in the world," he laughed, "but still I can't take your money, friend."

"Will you tell me why my money is worse than any other man's in the valley?" asked Pleasant.

"I'll tell you why, if you won't take it hard. There's blood on your money, friend!"

"Blood?" cried Pleasant, aghast. And he stared at the slip of paper curiously. Certainly it was not altogether fresh, but there was no stain that even faintly resembled blood.

Then, with a start and a shock, he understood what was meant.

The old man stood in the shadows of the corner, his hand resting on a shotgun—not as one ready to give offense, but as one standing resolutely on his rights.

"You're right!" cried Pleasant bitterly. "You're all correct. There's blood on every damned cent of it, and God help my miserable soul!"

And he strode on out of the doorway and found his horse and rode in blind haste towards the cold heights of the distant mountains. They were barren and stark, to be sure, but they were less dangerous and less cruel than the tongues of men!

CHAPTER 39

FOR a week he marched steadily, taking fine care of the Leinster Gray, which stood up like iron under the punishing work of the journey. All that time he saw no human face, and so he found himself again on the edge of the lofty table-land overlooking Fisher Valley. And there was an ache of sorrow in his heart as he looked down upon the trail up which he and Sally had ridden so long ago. He smiled faintly as he remembered that there had been greater trouble in his heart than the mere fear of danger. He had been in love, and like a perfect dolt, he had not known it. For had he known, he swore to himself that he would have found some way to persuade her in time.

Now she was riding somewhere through the dark of the valleys, hunted like him, and carrying in her heart a great load of hatred for the slayer of Long Tom Rizdal.

In nothing had he done well. All things seemed to him a blank except for the dead days when he had worked with his horses, and that one glorious time of struggle and labor when he had carried Sally through the lines of the law.

When he was through with his camp chores, he sat and dreamed not of the future but of the past, for hope was gone from him; and every small moment of the time with Sally was traced and retraced until the lines were made thick and strong indeed.

Danger itself had become a small thing to him. He had turned hard. From the bright steel of this new nature of his, the face of peril seemed to slip away; it had no cutting edge against him. Only two days before he had wound through the Cameron Pass despite its guards set to catch him. Men talked much of this and of his other deeds, but he regarded them not. There was no past, there was no future to him. There was only the dreadful sense of loss. And as for what was to come, he would meet it a step at a time and never walk far afield in his speculations.

But, as he sat with his cigarette on the edge of a rock that hung above the valley wall, he heard a slight sound as of a cracked twig underfoot, in the brush behind him. It was not enough to have reached the ear of an ordinary man. Certainly there was nothing suspicious about it, but Pleasant heard it with a sudden brightening of his mind. He became alert, and almost anxious for it to turn into an actual danger.

He did not move. He went on calmly smoking, with his head apparently directed down towards the valley lights of the evening, but turned enough to scan, from the tail of his eye, the brush wall behind him.

And presently he saw the tops of the bush bending, slowly, softly, noiselessly, pressed to either side in such a manner as the wind could not possibly have managed it.

It was enough for him.

He jerked off his boots and in his stockinged feet he slipped back to the verge of the brush and waited. The faintest of rustlings came towards him. And suddenly a half-mad notion came to Pleasant to meet this danger with his bare hands.

Somewhere from an eminence above this stalker had marked him down and determined to work nearer for a point-blank shot that would send Pleasant Jim sliding from the rock and toppling with loose arms and legs through the void and down into the valley beneath!

With a cruel satisfaction, Pleasant considered this, and then he slipped his revolvers into their clips beneath his arm-pits.

The noise came a little closer; prying eyes might almost look out, now, and discover him crouched.

Then he hurled himself forward. One crash drove him diving through the bushes; a gun flashed and roared in his face; and then the weight of his shoulder struck down the stalker and stretched him on the ground.

Pleasant whirled like a tiger, fumbled for and found the hands of his victim, and dragged him out into the open.

"You damn head-hunter!" said he. "I'm gunna pitch you over the cliff here and let your bones rot underneath, my friend!"

A staggering voice answered him: "Do and be damned! I got no luck, or else you got ears a hundred feet away from you!"

"Hello!" said Pleasant. "Wait a minute—"

He brought his face close to the face of his prisoner.

"Fisher!" he exclaimed.

"It's me," said Lew Fisher bitterly. "A little turn of luck   and I'd have turned you into pulp, you swine. Go on and finish me, now. You're too damn strong for me!"

To prove his own words, he threw himself frantically back, but the hands which held his were remorselessly powerful. He could not dislodge that grip.

"All right," said young Fisher. "Go on and turn the trick. *I* ain't going to holler!"

"Where's Sam Lee?"

"None of your damn business."

"Ain't he coming right up behind you?"

"D'you think I'd squeal if he was?"

Jim Pleasant whistled.

"All right! All right!" said he. "Don't lose your shirt about it. But you're game, kid. You're dead game!"

"D'you think so?" said the boy, eagerly.

"I know it. Now, Fisher, I got to polish you off, because I'm afraid to leave you loose on my trail. Sam Lee and the rest   let them go. But you—you've trailed me down twice. The third time it would be me that was done for!"

"By God, I think it would!"

"Now, Fisher, you tell me what I can do for you, and what sort of message you want to send to your uncle, say. Or is there a girl, somewheres?"

"Aw, let the old boy rot; and I never give a damn about the women. I ain't that kind. Only—Pleasant   "

He seemed half choked with emotion.

"Yes?"

"Would you do one thing for me?"

"Sure I would."

"Now, look here. Me being dead, it wouldn't hurt you none to do it. But write down and mail to some newspaper that you was afraid of me   just like you said to me   not of Sam Lee and the rest, but only of me."

"I'll do it."

"Will you? My God, that'll make me die a happy man. That'll show people that I was something more than a damn bank clerk and the nephew of crooked Lewis Fisher."

"Crooked?"

"Sure. A snake has got a bigger soul than him!"

"You wouldn't run the bank the way he does, maybe?"

"If I lived to have it? No, damned if I would. But what's the use of talking like that? What are you doing? You don't have to tie my hands. I'll take the jump myself and never yip."

But Pleasant Jim secured his hands firmly and then searched him and removed a veritable small armory of weapons.

"Where's your horse?" he asked.

"What's that to you, Big Boy?"

"I ask you, where's your horse?"

"Well, it'll be no use to me, and he's a jim-dandy. Back of the hummock, there. Favor him a little; he's got a tender mouth."

"You like horses, son?"

"Me? What fool doesn't? I mean, except Uncle Lewis! He likes nothing but cash."

"You know horses, too?"

"Not a bit, hardly. But some day I will. I mean, I would have!"

"Son," said Pleasant, "turn around and start for your horse."

"What's the idea?"

"Do what I tell you!"

The boy turned obediently, swallowing his wonder, and they went slowly back around the edge of the brush. A soft whistle brought the Leinster Gray glimmering towards them, beautiful beyond belief even in that soft, dim light.

"They'll never catch you   not with your pair of ears and that horse," said the boy.

Behind the hummock they came to the waiting pony, and Pleasant helped the lad to mount him.

"You left Sam Lee and came on by yourself?"

"Yes."

"How come?"

"Why should I split up a little reputation with six others?"

"Besides, you were able to find me once."

"Yes, and I found you again   except that you found me first!" He swore softly. "I should have tried the long-range shot," said he, "but in the half light   I wasn't quite sure of myself. And I wanted to make sure. Pleasant, how could you possibly have heard me? I didn't make a sound coming through the bush."

"Only one," admitted Pleasant. "You did a good job. But then, I have to live by my eyes and ears, and that makes a difference."

"Aye, it does. Now what?"

But Pleasant had swung into the saddle.

"Never mind asking questions. You ride straight ahead and turn when I tell you to turn."

"I'll do it. Only— I'd like to have the business over with. Mind you, I'm not whining, though. Damned if I'm whining, Pleasant!"

Jim Pleasant laughed a little. His heart was freeing itself of a peculiar pain. There was something about this strange youth that delighted him.

"Suppose that I don't murder you, Lew?"

There was a long silence. The horses went slowly ahead down the trail, the stirrup leathers creaking.

"What d'you mean by saying that?" asked the boy in his sharp, ugly voice.

"Why, kid, I never shot a man in cold blood in my life!"

And he added savagely: "No matter what Charlie Rizdal said!"

"Aw, Charlie's a hound dog," said the boy with unutterable scorn. "Sam Lee says so. Sam ain't on your trail any longer, you know!"

"The devil he isn't!"

"No, he says that the main part of his work you've already done for him. The killing of Tom Rizdal, I mean."

CHAPTER 40

THUS a new idea was presented to Pleasant Jim, and one which he did not greatly relish; and Lew Fisher developed the theme as he rode on down the trail, his hands tied in front of him, but free enough to use the reins of his pony.

"It was a great stroke that the old marshal put in," said Lew. "I mean, sending you word that would get you into trouble with the two Rizdals. Look how it worked! What good was the catching of Tom? He'd been caught before but never held. Now he's dead, and that's a little different. Then there's Charlie. Well, Charlie is caught and it'll be queer if Charlie ever gets away again. They've got enough against him to hang him ten times over, and this time he'll hang, all right, because he's used up all of his good luck. A fellow can't go on forever like that—slipping away from trouble, I mean. He may dodge for a while, but at last they get him. And what's the use of all his good time, if he's got to pay for it with a rope around his neck in the finish? That's what I heard Charlie Rizdal say. He ought to know!"

The boy chuckled grimly, and big Pleasant grew more and more serious. For, after all, this was a fairly accurate description of his own position in life, and beyond doubt he would come to the same evil end.

All that night they worked down from the edge of the plateau and into Fisher Valley; and by the morning they were well up towards the town. There Pleasant made camp, tying himself to the youngster as he lay down to sleep, though Lew Fisher said with his chuckle: "What's the good, Jim? Am I gunna be crazy enough to tackle you with my bare hands?"

However, he took no chances; a great and forlorn hope was forming in his mind and he meant to stake everything upon a strange cast of the dice.

After that, if all went well, the way would be cleared for him

206

to reach into the darkness of the unknown criminal world and try to find Sally.

So he went to sleep and dreamed all night tht he was struggling against a dreadful monster of many heads; and as fast as he throttled one, other heads appeared and fastened their teeth in him.

In this manner, therefore, big Pleasant slept through the middle of the day.

Before dusk, hungry and tired, he was on the way again with Lew Fisher, pressing recklessly ahead through the woods, risking much.

"You've been seen about six times," said Lew, shortly after sunset. "D'you know that you've been spotted, Pleasant?"

"They see the gray and me on it," answered Pleasant. "But they'll never expect to see me riding along like this, in this direction, and at this time of day. And folks only see what they want to see."

The boy nodded with admiration.

"Where are you going, Jim?"

"Some place you've been before. Wait and see."

They cast a slight circle around the town and so came out in the thick of the dusk above Fisher Falls so close to the residence of Lewis Fisher himself.

The house of that celebrated man was retired a little from the rest of the town; just as his reputation was greater than that of any other in the valley, so his home was more largely planned and built. He had surrounded an extent of hills and woods with a strong stone wall, and behind the wall transplanted trees had now grown up into a veritable jungle. Passing by the huge gate of wrought iron, one had a swift glimpse of the imposing façade of his house on the distant hill, and many wondered that the owner of so great a mansion should deign to remain in so small a community. In one thought, however, Lewis Fisher agreed with Caesar.

As the two riders came near this house, Pleasant dismounted and brought the horses into a thick grove and secured them there. After that he found an easily climbed section of the wall, went up himself, and helped Lew Fisher after him. This done, he headed straight across the grounds towards the distant house.

"You know, Pleasant," said the boy cheerfully, "that I could let out a yell and have half a hundred people swarming on top of you in no time!"

"You know, son," answered Pleasant with almost equal good nature, "that I could send a bullet into you or cut your throat before the help came."

"You wouldn't do it," said the boy with a perfect confidence. "Sam Lee said that you'd never do a murder; and that you never would, unless you were driven into a corner! Sam says a good many fine things about you, old timer."

"Sam hates my heart," answered Pleasant bitterly. "It was Sam Lee that dragged me into hell, and one of these days Sam and me are going to fight it out!"

They had crossed an open meadow; now they passed through a grove of trembling poplars and went on under the very shadow of the house.

They knew Mr. Fisher was close before they laid eyes on him, for they heard his loud voice from the side veranda. Crouched in the brush, they stole closer, and it seemed to Pleasant that the boy put as much zest and care into this maneuver as did he himself.

They could see Fisher at last, and the red round point of light which was his cigar. He was calling out servants from his house, one at a time, and dressing them down in the most severe manner.

"He's sore as a goat!" whispered young Lew to his captor in the darkness. "There's poor Johnson. He'll catch hell worse than all the rest."

Johnson was the secretary-clerk-stenographer who performed like a slave for the banker; and like a slave he was lashed by the words of the elder Fisher now—until a sudden change came in the voice of the banker.

"Johnson," he said, "what's the news about the boy?"

"About your nephew? There's no news except bad news. The marshal has come in—and your nephew is not with him!"

Utter silence greeted that remark, and then: "What report did Sam Lee send?" asked Fisher in a shaken voice.

"He sent in word, it's said, that your nephew went off by himself and swore that he never would come back unless he brought Jim Pleasant with him."

"The fool!" shouted Fisher, Senior. "The jackass! He wants to make the world think that he's a hero   and he's only a baby a rabbit—and yet—"

He checked himself again.

"Johnson," he said at last, "the lad *is* a hero. And I never have appreciated him! Go down to the town, make the telegraph hum. Find out more word about him!"

Johnson hastily retreated, and young Lew touched the arm of his companion in the darkness.

"That beats me," said he. "That sure beats me, Jim! I think maybe he's fond of me, and not using me because he simply hasn't any other heir!"

"Keep before me," said Pleasant, and added, as they stood up: "Walk up to the veranda and warn him in a quiet voice that he mustn't shout or do anything to attract attention."

So they approached the veranda, and as they drew nearer, they heard Fisher call out briskly: "You there, Tucker? That you and Bliss?"

They stepped still closer.

"What the devil—" began the banker as if in alarm, and stood up.

"Uncle Lewis," said the warning voice of his nephew, "don't make a noise. Be quiet."

"Merciful God," breathed the man of money. "Are you there, Lew? Are you there, and safe?"

"Softer, softer!" said Lew Fisher. "I'm here, but I'm a prisoner."

"To whom?"

"To Jim Pleasant here beside me."

They had come up quite close, by this time, and Lewis Fisher as he heard the name cried out in a stifled voice and stumbled back.

"Keep close and keep still," said Jim Pleasant. "I haven't come here to shoot you."

The alarm of the older man for himself was instantly swallowed in concern for his nephew.

"You've been hurt, lad! You've been shot down and you're bleeding to death, I know!" murmured Fisher. "Otherwise, how could he ever have taken you?"

"He took me the way a tiger takes a goat with his hands. He's brought me here and he wants to talk to you."

Fisher spread out his legs. Instantly he was the business man striking a bargain.

"Leave the boy here with me, unharmed in any particular," said he, "and I'll guarantee not to turn in alarm on you. Do you hear?"

"I hear."

"But if not, I call one word and the alarm goes out and the place will be surrounded and you will be   "

"Fisher, I walked through a Fisher Falls alarm one night. Now I have a horse to get through it. Besides, you don't understand. I'm not in your net. You're in mine. My gun is in my hand. I have you covered from the hip. Are you talking alarms to me, Fisher?"

The banker said quickly: "Very well. You have a certain business sense, my lad. Now what is your point of view?"

"That I have the drop on you."

"I suppose that you have, in a way, owing to the idiocy of my nephew in letting himself be captured."

"Friend," said Pleasant coldly, "there have been some hard men and some rough men on my trail lately, as you may know. But there's never a one of them that give me as much to worry about as your nephew."

"Is it true?" cried Fisher, Senior, in delight. "By heavens, Lew, I'm proud of you. There's been a great deal about you that I never understood or knew about!"

"There's been a great deal of you," replied Pleasant, "that your nephew never knew. I'm going to tell him now. Lew, listen to the yarn of how I went bad. I was working to clear away a mortgage on my little farm; I nearly had turned the trick by working like a dog on the place, taking my luck and making my luck, and even by getting blood money from the law. Then I met Long Tom and he offered me a thousand for what looked like an easy thing to do. I did the job. I sent in the thousand to the bank—and your uncle, here, found out that the money was counterfeit. Right there he made up his mind. He decided that here was his chance to get for next to nothing the farm that   "

"You lie!" panted Lewis Fisher.

"Wait a minute," said Jim Pleasant. "I was jailed for passing counterfeit; while I was in jail your uncle foreclosed on me when he knew that I was helpless, and he scared out the other bidders at the auction, so that he got everything on the place for twenty-five hundred. And there you are! I was cleaned out of my life's work. What I did then was to break jail, and the next thing I did was to crack open a bank. Notice, that it was Lewis Fisher's bank. I felt that that sort of squared things between us, in a way. Now I'm hounded across the world and some day I'll have to start killing to avoid being killed. Part of the fault is mine. I never should have taken a job from a known crook like Long

Tom. I can see that. But who was it that put the slide under me and shot me down into hell? Why, your uncle, there!"

"Every criminal tries to sneak the blame on the shoulders of another!"

"Uncle Lewis," said the boy in a fury of disgust and scorn, "he's told the truth!"

"You impertinent young scoundrel!" cried the banker. "Are you daring to dispute what I—"

"Quit it," said the boy curtly. "I'm not what I used to be, and I don't swallow that sort of talk from you any longer. I've done a man's job once; and I'll never go back to boy's work again. That's flat!"

Lewis Fisher was silent, amazed and bewildered.

"Are you daring to throw away—" he began.

And the boy said fiercely: "Hell, Uncle Lewis, what am I throwing away? The life of a bat for the life of a man! D'you think there's much to hesitate over in that choice?"

And again Lewis Fisher was silent.

His nephew added suddenly: "I've talked pretty hard to you. Confound it, Uncle Lewis, I mean to talk better than that. You'be been mighty kind to me in a million ways. Only—maybe you understand that everything hasn't been so very easy for me! I'd like to be your nephew and your friend; but I'm never again going to be your slave!"

This declaration of independence caught Mr. Fisher behind the knees, apparently; for suddenly his legs bowed and he sat down heavily in his chair, with a great creak of wickerwork.

"So that's the end of years of nurture and care and forethought for your sake, young man?" he asked savagely. "That's the end of it all?'"

"Or maybe it's the beginning," broke in Jim Pleasant. "D'you want a soft-head or a man to take your place when you die?"

He added: "Now we'll get down to *my* business. Fisher, you can tell me what stands between me and a chance to get back inside the law?"

CHAPTER 41

THE banker seemed to take enjoyment in this sudden turn of the conversation, for he turned the words slowly over his tongue.

"What keeps you outside the law? Only a few little things, my friend Pleasant! You've passed counterfeit money, in the first place, and in the second place you've broken jail. In the third place, you've taken a million dollars from my bank. I think those are three counts. Beyond this, you've done little things such as shooting down men in the act of enforcing the law against you but I suppose that hardly counts!"

"Very well," said Pleasant. "I've got three big counts against me. Start with the last first. It wasn't a million."

"It was nearly nine hundred thousand."

"You got a quarter of that back at once."

"A third of it," said the banker.

"How is that?"

"You don't know the story of the satchel of money left on my doorstep?"

"Sally!" cried Jim Pleasant suddenly. "She's turned in her share!"

"An admirable young woman—if it was she," said the banker. "And if you could let her know   I'd arrange to have all danger of arrest removed from her. Sam Lee says that it can be done. We're above persecuting women, in this part of the country," continued Fisher nobly.

"You're still out five-eighths of the money you lost."

"Yes."

"Now, Fisher, suppose that I lay down that money   more than half a million—here on the veranda at your feet?"

Mr. Fisher rose, electrified, to his feet.

"Good God!" he breathed. "That ain't possible!"

212

"What would you pay for that, Fisher?"

"Pay? I'd have the indictment quashed! I'd I'd arrange everything! You would have to have no fear, my friend! As for the passing of a thousand dollars counterfeit Sam Lee is a sensible man. We could see to it that he kept his hands off you. As for the men who were injured in trying to stop your escape a little money judiciously spent on their families well, everything could be arranged. Pleasant, do you mean what you say?"

"I mean that I'll come back," said Jim Pleasant, "if I can step in right where I stepped out. I stepped out from a farm stocked with fine horseflesh. I want that farm back and all the horses, Mr. Fisher!"

Lewis Fisher groaned. That little farm had become the very apple of his eye.

"A business transaction " he began.

"I'm offering you half a million," said Pleasant.

"Of my own money!"

"For a thing you stole. Stolen fruit for stolen cash, my friend!"

"I'll see you damned first, Pleasant! It it's not business!"

"Is that final?"

"Absolutely."

"Then good-by."

He turned briskly away, taking young Fisher by the arm.

"Hold on," said the banker. "Do you take Lew with you? Do you dare to "

"D'you think that I'll take to the trail and leave this here young bloodhound to follow me again?"

"Pay down the money and set Lew free," said Fisher suddenly. "I'll give you what you want."

"What's your security?" asked Lew Fisher curiously.

"You are," replied the outlaw. "If he breaks his word to me, he'll be less than a cur in your eyes, and he knows it. Besides, if he double-crosses me, I'll kill him if I die trying!"

The banker was breathing hard, rubbing his handkerchief repeatedly across his forehead.

"I'll leave the money with you," said Pleasant. "I'll leave your nephew with you, too. If everything can't be arranged the way I want all the law-dogs called off and the farm given back to me—I expect that half million to come back. Is that straight?"

There was a pause, and then Lewis Fisher groaned.

"That's straight!" said he.

"You're a witness, Lew?" asked the outlaw.

"I'm a witness to every word, Jim. Why, if Uncle Lewis even dreamed of double-crossing you after you've played so white with me, I'd write him up in the newspapers myself!"

"Good night."

"How'll we keep in touch with you?"

"I'll be not far from town. If you want me, send Lew up the valley to The Three Sisters. He can send a smoke signal by day or a fire signal by night, and I'll not be far away."

So he turned from them and crossing the ground rapidly, climbed the wall, found the Leinster Gray, and rode off through the night.

CHAPTER 42

THE mental reaction of the banker was instant and powerful.

"Now I've got the cash—where's Sam Lee to throw this scoundrel of an outlaw into prison? Send for Sam Lee!"

"Send for him, then," said young Lew. "I'll ride down to The Three Sisters and warn poor Pleasant."

"You! Lew, you've lost your head! You're out of your wits!"

"Or else send for Sam Lee," said the boy firmly, "and ask him how we possibly can save Pleasant from jail."

His uncle listened to this speech in the deepest amazement, but suddenly he nodded in acquiescence.

"Get Sam Lee!"

They got the marshal.

He rode up on a tough mustang and came cheerfully to the banker that morning.

"I want to talk about Jim Pleasant," said Fisher.

"Everybody does," answered Sam, with a grin.

"Look at this!"

"More bank loot," said the marshal, glancing at the heap.

"All that I've lost now," said Lewis Fisher, "is a good deal of sleep, and a paltry few thousands in hard cash that was spent along the way. Now, marshal, this money is left with me in trust. If Pleasant can be kept out of jail, it's mine. If not, it has to go back to him. You see where I stand?"

"Did Pleasant do that?" murmured the marshal, a glint of fire in his eyes. "Did he dare to ride down to Fisher Falls again? By God, that man has nerve!"

"He brought down my nephew," said the banker. "Lew was head-hunting. Pleasant caught him and brought him down, and turned him over to me along with the money. What do you say, Sam Lee?"

"I've heard a good deal about bank robberies," said he. "And I've never heard of a neater one than this, and damn few bigger ones. Everything worked off well: They got away with the bigger part of a million; and most of them broke through my hands. Well—what happens? They all go crash, except two. Somewhere there's the girl. And somewhere there's this Jim Pleasant. But all of the money comes back to Mr. Lewis Fisher like homing pigeons. How do you make that out, sir?"

"Who killed the Rizdals?" asked Fisher.

The marshal nodded.

"It was Pleasant," said he. "He's done more work for me than my whole posse of hand-picked gun-fighters! But as long as Jim Pleasant is free to get away with this job, I'm done for. People will laugh at me. I've failed a good many times. But I've never been made a fool of before!"

"Listen to me," said Lewis Fisher. "I don't want to pay the price for my own money. I'd be glad enough if you could rake in Pleasant and put him behind steel bars that he couldn't cut through. But I'll tell you what, my friend, you'll never catch Jim Pleasant without causing a lot of brave men to die. He's proved what he can do in a pinch!"

"Let him prove it again," said the marshal savagely. "I've said my last word about him!"

With that, he hurried down the steps and away from the house, with Lewis Fisher vainly following and protesting that this decision was costing him half a million.

Sam Lee with a sort of guilty haste mounted his horse and rushed back to the town and to his own little private office, which had been built to the side with a separate entrance upon the lane that wound sinuously from one main street to another. A huge and overarching tree kept the little room fairly cool.

There the marshal sat down, his jaw set and his eyes keen, like one about to fight a battle. And a battle, surely, soon would come. His tried and trusted trailers were at work running down the traces of Jim Pleasant. And when they located their quarry—

There was a knock at the door to the lane.

"Hello," said the marshal. "Come in!"

"I'll talk to you through the door," said the voice of a girl.

"You will?" exclaimed the marshal.

"Yes. Stay where you are. I simply want to have a little chat with you."

"Who are you?"

"My name doesn't matter, to begin with. Later I can tell you."

"Go on," said the marshal. "What have you got to say?"

But as he spoke, he glided softly, softly forward, and then seized the handle of the door with a tremendous wrench to tear it open.

He almost broke his wrists, but he did not budge the door.

"I knew that you'd try that," said the girl's voice, without triumph. "So I tied the door on this side. More than that, I can watch you through a bit of a crack, Sam Lee, and if you try to slip around outside your office, I'll just climb into the saddle on my horse which is standing here, and I'll be off among the trees before you can possibly get a shot at me."

"I don't shoot at women," said the marshal a little in anger.

"Maybe you don't," said the girl. "And I'd like to think that you don't, of course. But I haven't come here to talk about women. I've come to talk about a man."

"Ah," said the marshal, "you've got a sweetheart in trouble through me. Is that it? And you've come to beg him off? Is that the idea? Or maybe to find out what my price may be? Lemme tell you, honey, that I got no price, and that I never let no man off once the law has fixed on him for wrong-doing!"

"I'm talking about Jim Pleasant," said the girl.

"By the Eternal God!" groaned the marshal. "Has the whole world gone nutty about that man? What about him? And who are you?"

"I want to know what you'll take to let Pleasant go free."

"You, too! Why," said the marshal, "I wouldn't take ten billion dollars!"

"Because men would say that you'd failed?"

"Yes."

"You're honest. But look here—suppppose that we arrange a little exchange. Jim Pleasant is pretty well known, but in his place I'll give you a much worse criminal than Pleasant."

"That's interesting," said the marshal. "Who might the criminal be, that's done more than Jim Pleasant? Will you tell me that?"

"I have," said the voice of the girl.

"You? A woman?"

"Yes, and a young one."

"By heavens!" said the marshal. "You'd give yourself up for the sake of Pleasant?"

"Yes."

"And who are you?"

"I'm Sally."

CHAPTER 43

THE marshal clung to the door for a moment, bewildered.

"Untie the door," he said at last. "I give you my word I'll not try to make an arrest unless you give me the word. I want to talk this over."

A slash of a knife the door sagged open and Sally stood before him, her pretty face shadowed by a wide-brimmed sombrero.

"Nothing but nerve! Nothing but nerve!" said the marshal, inviting her towards a chair. "You've rode in right through Fisher Falls, and nobody recognized you! Well, Sally, you want to give yourself up for Pleasant Jim?"

"Yes."

"He'd never let a woman pay that price for him."

"He doesn't care," said the girl bitterly. "All that he cares about are horses. He likes the Leinster Gray better than he likes any man or woman."

"But what sort of a price?" said the marshal. "You want me to make Jim Pleasant a free man. Well, it might be done by getting a pardon from the governor, you know. It might even be worth while. But it would have to be an equal value in exchange. What have you done, Sally?"

"I'll tell you a few of the main things," said the girl. "I did the inside work in the Ponting robbery. I brought the Cushing emeralds through without customs. I—"

"You did the Cushing job! And they always thought it was the old man—"

"I used him for a sort of a blind and he didn't know that he was being used. I got to Duncan and Leicester the tools they used when they broke jail—"

"How did you do it? How did you manage that?"

"I'll write it all out. I'll confess all of those things, Marshal Lee. And a lot more. Oh, a lot more. That's not even half of the headliners, because I've been a bad one! But will I do to take the place of Jim Pleasant?"

The marshal was silent, moistening his lips.

Then he murmured: "Ponting Sally, will you sit down here and write that confession?"

"I will."

"There's a fountain pen. There's a stack of paper. And you can have all the time in the world! Want to start?"

"First would I do to take the place of Jim Pleasant?"

"Sally," said the marshal, "the brutal truth is that Fisher has withdrawn his complaint; there'll be no pressing of the robbery charge and the worst that stands against him is an accusation of passing a thousand of counterfeit. And as a matter of fact, we all who are in the know understand that he never dreamed it was counterfeit! Write the confession, Sally!"

And Sally sat down to write.

So it was that a smoke signal brought big Jim Pleasant to the rock of The Three Sisters, where he found young Lew Fisher waiting for him.

"It's all fixed," reported Lew. "All you got to do is to ride up the valley to your farm. That's all. You'll find the same two greasers there that was running the place before "

"No, I won't," said Pleasant Jim with a grin. "One of those greasers is south of the Rio, already. But tell me on the level, Lew, is it all fixed?"

"It's all fixed," said Lew Fisher. "You might as well ride right on down through Fisher Falls, and stop off at the marshal's office there. He wants to see you to arrange a couple of things."

Down through the valley, towards Fisher Falls they rode. And a strange ecstasy swept up through the body and the brain of Pleasant Jim as he approached those lights and began to feel that they were not like hostile eyes watching him.

They hardly had entered Fisher Falls when he was recognized by the silver beauty of the Leinster Gray and the grand manner of that noble horse.

A cloud of small boys instantly closed around them. They were in danger of trampling the fearless youngsters under foot; and the men and women came out. Windows and doors were filled, and a wide wave of murmuring went through and through Fisher Falls.

They passed the imposing front of the bank, and behold! the door opened and there was President Fisher standing forth with the broadest of smiles and with extended hand.

Pleasant Jim waved to him but did not pause.

"I'd rather shake hands with the devil," he said bitterly to Lew.

And so they went on until they came to the office of the marshal.

He stood at the door of his office and waved the others back. Only Pleasant Jim advanced to meet him; and formally they shook hands. The crowd in the distance shouted.

"I suppose that I ought to say that I'm glad to see you back," drawled Sam Lee. "Anyway, Pleasant, you've been bought and paid for, and you're free."

"Bought and paid for?" repeated Pleasant sternly. "What you mean by that, Sam Lee?"

"The law can't give something for nothing," said the marshal. "So it gives up you and it takes the girl, instead. She's written out a full confession—"

And he opened the door of his office.

Pleasant, springing in, saw the pale face of Sally, on the farther side of the chamber, pressed into a corner.

"Sam Lee, you traitor! You traitor!" she cried. "You swore that you wouldn't tell!"

"She come down here to sort of drink up the sight of you and to hear you and to see you," said Sam Lee, with something like a sneer. "She wanted to enjoy the sight of magnificent Jim Pleasant ridin' in to the freedom that she'd paid for with the rest of her life in jail. So she swore me not to show her to you. But I thought that maybe you was man enough to sort of want to have a look at her. And here she is!"

"Get out of the room!" said Pleasant Jim, and he swept the marshal back towards the door, and then advanced upon the girl.

"The governor sent this," said the marshal. "Maybe you'd better see it."

And he slammed the door heavily behind him as he went out.

"That means something!" said Sally. And she darted forward and picked up the yellow form.

It was a long message: addressed to Marshal Sam Lee.

"USE YOUR OWN DISCRETION. BUT IF THE GIRL IS WILLING TO

SACRIFICE HERSELF FOR THE MAN AND THE MAN IS WHAT YOU SAY
ABOUT HIM I PROPOSE TO PARDON THEM BOTH IF THEY WILL
PROMISE YOU PERSONALLY TO BE GOOD HEREAFTER. LET ME KNOW
DATE OF MARRIAGE."

Half a dozen times their blured eyes strained through that
message, Sally in the arms of Jim Pleasant, holding the paper in
shaking hands.

"Call Sam," said Pleasant in a choked voice, at last. "Call
Sam Lee, God bless him! I want to promise to be good!"